W9-DET-044

LAUREL ULEN CURTIS

Quirks & Kinks
Published by Laurel Ulen Curtis
© 2015, Laurel Ulen Curtis

Cover Design by Stephanie White of Steph's Cover Design
Formatting by Champagne Formats

Champagne
Formats

All rights reserved.

Without limiting the rights under copyright reserved above, no part of this publication may be reproduced, stored in or introduced into a retrieval system, or transmitted, in any form, or by any means (electronic, mechanical, photocopying, recording, or otherwise) without the prior written permission of both the copyright owner and the above publisher of this book.

This is a work of fiction. Names, characters, places, brands, media, and incidents are either the product of the author's imagination or are used fictitiously. The author acknowledges the trademarked status and trademark owners of various products referenced in this work of fiction, which have been used without permission. The publication/use of these trademarks is not authorized, associated with, or sponsored by the trademark owners.

ISBN-13: 978-1514681640
ISBN-10:1514681641

Dedication

To the ladies of Bx3. You guys are *legiterally* a bright spot in my day and kept my chin up during the writing of this book. All of my love to the neighborhood.

PS- Don't let this dedication go to your head, bitches. I'm still clearly the most important person. ;)

PPS- Fuck Isaac!

Author's Note

Dear loyal and brand-new readers alike,

When I got the idea for and started writing this book, I saw it going a very distinct direction. Lighthearted. Easy-reading. Funny as hell and riddled with slightly uncomfortable, untapped situations.

What the characters gave me was something a little bit different and a whole lot more. While I'm still hoping this book makes you laugh out loud and reads easily, the story isn't what I'd call lighthearted. At least not for the entire book. What it is, is Easie and Anderson's. I hope they stick with you the way they ended up sticking with me.

Also, now that I've prepared you for the unexpected serious nature of portions of this book, please be aware that it briefly features clowns. I'd tell you that no clowns were harmed in the making of this book, but I'm pretty sure that'd be nothing but a disappointment.

All my love,
Laurel xx

PS- When you get done reading, come hang out with me in a very relaxed setting in Books, B*tches, & Balderdash.
https://www.facebook.com/groups/1001568759857518/

Part 1

Easie

"To share your weakness is to make yourself vulnerable; to make yourself vulnerable is to show your strength."
— Criss Jami

Prologue

"I JUST GOT WIND OF a great part. A really great opportunity," my sister Ashley chirped through the speaker of my phone smashed firmly to my ear.

Glancing over my right shoulder to check for traffic, I swerved my rusted out Honda Civic from my lane to the next. A cigarette hung precariously from my mouth, and since my right hand held my phone, that left only my left one to do the steering. A mirror probably would have been helpful too, but it had long since been busted off.

Money didn't come easy, and as long as my old beater was still coughing and sputtering its way from one place to the next, I pretended I couldn't hear the hiss of its barely there exhaust or see the proverbial lung it hacked up on the asphalt right in front of me.

Expert multitasker that I was, my eyes narrowed regardless of the fact that no one could see me. At least, *Ashley* couldn't see me. I wasn't fucking invisible. Though, if I could swing it, I was pretty certain that would be a handy little trick.

"I know this voice," I mumbled, belatedly grabbing the cigarette with my left hand and steering with my knee. "This is your fake voice. The one that tells me every time you say great, I should replace it with shitty. So tell me. What's this shitty part? This really *shitty* opportunity?"

"Okay, look," she conceded immediately. She had always been the good girl to my bad. The Angel to my seriously deranged Devil. "So it's not one we've been specifically going after—"

"What is it?" I cut her off just as I did the same to a car blocking my way to my exit. Forefinger and thumb tightly clutched on the smooth paper of my smoke, I threw up my middle finger in the Southern California Salute. Flipping people off on the freeway was practically part of the driving test. His horn barely even squeaked in response. Obviously, his level of commitment to being pissed at me was substantially low.

"It's a recurring spot. A whole season deal," she hedged, doing her best to make it sound better than it was.

"Ashley!"

"It's the lead reenactment actor on Quirks and Kinks."

What the? What in the actual *fuck* was a *lead* reenactment actor?

"Why don't I like the sound of that?"

Her voice was solemn. "Probably because you have more than one working brain cell."

"Ashley—"

"Look. You need this. *We* need this." Normally, the desperation in my agent's voice would have gone unnoticed. *Normally,* I would have snapped at her for putting a fancy spin on something in order to con me into it.

But that would have been in the days when my agent wasn't my sister, and I wasn't spinning a tale of my own by calling her both.

"Fine. What are the details?"

"Honestly, I don't know them."

"Okay—"

"But Larry does, and you have a meeting with him in two hours."

"Wahhhh," I whined dramatically, making use of my one free foot by stomping it on the floorboard like a petulant child. "Larry? That guy is *such* an asshole."

She scoffed. Choked a little on her saliva. Apparently, what I'd said was *that* funny. "You don't get along with anyone."

In other words—the punch line—maybe *you're* the asshole.

True.

It wasn't intentional, but that's the part of the Easie pie chart I seemed to show everyone. I was sixty percent self-preserving humor and forty percent unrealized vulnerability. So far, I hadn't been able to figure out how to reload the scales.

"But I *really* don't get along with Larry."

He was ornery and brash, and never, ever tried to sweet talk his way around my bullshit. Instead, he called me on my antics when I committed them and made them up when I didn't. Our relationship wasn't close, and we hadn't spent years forming grudges to hate each other for.

We just never seemed to get along.

Perhaps it was the melding—or lack there of—of two completely alpha personalities or my inability to be mature.

But, whatever it was, I preferred to blame him.

"E. We need money. He has the ability to give it to us," she explained phonetically, treating me like a child. Appropriate, since I was so good at acting like one.

"Fuck!" I huffed out a disgruntled breath, knowing I deserved her condescension about as much as a child genius deserves an A. Ironically, the amount was also the exact opposite of my chances of getting out of this job. "Fine."

Screeching all four tires to a sliding stop, I gave a half-assed glance both directions before pulling an illegal U-turn and swinging right back onto the on ramp for the Freeway I'd just abandoned. Time in Los Angeles was like dog years—completely disproportional with reality. If I needed to meet Larry in two hours, I needed to be on my way now.

Right back in the direction from which I had just come.

I didn't realize then, but apparently, despite what physics would have you believe, you *can* both move backward and be propelled forward at the same damn time.

Chapter 1

MY SISTER SPENT THE whole drive here jabbering away in my ear, trying to coach me out of fucking us both over. "Don't let him bait you," she said. "Just nod your head and smile," she said.

It all sounded good and easy—until I got here and saw Larry, blond hair glistening in the fluorescent overhead lights, sitting at the table in the conference room, tapping his foot with annoyance like I was late. I had arrived fifteen minutes early, fuck you very much.

Granted, I'd stayed outside to smoke another cigarette before coming in, so now I was only *five* minutes early, but qualifying variances or not, early is early.

Three out of four walls of the conference room were comprised of floor to ceiling glass, and a sleek, dark wood, modern table stretched from one end to the other. One crystal vase sat centered on the table and was filled with creamy white calla lilies. If I didn't know any better, the illusion might have fooled me into thinking this production company *wasn't* the armpit of the industry. That the grandeur of their office surely pointed to a successful track record and potential for a sustainable income.

But I *did* know better, and my knowledge came by way of experience. The sticky glue of their honey trap had secured me once before, back when I was naive and hopeful. Back when I thought I'd find my way to the glory and fame at the top one percent of the industry.

Back when I was an idiot.

What I got instead was a backlot commercial directed by a gold-chain-wearing guy named Joe Bernstein that never made it to TV.

And yet, at the prospect of being broke and homeless, here I was again. Meeting with Larry in the fancy room and hoping he could hitch my star to something great.

Gripping the cold metal handle of the door, I shoved forward using the weight of my body before I could back out. My entrance didn't make any noise, but nevertheless, Larry noticed.

Maybe he was acutely attuned to the barometric pressure of the room, and the sudden breach of the seal tipped him off.

Or maybe, he just got lucky.

"Ahh, you're here. Good. I wasn't sure how much longer I could wait," he barked out immediately, glancing at his watch derisively and raising his eyebrows into an even more prick-like position.

Ashley's words choked my own, cutting off my long-winded rant about how very fucking on time I was and replacing it with a smile and a nod.

My bubblegum-pink-nailed hand shook as I channeled all of my anger into tucking my shoulder length blond hair behind my ear. The nails and hair—frankly, everything about my appearance—did nothing to speak for my real personality. But, really, that was the whole point. Casting directors and producers weren't looking for the ugly display my inner workings would translate into. They wanted the bubbly girl, the perfectly busty blonde that would sell their show with sex. Of course, there were millions of us just like that, swarming casting calls and mistaking one another for a reflection of ourselves in a room of mirrors. You needed to be that girl on the outside with something extra underneath.

I'd like to tell you that was me. That I was the special one. The girl in the sea of girls that had *it*. Of course, if that were actually the case, I'd probably be employed gainfully enough to support a decent drinking habit.

But I wasn't, and I had noticed. Trust me. Reality is a lot harsher when you're stone cold sober.

"Sit," Larry ordered, eyeing the opposite side of the table and waiting for me to obey.

There was no point in arguing this early in the meeting. I was almost certain I would need to voice my opposition more later, and I really wouldn't mind taking a load off.

See?

I could be reasonable.

Rounding the table quickly, I took my seat, slamming my purse and keys onto the surface of the table gracelessly enough to make Larry wince. I took secret pleasure in his pain.

The sparkles of my pink Hollywood keychain mocked me with my long-beaten naivety, looking every bit as used up as I felt. Little jewels from the crown were missing and the edge of the trademark 'E' was starting to chip off.

Hah. I'd thought I was really going places. I'd thought it strongly enough that I'd taken my sister down with me.

To here. This place.

Washed up—or, at least, *feeling* like it—at the plump old age of twenty-five. Seven measly years into my adult life, and my woes were already feeling heavier than my dreams. I just barely stopped my self-deprecating snort.

"I'm going to be honest with you, Easie. You're not the girl I wanted for this show. In fact, you're pretty much last on my list." His eyes held real malice, and the fight to stop myself from checking to make sure I was indeed myself and not, in fact, shit on his shoe was equivalent to the championship round of a Heavyweight Tournament.

Okay. Apparently, Larry hated me even more than I hated him.

Impressive.

"You better watch blowing all that smoke up my ass, Larry. Might start a fire," I told him sarcastically, all of my good behavior officially used up. If he was going to be mean to me, I could sure as shit be mean to him.

"A fire in your ass seems like just the right start to our partnership."

When I quirked a brow, he elaborated. "You may as well get used to having weird things in unexpected places."

Uh . . . what?

Freaky meter reading? Too freaky.

Plan? Ignore it for now.

"I'm a little nervous to hear about this job that apparently lacks any kind of appeal. Don't tell me, you want me to reenact the Anti-Christ? Maybe sell the souls of my unborn children to pedophiles while I'm at it?"

Larry ignored me—like usual—and instead went on to explain the actual job. "It's a new show, Quirks and Kinks. We've already selected a male reenactment actor to be your co-host, so you're the last piece of the puzzle. There's some seriously fucked up shit out there that people are into, and the two of you are going to be the face of it."

Suddenly, his weird things in my ass reference was busting through my forcefield and making way too much sense. And I didn't like it one bit.

"I'm going to be the face of people's freakish fetishes?" I asked disbelievingly.

Larry shrugged his nonchalance, shoving it directly down the throat of my panic. "Half of it."

His chocolate brown eyes held mine intently, and the severity of his serious face only heightened when he leaned his weight into the table.

Moisture pooled in the palms of my hands as nerves made my heart beat faster. I felt like this meeting was doing nothing to assuage my fears, and the eerie calm I'd been hoping to find in the words of a bullshitting producer was nowhere in sight.

I licked my drying lips. Forced a rough swallow a couple of times.

"Shouldn't you be pitching this harder? Telling me what a great opportunity it is, how it could be my breakout role, how it could lead to bigger and better things?"

The sound of the mixture of a male chortle and snort was not attractive. Larry's reaction provided solid evidence.

"Give me a break, Easie. Anyone but you, I'd do the walk, talk the talk. I'd song and dance you until you thought you were on the set of a fucking musical, but with you, it'd be a waste of time. You're combative, hard to work with, and rarely ever listen to direction. But I'm out of options and you're attractive. Your prospects are hovering right around the same number as mine, and I know you like to feed that pretty sister of yours. So I'm saving us both the time and effort that we could be spending on bullshit, and laying it out for you."

"What makes you so damn sure I'll take this job instead of one of my other offers?"

His response was to laugh maniacally in my face. It was a wonder he was still alive by the time he got control of the laughter and took a full breath again. He must be one of those people who could hold his breath under water for freakishly long amounts of time.

But he laughed because he knew the truth.

If I had any other offers, I wouldn't be in this cocksucking conference room.

Bottom line, I needed the job.

Bottom line, I liked to eat, and people generally expected you to pay them for food.

Bottom line, my sister was counting on me.

Bottom line, I was fucked.

Still, I felt it prudent to dip my toe into the informational pond and get a feel for the temperature a little before cannonballing my way into the deep end.

"Are we talking "Oops, we got a little too wild having sex against elevator doors and fell into an empty shaft" or "I eat six rolls of toilet paper a day, every day" kind of thing?

"Both."

Shit.

Tap, tap, tap, my nail played out in a rhythm on the edge of the table. My toe bounced too, but the timing was off, proving irrefutably that music wasn't one of my natural gifts.

"So you're in, right?" he asked just for the sake of asking. We both knew I had no other option. He had my metaphorical balls in a fucking vise, and I could already feel them bruising.

I just barely managed to choke out my answer through an uncomfortably tight throat. "Yes."

"Good," he nodded, pushing my contract and a pen across the table in front of me, and then tossed a red-bordered package on the table in between us with a thud. "Here. Your signing bonus."

Reaching slowly to the middle of the table, I picked it up and turned it over as his retreating back moved toward the door with purpose.

Namely, getting the hell out of the room that I inhabited.

My thumb glided smoothly along the words on the package as I read them to myself.

Blueberry muffin mix?

"I have to bake my bonus?" I called out quickly, jerking my gaze from the package to the smooth line of his tailored gray suit. Muscular but lean, his body wore the fabric instead of the other way around.

I had a feeling if he smiled a little more and, you know, didn't have the tarnished soul of a devil worshipper, he'd be pretty attractive.

His eyes flashed over his shoulder in mocking triumph as he taunted back, "You're rolling in the dough."

Sputtering and clawing my way out of my chair, I just barely got off a response before the door clicked softly behind him. It didn't do me a hell of a lot of good, but it sure made me feel better.

"Muffins are made of batter, asshole!"

Chapter 2

"I'M STILL NOT EVEN sure what we're doing here," I told Ashley as I glanced around at the cheap Tex Mex themed decor of El Loco Restaurant.

All around us, business-suit-clad, young singles chatted and laughed, sinking deeper into their margaritas and each other. A life untraveled stared me in the face, but it didn't make me feel bitter or regretful. All I felt was stupid for being out and spending money that we didn't have.

"You just landed a job," she cooed before sipping delicately from the free water.

Giving her my undivided attention, I narrowed my cat-like blue eyes.

"Granted, it's not a job you're exactly thrilled about, but it comes with money, and that's worth celebrating a little."

"Pff," I huffed. "So far, all it's come with is a bag of muffin mix and humiliation." Exaggeratedly, I checked my purse. "Nope, no money."

Ashley just shook her head. "We're eating one dollar tacos. Peanut butter and bread are more expensive. Relax."

My fingers itched for a cigarette, and astute twenty-three year old lady that she was, Ashley didn't miss it.

"Besides, if we're going to get on the money discussion, you're going to have to take a closer look at some of your other expensive habits."

Ashley had been trying to talk me into quitting for years, and I knew my lungs would thank me if I somehow managed to follow through. But as desirable as it sounded, I just . . . couldn't. It wasn't so much the addiction and the work it would take to kick a years-in-the-making habit. It was that smoking had become my emotional crutch. My timeout in any moment of need and my excuse to busy myself with something other than being a bitch. I was scared of the chasm I'd fall into, the inescapable hole I'd create with my auger-like anxiety without it.

My sister didn't know any of that. No one did.

"I smoke for my career."

Her eyes practically rolled all the way out of her head. "This ought to be good."

"You know this industry is unbelievably vapid, and vapid means skinny. Smoking keeps me that way."

She shook her head in disdain.

"And it's cheaper than a gym membership."

"Global warming, anyone?" she called dramatically. "You're argument is balancing on some *pretty* thin ice."

"Shut up," I poked, shoving her in her petite, narrow shoulder with our usual sibling playfulness.

Suddenly, warmth wafted up into my face as our waiter shoved the toasty basket of complimentary chips into the center of our table. My eyes drifted naturally from the basket to the hand holding it, where a large, oval, heavy metal ring sat in blazing contrast to the tan expanse of his long ring finger, up the line of his muscular—*deliciously* veiny—forearm, to the cuff of his rolled up black sleeve. On a runaway mission of their own, my eyes wouldn't stop, eating up the expanse of his bicep in an instant, stutter-stepping up the corded column of his slender throat, and landing on one of the most attractive male mugs I've ever seen.

A mixing bowl of ethnicity, his naturally tanned skin and dark features stood in stark contrast with the minty green of his eyes. Directly on me and smirking, they were mesmerizing.

And mocking.

Ashley spoke, as I'd apparently lost all of my normal snarky ability.

"Thanks."

A small glance from me to her preceded his polite answer. "You're welcome."

She smiled her prettiest smile, the one that infused her entire being from chest to eyes, and the corner of his mouth notched higher in response.

A foreign heaviness settled in my chest as I watched, and its completely unwelcome presence nearly made me sick.

He turned to leave slowly, one last lingering look in my direction making my nerves ratchet up to an eleven.

Fuck. I did *not* like to be rattled. Confident words were my modus operandi, but a good earthquake could wreck even the strongest of routines. My table at El Loco, tonight—this *guy*—was the epicenter.

The man in question had just earned himself automatic placement on my shit list.

Straight, white, top teeth just barely teased the plump pillow of his bottom lip. It was unintentional, completely innocent, and hot as Jesus' sauna.

Shit list position confirmed.

"You're, like, really attractive," Ashley noted, evidently drunk on her water and speaking via a direct link to my brain.

His chuckle was like a full body vibrator, skating through the nerves on every inch of my skin. One long-fingered hand shot straight to his neck, rubbing the uneasiness of Ashley's compliment out quickly.

"Thanks."

"Are you an actor?" she continued. "You've got to be, right?"

Los Angeles. Every attractive person you meet *must be* in the business.

I would have laughed at Ashley's assumption and how ridiculous it was if I hadn't been thinking the same thing. I tried to avoid making fun of myself when I could.

He looked slightly bashful, his flighty eyes seeking comfort in the ground momentarily, but fought straight through the discomfort and answered her frankly. "Uh, yeah. I mean, I'm trying anyway. I'm not particularly successful."

Distracted by my reaction to him and his honesty, I didn't run a pre-check on anything coming out of my mouth. Not that I normally had the best filter, but this particular faux pas really took the cake. "So you're another one of those actors, waiting tables to pay the bills and pass the time?"

He bristled, and rightfully so.

I really had been out of line with that comment, but I couldn't seem to call upon the tools so desperately needed to call it back.

But he did it with an otherworldly calm, meeting my eyes directly and speaking in a soft, polite—if only slightly teasing—voice.

"One of those? Oh. No. Waiting tables is my dream. I just act to fit in."

My cheeks felt hot with embarrassment and shame, and the glint in his eyes told me that he saw it.

Sometimes I hated that my default setting was bitch. Such a dominant trait was hard to overturn. "Okay, so maybe that was a little rude."

One corner of his mouth—the smug one—rose just slightly. "It's a distinct possibility."

Silence hung between us, but while my time was spent avoiding eye contact, his was spent calculating his next blow.

"I guess you must be something really impressive then?"

"Huh?" My wandering eyes shot to his with the focus of a

heat-seeking missile.

"Well, you obviously aren't on the waiting tables slash acting track that the rest of us losers are."

"Um—"

"I mean, you must spend your time doing something that really matters, right? Educating orphaned kids. Curing Cancer. Coming up with the way to end all of the world's unrest." Attractive arms crossed over an equally nice chest. "Am I right?"

As confident as I usually was, and as many comebacks as I normally had, I couldn't think of one single thing to say. I'm talking silence. Not even a stutter.

Unfortunately, my sister wasn't suffering from a similar problem.

"Hah! She's an actor too. But she's too busy to wait tables."

"Working?" he asked, one manly eyebrow cocking in time with his question. If I wasn't mistaken, he actually looked impressed for a minute.

I was ready to leave right then, get out while I was ahead, but Ashley, being the one of us with a conscience, had a knack for ruining a good thing.

"Oh. No. She's just too busy being her. You know, cutting people like you down in her spare time." She looked away, bopped her blond head to the music in the background. "But, she doesn't do it on purpose. She was born this way. Cold, dead heart and all. I guess that's why people like me still love her."

I tried not to let her words hurt. After all, if I were describing myself, I probably would have chosen the exact same phrasing, and because I knew her so well, I knew she was just trying to make a joke and bail me out of a situation of my own making.

And yet, I still couldn't stop the smile from slipping and sliding its way off of my face. Eyes on the table, I blinked rapidly, pushing the emotion back inside forcefully.

I wanted to be nicer. I really did. But I couldn't seem to figure out how to be emotionally exposed and strong at the same time. And when

I had to make a choice between the two, strong always won out.

It only took a few seconds to recover, but when I looked back up at the waiter, he was looking at me differently. Assessing.

Uncomfortable was too cushy a word for what I was feeling. Bombs exploded and sprayed shrapnel, the sharp edges of his scrutiny digging into the flesh of my muscle and making it twitch just beneath the not-protective-enough layer of my skin. So much sensation at once made my eyes jump back and forth, struggling to compensate for the sensory overload.

I didn't like being judged. I mean, the actual process of it. Not just the result of someone's perusal, but the examination itself. This guy was reading me, studying the order and punctuation of my paragraph and piecing it together to understand my story. It felt invasive. Personal. Nearly intimate.

I knew it was a necessary part of life, and unfortunately, with acting, it came as a pretty regular part of the job. But for the most part, when it came to my professional life, people did it behind my back. Some might call it underhanded. I just called it preferred.

"Anderson," he said, offering his hand to Ashley first.

"That's your first name?" I asked, interjecting myself back into the conversation just in time to sound like an asshole. Obviously, it was.

Jesus.

I was on a goddamn roll tonight. Next I'd be implying that he walked and talked wrong. Or maybe, if I really got out of control, that his penis somehow didn't measure up to societal standards. I didn't know how I'd make the geographical leap from simple insults to belittling the most essential part of the male form, but if anyone could do it, it'd be me.

Plus, I had absolutely *no* room for making fun of someone's name.

My parents had named me Easie. Seriously, Easie—said just like 'easy.' And no, it wasn't a cute nickname for something far more elegant and sophisticated.

I can't even count the number of times I heard my parents tell the story of my name. How they knew their first child wouldn't be easy. That even though everyone thought they were young and naive, they knew I would be the biggest challenge of their lives. But that didn't mean they couldn't try to sway the odds in their favor with my name.

It was a pretty annoying name to be saddled with as a kid, but even I had to admit it was clever for a couple of sixteen year olds.

"Well, I'm not Bond. I don't make a habit of introducing myself with just a last name."

"Ashley," my sister introduced herself, ignoring my stupid comment. "And this is Easie," she explained, pointing to me.

His eyes lit up like fireworks, sparkling and splaying with mischief and mirth in a riotous explosion of green that sucked at my attention just like an unexpected explosion in the dark, night sky would have.

Fuuuck.

I needed a cigarette. Stat.

Ignoring his imploringly naughty green eyes and Ashley's smug yet innocent smirk, I pulled the strap of my bag off the back of my chair and rummaged through the contents of my purse recklessly. I knew that being a disorganized mess would come back to bite me at some point, but I never would have guessed it would be in a moment like this.

Thin, sturdy cardboard met the tips of my fingers surprisingly quickly, but the churning whoosh of my panicked blood made it feel like a lifetime.

By some mini miracle, my hand emerged uninhibited, though the thrill of victory didn't last long.

"You can't smoke in here," Anderson informed me swiftly, his words completely devoid of flirtation. He didn't mean it as a suggestion.

Fucking fuuuuck.

Were there no lung-destroying people like me left in this world?! I missed the days when you could actually light up indoors.

"Alright," I agreed in the name of expediency, hopping down off of my stool height chair. "I'll just pop outside real quick."

"Or you could stop smoking," Anderson suggested, cocking a brow with interest he had no right or reason to have.

Who the fuck did this guy think he was?

Hackles fully risen, I snapped back, "Right. I'll just go outside," moving to skirt my way around his imposing posture.

His eyes lingered on my face, scanning the line of my mouth and trailing their way up to my eyes. The set of his jaw sharpened noticeably from the exaggerated clenching of his teeth, but he didn't move. Not with a turn of his shoulders or his hips, and certainly not to take a step out of my way. His body acted as a literal barricade, a fortress I would have to escape should the cigarette be that important to me.

If I hadn't found his highhanded response so fucking irritating I might have given in. I was all about expending the least possible effort.

Of course, I *did* find it irritating—on a fairly epic level—so I shoved my way past, practically body checking him with the full weight of mine as I did.

His green eyes followed me, yielding to my movements when his body refused to do the same, and for some God-awful, weak-willed reason, my traitorous bright blues looked back and held them.

Like a twisted turn of fate, the features of his face were made to smile but instead sat stagnant, weighted down by years of sadness. I didn't know him, but I knew what I saw in his frighteningly open expression—pages and pages of irreversible history waging a war within his story.

I didn't break the contact quickly enough, and not looking where I was going, I tripped over the leg of a chair and fell straight into another man. Big hands gripped the skin of my upper arms, righting me to standing again and pulling my attention away from Anderson once and for all.

"Excuse me," I murmured quickly before gathering my will and barely surviving dignity and bolting for the safety of outside. Located in one of the less desirable neighborhoods of Los Angeles, the irony of being safer *outside* of El Loco rather than *inside* of it wasn't lost on me.

The hot, muggy air of the urban outdoors hugged me oppressively as soon as it hit my air-conditioner-cooled skin, but compared to my burning rage, it felt like a fucking freezer.

Shaking the package violently, I freed one cigarette, tucked the pack back into my bag, twitched the wheel of my lighter with my thumb, and touched the brilliant orange flame to my eagerly waiting paper.

What an unbelievable *asshole*. Jesus. The fucking *nerve* of that guy.

Adrenaline only fed my temper, making me shake and mutter to myself nonsensically until it abated.

The smoke had just settled fully into my lungs, warming me on the inside and smothering the bright lights of my anxiety, when the front door of the restaurant squealed open.

Curious and cautious, I looked up, drew in another hit of nicotine, kicked one foot against the rough brick of the building, and turned my head to greet my newfound company.

Unwelcome green eyes struck me as physically as a healthy slap to the face almost instantly. They were like the underside of a leaf in both color and omen, pointing to an upcoming storm that was sure to do nothing but rage.

"Oh come onnnn," I grumbled, straightening from the building and blowing all of my recycled smoke right into his stupid, meddling face.

I had to give him credit. He just barely cringed at the smoggy intrusion, throwing up his hands and promising, "I come in peace. I swear. No more undeserved lectures from some guy you don't know."

"Yeah?" I asked skeptically, letting myself take another drag but making sure to aim my blown smoke elsewhere.

"Yeah."

"Then what the hell are you doing out here?"

"Apologizing," he admitted sheepishly as he leaned back against the building next to me. "At least, I'm trying to."

Thoroughly washed, my thoughts chattered and splattered against the walls of my mind in an all out mental rinse cycle. I didn't understand anything that had happened tonight. Why my smoking meant so much to him in the first place and why he felt the need to apologize.

He didn't know me. And I sure as fuck couldn't get a handle on him.

"Why?"

Surprised at my unwillingness to blindly accept, his head turned toward me in question.

"After tonight, you'll probably never see me again. There's what?" I raised my eyes to the sky and thought back on the latest statistics I'd seen. "Something like four million people in Los Angeles alone. If I don't come back here, to this restaurant . . . don't seek you out intentionally . . . our paths will probably never cross."

He shrugged. "Seems to me you answered your own question."

Confused, my face scrunched slightly and my cigarette-holding hand dropped to my side.

"If I don't apologize now, I'll never get another chance," he explained. "I've got enough sins to live with already. I try not to add to the list."

Sins? What the hell was this guy talking about?

At a loss for what to say, I offered what I thought was a simple question. "You're religious?"

His laugh cut harshly through my ears.

"My sins have *nothing* to do with God and *everything* to do with regret."

The intensity of his words left me speechless—gave me time to study *him*—and in the silence that resulted, Anderson shoved off of the building and stepped back to the door.

"It was nice to meet you, Easie," he said with a smirk, pulling the door open and stepping back into the chaos that waited inside.

"It was nice to meet you too," I said to the space where he used to be, throwing my half-smoked cigarette to the ground and stubbing it out with my toe. "You fucking lunatic."

A chill swept down my arms, raising the hairs and bringing my hands up to rub the goosebumps away. The previously busy street seemed quiet, and the light from the door beckoned like a lighthouse. I hated to follow him inside so quickly, but now that my rage had dulled, being out here alone was giving me the creeps. And the whole rape/murder combination completely lacked appeal.

A wave of noise hit me as I pulled the door open and jumped back inside. I worked hard to reorient myself, pausing to let the hostess gather menus and take a waiting couple to their table. Laughter rang out and people mingling throughout the bar jostled and moved, waving at lesser known acquaintances across the room and signaling the bartender to help them sink into the night just a little bit more.

When the crowd parted, a lone Ashley sat perched on her chair typing away at the screen of her phone with a crease of concentration between her eyes. There was no sign of Anderson anywhere, and believe me, I looked.

Feeling the coast was as clear as it was ever going to get, I power-weaved my way back to the table, anxious and uneasy about the fact that we had *yet* to even eat. There was no way Ashley was going to leave without eating her tacos. At least not without the help of chloroform or Rohypnol.

"Hey," she greeted, the sound of my chair legs scraping the floor bringing her attention up and away from the screen of her phone. "You made it back alive."

"Yeah," I confirmed, trying to dig up some sort of witty response but coming up painfully empty.

"Are you okay?" she asked and narrowed her eyes to assess me more closely.

"Yeah, I'm fine," I lied, feeling completely twilight-zone-level out of my skin. All I needed was to get my fucking focus back.

Using the first thing I saw as a contextual crutch, I asked, "Who are you talking to with so much concentration? I could see your frown lines from all the way across the restaurant."

"Larry," she muttered easily, throwing me for my forty-second loop of the night.

"Larry? What the fuck are you talking to him about?"

Her face was incredulous yet faintly pink. "Um, your call sheet for tomorrow. What else would I be talking to him about?"

"Tomorrow? What do you mean tomorrow?"

"You start shooting tomorrow," she said, but the combination of words sounded strangely like *what the fuck is wrong with you?*

"WHAT?" I shrieked. Unknown wide eyes blinded me from several directions.

"Are you on drugs?"

"No, I'm not on drugs! But I am probably going to end up in prison!"

"For what?"

"For killing that prick, Larry!"

"He didn't tell you we start tomorrow?"

"No!" I screamed. "Obviously fucking not!"

"Okay, relax. Jesus," she placated. "He told me, and now I'm telling you. No harm done."

"No harm done? NO HARM DONE?"

"Shhhh!" she commanded, grabbing the first waitress that walked by at the elbow. "I'm sorry, can you *please* bring us our tacos to go?"

Huh. Look at that. Apparently, an inappropriate outburst will get my sister to leave just as effectively as kidnapping drugs. Good to know.

The poor, random server was surprised, but the imploring look on my sister's face went a long way to ease the awkwardness. With a nod and a fake smile, she scurried off to get our tacos. Or, presumably, to disappear until we did.

"God, you're ridiculous tonight. What's got you acting so dramatic?"

Anderson.

"This. Larry. Stupid. Surprised," I evaded nonsensically.

"Riiiight."

"Sorry. I'm calm. I swear." She eyed me skeptically. "Really," I promised. "Meditation's got nothing on me."

Fearing that anything I said could or would be used against me in the Ashley court of law, I sat silently, staring down at my fiddling thumbs instead of looking around. I blocked out time, letting it pass without inspection.

Warm fingers brushed my arm as Anderson reached between us to set our bag of to-go tacos and the bill on the table.

"Ahhhhh!" I screamed in surprise, my promise becoming nothing more than a broken memory in record time.

Perhaps sensing my instability, Anderson didn't say a word, instead opting for a simple nod and masculine salute before taking off again.

Ashley didn't know what the hell was going on, but she knew it wasn't good. Fishing around in her purse for enough money to cover the bill, she threw it on the table and grabbed me by the arm to lead me out of there before I could start a brawl or wave my vibrator around. That's the kind of gesture it would take to make even bigger fools out of us.

"Let's go," she instructed, moving me through the restaurant and out the door with precision.

Electing to drive herself rather than chance me under these circumstances, she settled me into passenger side and rounded the hood on her own.

As soon as the ignition fired, my tired brain outlined the next twenty-four hours of my life aloud and prayed it would go better.

"Tacos. Sleep. Start over. Quirky Kinkery."

"Needlessly concise, but accurate." She shrugged, ready to put this night behind us too. "Sounds like a plan, E."

Chapter 3

"**D**IDN'T LARRY EXPLAIN THIS to you?" Ashley asked after the third time I required detailed instruction about where to go, what to do, and generally any-fucking-thing about my new job since we'd arrived this morning.

The set wasn't big, and the accommodations weren't exactly five-star, but I had my own dressing room with a light, mirror, and locking door. Considering my expectations, I was declaring it a win.

"Does it look like he explained any of this to me?" I asked, standing in the middle of the room for the millionth time and looking around aimlessly.

"Well, no, but—"

"You're surprised? I didn't even know that we were shooting today! Of course that asshole didn't tell me anything."

"I'm not sure why the two of you rub each other the wrong way so much," she said, digging around in her big bag full of answers. She was the woman with the information while I was nothing but a puppet strung up helplessly on its strings.

I shot her a surprised glance which she read immediately upon looking up from her rummaging.

A delicate laugh puffed the air around her and moved one stray blond hair away from her mouth. "Oh, no. I know why *you* rub *him* the wrong way, but I don't know why he buys into it. I have no trouble talking to him."

"Yeah, I get it. You're nice and I'm not. Can we cut to the chase about what I'm supposed to be doing with myself?"

A knock on the door interrupted my bitching, and Ashley turned to open it.

"Oh, great!" she said into the small opening, accepting something I couldn't make out and shutting the door.

"Well, here's the script," she declared, handing it to me with a small flourish. "Abby and Mike are real people, and they're here on the set." She made sure I held her eyes as she explained, "Your main goal is to be as respectful of them as possible. They're volunteering their story for our use on the show with absolutely no reimbursement, so the last thing we want is for them to feel uncomfortable."

"Larry didn't even think I should have the fucking script before now? Does he actually *want* me to fail?"

"You're reading too much into it and, frankly, giving him too much credit. He's just human, and the success of this show is all on him. If he didn't get you the script before now, it wasn't on purpose. It actually says something really positive that he was willing to take the risk on you."

"That he positively hates me."

"Easie, there's a very good possibility that if this thing goes under, Larry loses his job. He loses all the years he's put into this industry, this company, and he has enough faith in you to believe you're not going to let that happen. Honestly, you guys fight like brother and sister." She heaved a deep breath.

"Besides, the show's going to be shot in short, choppy segments, so memorizing a piece at a time shouldn't be any trouble at all."

As she spoke, I cracked open the script to get an idea of what I was in for. Before I knew it, my eyes were making a valiant attempt to bug all the way out of my head.

"Clown sex?! These people are into clown sex?! Jesus."

Ashley's eyes widened comically as she pursed her lips, but her normally quippy mouth stayed closed. Reading further, I let my mouth run, venting about the ridiculousness of this show now so that I wouldn't do it later in front of Mike and Abby. Heaven forbid I run off the people with a fucking *clown* fetish.

"Red noses?! The last time something that red and shiny tried to come close my vagina, I ran the other direction and wound up going straight to my doctor's stirrups for an STD test."

"Larry thought that this show would be more successful getting us off the ground if we linked it with Red Nose Day and tied it back into charity. When he asked my opinion, I agreed."

"Since when is Larry asking your opinion on this stuff?" I asked skeptically. She was awfully close with a guy I didn't like.

"Believe it or not, Larry and I share a common goal. We both want you to succeed. We talk."

"Pffttt!" The thought of her having a serious consultation with Larry about *my* success was enough to make me scoff. But I had other stuff on my mind at the moment. I didn't have time to waste hashing out stupid stuff about Larry. "Whatever. If you can stand him, good for you."

Focusing back on the script, the next line jumped out at me like a bag of bricks in mid-swing approach to my face.

"I"m pregnant?!"

"WHAT?" Ashley screamed, dropping the papers in her hands and sending them flying all over my dressing room.

"Not 'I'm pregnant' period!" I yelled. "'I'm pregnant' question mark." When her saucer like eyes didn't narrow, I shook the papers in my hand. "In the script!"

"Oh, thank God!" she swore, clutching her now empty hand over her heart.

"Jesus, Ash," I grumbled, bending down to collect some of her paperwork, "I actually have to have sex to get pregnant, and that sure as hell hasn't been happening."

"I know, I know. I just panicked. I mean, *you,* with a baby." Her body gave a full height shudder, and I froze as a pang gripped my chest.

In order to distract myself from the shame I felt—the upset of the brutality of my sweet sister's opinion of me—I stopped picking up papers and went back to reading the script.

Wanting to stop the toxically spreading ache, I forced myself to hold on tight to my quickly fleeting joviality.

"I swear to Mary, Mother of Jesus, my willingness to get freaky with some dude in a clown nose will significantly diminish when I'm with child." She looked up from her position on her hands and knees and met my eyes. "And it's already pretty low to begin with."

"Why Mary?"

"Huh?"

"Why did you swear to Mary instead of Jesus himself?"

I hadn't even been conscious of my choice, but in the face of her questioning, the reason became abundantly clear. "Because Mary is a sister, she's had the kid high-jumping on her bladder, and she would understand."

"Shit!" she yelled, jumping up from the ground to point at the clock. Two quick steps to the side had her grabbing my robe from the hanger on the door and throwing it at me. "Put this on! We're late!"

"Late for what, goddamnit?!" Pointing angrily towards the floor, I laid out my demands. "From this day forward, I want a printed itinerary! I've been like a hooker without a john all morning, and I'm fucking sick of it!"

"A hooker without a john?"

I rolled my eyes. "A little lost, a lot desperate, and constantly begging you to give it to me. 'It' being information."

"Fine," she conceded. "You can have all the printouts you want, but for now, just get in the robe. You've got hair and makeup, and wardrobe, and you've got to meet your co-star."

"Great." I fake smiled and stripped off my t-shirt and yoga pants.

"All things I can't wait to do since I found out I'm going to be clowned up, carrying thirty extra pounds, and pretending to hump some stranger."

Settling my arms into the sleeves, I tied the sash, slipped my feet back into my flip flops and scooped the script up off of the table. "Ready. Let's go."

"It won't be that bad," Ashley soothed as she ushered me out the door. "I've never seen you this out of sorts. Take a deep breath, calm down, and find the confident inner bitch you've got living somewhere in your body."

"Right."

She was right. The sooner I stopped freaking out and put on my game face, the better off I would be.

Preparing, I steeled my face and hardened my eyes.

"But not too bitchy," she amended, obviously worried that she was going to push me into being unreasonable. Her micromanaging panic was enough to bring me back to my happy place. A place where I could handle anything and had the awareness I needed to tell *her* everything was going to be alright.

"Relax, would you?" I teased. "Everything's going to be fine. I'm going to be the best pregnant clown sex deviant you've ever seen."

She giggled softly, sounding the youngest I ever heard her these days. Being my agent came with too much responsibility. She'd started too young, become jaded too fast. I liked any time I saw a glimpse that I hadn't completely ruined her youthfulness.

"You'll be the first pregnant clown sex deviant I've ever seen."

"See? I'm betting you're not the only one. I like things where I have a built in winning streak due to a lack of competition."

This time both of us laughed, looking at each other as we entered a random room. At least, it was random to me. Ashley had been the one to lead us here.

"It's about time you showed up," Larry barked without preamble, turning away from the guy next to him. I couldn't make out any of his features other than a dark complexion and hair.

I was all fired up to lay into him when Ashley touched my arm in warning instead. She didn't bristle or yell or turn any of the many shades of red I'm sure graced my face.

Nope.

She *smiled.* Sweet and innocent and completely unlike me. She obviously got the good set of genes from our parents.

"My fault, Larry. Sorry about the wait," she cooed softly, tilting her blond head just so and blinking her navy blue eyes daintily.

Was Larry actually fucking blushing?

"No worries, Ash. We have plenty of time," he said with a genuine smile.

Okay . . . what?

His eyes lingered just noticeably before turning to me and hardening. "Come here, Easie. I'd like you to meet your leading man."

Confused and curious, I gave into his command, moving toward him and the shadowy stranger but looking back at my sister's face. She busied herself, looking everywhere but at me or the other occupants of the room. *Especially* one very specific male occupant of the room.

My sister and Larry? No way. He was, like, fifteen years older than she was, and she was too smart. *Wasn't she?*

Fuck. I didn't have time to follow this yellow brick road right now. I could only handle one ginormous, uncomfortable thing at a time.

Ha! That's what she said.

Shut up, brain.

Larry grabbed my hand and pulled me toward the man in the chair, introducing me in an effort to multitask as he did. "Easie Reynolds this is—"

It was as if time slowed down as my eyes followed the line of his hand to the mystery man. Black shoes and finely pressed pants disappeared into the abyss of his dress coat, the tan column of his throat flexing noticeably as he made an effort to turn toward me. Dark hair sat just perfectly askew, and in one heart pumping moment, recognition kicked in.

I could feel it coming, the slap of the Karma God's hand as it struck violently against the apple of my cheek—those torturous eyes. Those evil, world destroying—

Blue eyes.

Blue.

"—Ryder Thompson."

Not Anderson What's-his-name.

Oh shit. Oh *shit.* I was losing it. One completely discombobulating conversation, and the hot waiter at the restaurant had burrowed his way so deep inside my head I was mirage-ing his face onto the bodies of un-suspecting strangers. *Holy brown gravy, get your shit together, Easie.*

"Ah, nice to meet you, Ryder," I forced out, somehow pep-talking my way back out of the black vortex of a panic attack.

Unfortunately, when the panic was gone, the smarmy look on my new co-star's face remained. Mirth lit his eyes as he muttered, "Nice robe," but it wasn't the good kind. Under the scrutiny of his gaze, I felt naked. And dirty. Like, dipped in a vat of molasses, rolled in cow manure, buried in mud kind of dirty.

Skeeve-central.

"Easie, over here!" Larry called impatiently, and for once, I didn't have any desire to protest. Ryder's wandering eyes had traveled enough unapproved miles, thank you very much.

Helping me into the makeup chair, he spoke. "It's showtime, kid. For as much as we throw blows at one another, I know you're talented. So, read up on that script and add your flare. Snarky is good, as long as it's the charming kind."

Larry was nice, and I was speechless.

And just like that, everything was upside down again.

Chapter 4

"'M WORRIED," I MUTTERED, chewing on a nail as the makeup and hair people stepped away from my chair.

"About what?" Ashley asked with a huff. All of my yo-yo-ing was apparently trying her saint-like patience.

Lowering my voice to whisper, I explained. "Ryder kind of gives me the creeps."

"He's said two words to you."

"Yeah. A creepy two words."

"E—"

"And have you read this script? I mean really read it? He spends half of the episode with his face *this close* to my vagina!"

She cocked an eyebrow.

"That's a little personal, a little fast—"

"You have no problems when it's your gynecologist," she pointed it out.

"Well, I don't *like* it—" I started to argue.

"Or your waxer or spray tan lady."

"But—"

"At this rate the mailman—"

"Okay! I get it. You've made your point. My vagina's like Grand

Central Station. I'll be cool."

"That'd be great! Thanks!" she chirped like an annoying little bird.

"Five minutes, Ash," Larry called with a knock on the doorframe.

"Thanks," she called back, hustling me out of the chair and across the hall to the wardrobe room.

Grabbing a colorful skirt and stockings off of a rack, Ashley handed it to me and shoved me in the direction of a changing screen. "Hurry up and get changed. You heard Larry. We don't have a ton of time."

Scanning the clown-themed skimpiness of the costume, I realized something. "I think I need a new management team."

Seeing as my management team was her, Ashley reacted accordingly. "What?! Why?"

"Because Ryder is in a fucking tuxedo, and I'm in *this!*" I shook the flimsy, striped fabric in front of her face. "And he was in it thirty minutes ago, so he's obviously better informed."

"You know how it is, E. Sex sells and all that. During the opening of the show, Ryder will wear his tux and you'll wear a show-themed, sexy get up." I pretended to gag as she continued, "That's just the way it is."

The sour news contorted my face just as though it'd been actual candy.

"During the reenactment, he'll be in clown shit too. And I've seen it, it's even more ridiculous than yours."

"I'm holding you to that."

"Hold away," she offered with a shove. "Now get your ass behind that screen and pull the straps of your suspenders over your nipples. There's a limit to exactly how much sex we're allowed to sell."

"Cute," I mocked through a fake laugh. "Laugh it up now, but I'll get you back for this."

"I've no doubt you will," she agreed as I slid behind the screen. "Don't forget the stockings!"

"I won't," I grumbled. "Trust me." They were the most substantial part of the whole outfit.

I made quick work of the stockings first, and then pulled on the suspender style straps and smoothed my hands down to the edge of the bright red, fluffy, tulle skirt.

I could scarcely remember feeling more ridiculous, but even I couldn't deny that my boobs looked great. If you were going to get into the clown lifestyle, this was the way to go.

"I guess the silver lining is that I don't have to carry the pregnant belly yet," I said, stepping around the screen and back out in front of my sister.

As soon as the words cleared my lips, Ashley stepped forward and smothered my good mood with the well-timed placement of my bright red nose.

"I love your positive thinking, E," she praised through a smile, leaning forward to place a smug kiss on the apple of my cheek. "Breathe through your mouth, m'kay?"

Hustling out of the dressing room and toward the set, I pulled the script out of Ashley's arms for one last read through of the opener. It was a largely loose format, giving us guidelines and specific talking points, but leaving the extras up to us. I liked the idea of having some creative liberties—the chance to really tap into any and all talent I might have—but the idea of doing it with someone I knew nothing about shifted my nerves into overdrive.

Cameras and the crew sat waiting as we approached the set, and for the first time all morning, I took the time to take it all in.

I was doing it. Sure, it might not have been my dream job, but it was a job—and a real one at that. An actual director awaited our arrival by perusing the set and doling out orders, and cameramen sat patiently behind several cameras.

It was fairly low budget, just as I would have expected, but *real*. And about a million times better than Bernstein's backlot commercial gone wrong.

Ryder waved me over, looking attractive and far too normal in his tuxedo around the periphery of my big, red nose. His tux hugged the lean line of his body and the silvery blue of his thin, striped tie coordinated well with his eyes.

Turning to tell Ashley where I was going, I found her deeply enthralled in a conversation with Larry, so I nudged her with a nod to convey my point and walked *onto* the actual set for the first time.

A huge neon sign lit the back wall, and colorful lights tinted the air all around us. A simple wood floor sounded under my heels as I walked and at least three cameras pointed directly at our marks on the floor.

"Good God," Ryder breathed when I arrived, pulling me from my distracted perusal and staring at my chest unabashedly. Naively, I'd thought he was awed by the first day jitters too, but the direction of his eyes wasn't exactly promising.

"Thank fuck this show is about kinks."

Anddd neither were those words.

"What? Why?" I asked as I tried in vain to stand at an angle that didn't give him such a good view but not appear needlessly rude.

He chuckled and leaned dangerously closer. "Because if I'm going to have a boner from thinking about licking your tits all the time, at least I can blame it on my role."

Um . . . what?

His eyebrows popped upward just once, but it was enough to confirm the dishonorable intentions his words suggested.

Well.

I should have smoked another fucking cigarette this morning. That much was becoming clear.

I wasn't normally opposed to some brutal dirty talk, but this guy was a fucking stranger. *And* my coworker. Him saying that to me at this stage in the game was about as appropriate as wearing nothing but a ball sling to the Oscars.

"Excuse me?" I asked, impressed I managed to say anything at all. I'd never had any stranger tell me any part of my body was something he'd like to snack on. I mean, I'd had a few scenarios run through my fantasies, but trust me, none of them went like this.

"Your tits," he said slowly—the jackass—as though maybe I hadn't *heard* him.

Right. Because that was the problem.

He raised one too-well manicured eyebrow. "Look fucking edible."

Don't kick him in the balls. *Do not kick him in the balls.*

"You know that I'm not a whore, right? That I'm an actor?" I lowered my voice, speaking through tightly clenched teeth. "No matter the subject matter, this is a professional setting, and speaking to me like that is in no way appropriate."

"You're an uptight bitch," he murmured fake-thoughtfully, rubbing the line of his chin with his thumb and forefinger. "Got it."

Anger flooded my veins, but before I could cold clock the asshole, the director called for our attention.

"Listen up, people!"

As everyone huddled up closer, I made sure to shuffle my feet *away* from Ryder.

"Big show today. As the first show, this is the one we have to make count. This is the one that the network will use to determine whether or not we have jobs for more than a week."

Sandy blond hair sat ruffled atop his head and peppered with gray, and a week's worth of stubble coated the skin of his cheeks. His nose was slightly crooked, his clothes equally askew, but he had a kindness in his eyes. He seemed kind of like a good-natured but out-of-touch-with-cool dad, from his slightly rounded belly all the way down to the white sneakers on his feet.

Turning directly to me, he introduced himself, shoving one meaty hand out for a shake. "Easie, I'm Howie. I'm sorry we didn't get a chance to meet before now. But I've heard a lot about you."

Grrreeaaat.

My thoughts must have been painted all over my face because a smirk settled onto his. "*Good* things."

At the skeptical rise of my brow, he burst out laughing. Murmurs took hold around us as people tried to figure out what was going on, but I didn't let it bother me. Instead, I focused on his genuine smile and began to relax for the first time today. Maybe this wouldn't be such a terrible experience after all. Maybe there *was* opportunity to really enjoy myself on this show.

"Mike, Abby," he called, turning to address the real life clown-sexers, "I want to thank you for being here and letting us do a piece on your story."

They both nodded bashfully, surprisingly shy and normal looking compared to what I expected. Though, I guess the whole thing about kinks is that people normally keep them a secret.

"We're going to be taking a few liberties and dramatizing a few things for TV, but if you have any problems or concerns, don't hesitate to come tell me." Abby and Mike seemed grateful for his consideration, and I was impressed by it. Most directors don't check their egos at the door, and by offering to compromise his vision of the show for Mike and Abby, that's exactly what Howie was doing.

Addressing everyone again, he continued, "As for the rest of you, I'm going to need you to bring your all today. I expect concise concession to direction and an open mind and attitude. You're not here for *you,* you're here for *us.* Understand that or leave, but whatever decision you make, do it now."

People looked at one another, but no one said a word or made a move to leave. Obviously, despite Howie's illusion of a choice, there was really only one decision to be made.

"Great!" he cheered, surreptitiously congratulating us all on not being ginormous idiots.

"It's going to be a long day, so settle in. Ryder, Easie, get ready for the opening, maybe have a little chat about specifics and timing now while we get the lighting right. Go ahead and stand on your marks."

After a brief pause of unpreparedness, everyone scattered, moving to do their jobs and taking their positions behind specific equipment. Ryder and I both moved to our marks, and I made a promise to let his earlier words go and start over. Howie was right. Today was going to be a long day, and stressing over Ryder's brash come-ons would only make it feel longer.

"Let me guess," Ryder jeered before I could say one word. "You want to talk the whole thing out, plan our every move."

God, this guy was a *dick*. And just because I didn't immediately invite him to wrap my tits around his two inch cock, he was under the impression that I was some kind of uptight shrew.

Fine.

"Nope."

"No?"

"*No,*" I confirmed with emphasis. "I'm good. More than ready to do this."

Looking down at the script in my hands, I studied the talking points, familiarizing myself and preparing. I pointedly avoided any and all contact with the Micropenis, and instead, used my time to line up my thoughts and improvisational ideas. If he couldn't keep up, that'd be all the better. And if he could, well, I guess that'd be good for the show.

Blue, green, red, and orange lights strobed and adjusted to produce a glow on my skin, and after several minutes of moving around, finally settled into what I guessed was the optimal filming position.

Lingering techies cleared the set, and Howie's eyes came to his stars. "Ready?"

"Yes, sir," I agreed respectfully with a nod, eliciting a snort of sorts from my new arch nemesis.

"Good," Howie remarked, largely ignoring the snort but giving Ryder a meaningful look. "In the final cut, this will follow the intro music and graphics and is meant to not only introduce viewers to you, but to the specific episode. As much as this show is about the circum-stances, or quirks, if you will, it's going to be more about the two of you. You'll be there telling every story, so it's important the viewers connect with each of you as individuals." He chuckled a little. "In other words, be charming."

With one last smile, he moved to his place behind the playback screen and signaled the beginning of the end. This was it. The first episode. The first roll of the camera.

The first day of the rest of my life.

"Come on, Sweetheart. I know the situation isn't ideal, but you have to push," Mike (Ryder) coached me for effect.

We'd been going at this for hours—pretending to have sex, making weird clown giggles, and talking to Mike and Abby about what had actually gone down the day their daughter was born—and I had officially reached my Ryder-tolerating limit.

"What makes you think pushing a miniature human out of my vagina without the help of drugs or the expertise of a doctor isn't ideal, Mike?" I asked sarcastically as I pushed the sweat-soaked hair off of my face leaving behind some rusty dust from the bed of the old pickup I was weighing down.

"Don't worry, Abby. A woman's body is made to do this. It's natural."

"Fuck. You," I said through gritted teeth, which if you asked me, added to the realism of the situation and might have even made it more relatable for viewers.

I knew we were taking a few liberties and ad libbing a bit compared to the conversation that had played out between the real Mike and Abby, but Jesus, I was fed up with the jerk.

"Cut!"

Apparently, the director didn't appreciate the value of viewer empathy like I did.

"While telling Mike to fuck off might be the way of reality-"

So he *did* appreciate it.

"-the network won't allow it. So clean it up, please."

Ugh, fine.

Abby was a patient woman, spending her years going to great lengths to please her man. But she'd admitted to me, that night, in the middle of nowhere and in the midst of labor, she didn't exactly keep her cool. She just didn't do it with the same amount of vulgarity as I did.

"You think you can manage being a little gentler with my fingers?" Ryder demanded callously. "It feels like you're going to snap them off."

"Yeah, well, if I were Abby and you were Mike, your fingers wouldn't be the only thing I'd be snapping off."

"You just want to touch me," he taunted ignorantly, reminding me of the way he'd been touching me without reason and without my permission all freaking day long.

The saddest part of my psyche couldn't accept the fact that he probably had women crawling all over him. The pretty package of his exterior did a good job of hiding the stupid. At least until he opened his mouth.

"I swear on my future ability to bear children that I would rather bathe in a vat of acid than have any sexual contact with you."

He opened his mouth to spew some hate filled cut down, but Howie beat him to the punch.

"Action!"

Blocking out the less than appealing surroundings, company, and paraphernalia, I tunneled deep into myself and got that shit done. By some miracle, the determination I had to finish that take translated into the determination Abby had to deliver that baby.

Clown-sex day from hell: over.

Chapter 5

"**I**'M EASIE REYNOLDS, AND you're watching Quirks and Kinks," the TV version of me trilled obnoxiously from the far corner of my living room as the first episode aired five days later.

Hand resting protectively over my eyes, I moaned and cringed all at once. "Ughhh, *God,* I sound freaking ridiculous."

Ashley's chuckle was an interesting mix of disbelieving and amused. "Um, all you've done is introduce yourself. You haven't even had the chance to sound like an idiot yet."

"Give it time."

Her laughter rolled all the way out of her body and into mine, practically filling the space with her mood. "Geez. Maybe you should go outside and smoke or something. You're awfully critical for so early on."

"Good idea. But after the show. I don't want to miss anything."

If she laughed at me one more time, I was pretty sure I could charge her an admission fee for the comedy show tonight.

"You're not even watching. You have your hands over your eyes!"

"I'm listen-watching," I justified.

"You're crazy."

"I know," I admitted, squeezing my eyes so tight that my cheeks puffed and pushed up into them. "It's just scary."

And for most of the filming of the show, all I was feeling was a slow burning fury at my co-star. I didn't think that was really the quality of chemistry Howie was looking to achieve. I'd had major *fake* love for Ryder and his big obnoxious clown shoes. I was just hoping I'd pretended convincingly enough.

"Today we follow the story of Mike and Abby, and how their long-time interest in wearing clown paraphernalia during intercourse took an unexpected turn," my voice explained.

"Good job keeping a straight face during that one," Ashley commented.

The screen cut to a silhouette shot of Mike just as I uncovered my eyes. *"There's something euphoric about combining two positively emotional experiences."*

Editing perfectly transitioned to a darkened image of Abby, just as her voice called over the airwaves. *"I don't get pleasure from the clothes or personas like Mike does, but it didn't take me long to realize I got gratification from his delight."*

"Aww, that's kind of sweet in a freaky way," Ashley noted.

"I know." It was. I'd been slightly mystified by my growing understanding (so unlike me) the more I'd talked to Abby during filming. She wasn't into clowns. *Not at all.* But she *was* into Mike. And love like that was something I couldn't help but get behind.

"Can you imagine the day he dropped this bomb years ago?" Ashley asked, sinking into the arm chair, sitting sideways, and throwing her legs over the arm.

Laying back into the couch, I giggled, changing my voice to as deep of a timber as I could manage. "Well, uh, Abby, you see, I'm um . . . Well, I'd really love it if you'd honk my nose and call me Bozo."

"You want me to what?!" Ashley shrieked dramatically, playing along as the part of Abby.

"She obviously got over it," I remarked, watching the screen with a sort of detached attention as a white-faced Ryder pretended to sink between my legs. We'd evidently missed the rest of the intro and Ryder's lead in to Red Nose Day while we were having a little reenactment of our own.

"Understatement of the century."

We watched in silence for several seconds before Ashley's eyebrows made an attempt to climb into her hairline. "Did he just—"

"No," I lied, reliving the moment when Ryder had run his stupid red nose up the line of my sex and inhaled. It hadn't been for show, but I wasn't certain he was doing it because he genuinely wanted me either. He just seemed to get some sort of sadistic pleasure out of making me the epitome of uncomfortable.

Of course, I hadn't exactly let it slide, getting mine back by threatening to maim the next seven generations of his family with ragged shards of glass and "bumping" an elbow directly into his balls as soon as Howie had yelled cut.

There was a necessary level of intimacy when you were shooting scenes like that. And then there was a flagrant abuse of that necessity. Ryder's actions fell well within the latter scenario.

Airing on a network like TLE (The Learning Experience), it wasn't unexpected to have a show that pushed the boundaries in both subject matter and propriety, but this wasn't that.

Major editing did a great job of making everything feel real without making it necessary to move to a network like Skin-e-max, but my personal experience made things easier to notice. And I'd noticed that Ryder's actions made *me* look appropriate.

I watched as we portrayed the day that Mike had approached Abby about his desire to take their show on the road, making love (as clowns, of course) on a remote piece of property he owned. How the thought of her as a pregnant clown only heightened his excitement.

I could see my cynicism in the face of trying to be understanding of the man I loved. Which, from talking to Abby, pretty much nailed how she was feeling when he'd actually approached her that day. But she'd gone through with it, hoping not only to please Mike, but knowing that once the baby came there would be a significant decrease in their role playing opportunities.

Unable to watch Ryder's smarmy attempt at compassion during childbirth, I grabbed the remote and forced the screen to black.

"Hey!" Ashley snapped, surprised at the abrupt ending.

"Sorry," I semi-apologized. "I just couldn't take it anymore."

She chuckled. "He's not exactly convincingly sincere, is he?"

"No," I agreed. "He's much more plausible as a creepy clown."

"Well," she murmured into the crickets of our silent apartment. "What do you want to do now?"

"Sleep," I said simply. "I'm going to go to sleep."

Tomorrow would be another long day with Ryder.

"I'm going to expect my itinerary under my door by six AM."

"Ha!" she laughed. "Let me know how that goes."

Great. Tomorrow would be another *mysteriously* long day with Ryder. I couldn't wait.

∽୨ℂଡ଼

"I'm having the hardest time with the one with the beady eyes," I told Ashley during our brief break from shooting.

Anytime Howie called "cut" I added the words "and run" and got as far away from my co-star as possible. He'd already touched me several times today, and with the show we were shooting, there wasn't even a pretense of necessity to hide behind.

"Not the one that looks like it's watching you constantly?"

"Shit!" I panicked. "Which one is that?"

I hadn't noticed one that followed my every move. They were coming at me from every angle!

"The one in the corner, by the one in with the buck teeth."

"Cripes. I hope this isn't their actual collection."

"It's not," Ashley said, making me feel at least a little better about the situation. "Their *kids* are in school."

"Oh." Teased with an inkling of comfort, only to have it ripped savagely away.

"Yeah."

Today's show featured more of a quirk than a kink, and for that, I was thankful. But it was outside of my usual realm of normal, and if I was honest, it was creeping me out even worse than the clowns.

Frank and Lisa Hendross were a seemingly normal middle-aged couple. They'd been married going on twenty years, and the sight of them together was heartwarming. Very obviously in love, they actually looked at one another when speaking and touched more than necessary.

It was the kind of thing you rarely saw in today's world of smart-phones and stupid social media.

But they hadn't been able to conceive children, something that devastated Lisa. Frank's melancholy bloomed as a consequence of hers, and that led them to their circumstances today.

Proud owners of one of the most extensive doll collections in the country, each of which they treated as though it was an actual living and breathing child.

First confronted with the story line, I'd cringed. But when I saw the sadness in Lisa's eyes—the truth behind the madness—and Frank's willingness to do anything to stop it, I'd shed a few tears of my own.

In the privacy of my dressing room with no one around to hear, of course.

But I'd held onto that frame of mind, Frank and Lisa's sadness haunting my every move until I'd arrived on set and seen the first doll.

Beady-eye McGee. That's what I'd named him.

"Come on, guys," Howie called. "Time to go again."

"Good luck," Ashley said, sending me off with a wink.

Evil. She was pure evil.

Enemies starting to outnumber me, I did my best to avoid two freaky dolls and one freaky man, but I only had so many eyes for watching my back.

Figuring the dolls were more dangerous than the man, I turned my back to Ryder as Howie called us to action.

Sadness clung to my chest as I combed the strawberry blond hair of a doll named Belinda and wished for a life within her that would never be.

Something about this show caused a twinge of longing, the idea that I too had no prospects for having children whispering softly at the back of my mind.

I pushed it away, focusing on the task as Ryder recited his line at my back.

"Did Belinda have her breakfast this morning?"

"No. She wasn't hungry. I hope she's not coming down with something," I answered, resisting the urge to mention that she probably wasn't eating because she *couldn't*.

Leaning in closer, Ryder's back brushed mine.

I stiffened slightly, but relaxed quickly, telling myself I had to get over the aversion to our tight proximity. It was bound to continue for the entirety of the show, and the sooner I could school myself to accept it, the better off I'd be.

It only took five seconds for my new zen outlook to evaporate.

Wandering fingers descended the line of my side, and then, after only a brief pause, sought the inside of my thighs, brushing against the apex and making me jump enough to break the scene completely.

"Cut!"

Thankful for the reprieve, even if it meant I was the cause of the screw-up, I jumped to my feet and turned to face my offender.

"Touch me again and I'm going to slice a mouth into your penis, cut off your balls, and then feed them to it like a game of fucking Hungry Hungry Hippos."

"Howie," I heard Larry call. "Let me know when you're done here. I need to see Ryder in his dressing room."

"We're done," he responded, making me turn to him in question.

He shook his head slightly before looking to Ryder.

"Your dressing room with Larry. Go now."

After one last lingering dirty look, Ryder was gone and so were the others. Left with nothing to do and no one to ask for answers, I followed them off the set, headed for my dressing room right across the hall from Ryder's.

Chapter 6

"VIEWERS DON'T THINK YOU'RE genuine, Ryder." I could just make out Larry's muffled voice through the door.

Of course, Ryder's screaming reply was much easier to hear clearly. "Fucking genuine? I'm pretending to be someone else!"

Uncomfortable listening, I cringed, turning away from the door and running straight into Howie. His face was knowing but not censorious. If anything, he looked mildly amused.

Still, I felt the need to defend myself.

"Howie! I was just—"

"Eavesdropping."

My shoulders slumped in defeat. "Yeah."

His lips curled into a smile and slightly coffee-stained teeth dug into his bottom lip before coughing out one dry chuckle. "It's okay, Easie. The viewers don't like him, sure, but neither do I."

"You don't?" I questioned as innocently as possible. I hadn't said one word to anyone about my run-ins with Ryder. I didn't want to start problems. Now that I'd started to get money, I didn't think the show was such a joke anymore.

"Easie," he said softly, shaking his head. "I hear everything he says to you. The microphones pick it up."

As I thought back to all the things Ryder had said, my cheeks heated with embarrassment. Howie noticed.

"Don't be embarrassed," he commanded softly. "Listen, he's been harassing you, plain and simple. If I'd thought you couldn't handle yourself or he'd put you in a truly uncomfortable place, I would have done something about it sooner. These first few shows are really important for the future of the show—"

"Howie, I understand. I would never expect you to—"

"Easie. Let me finish."

I gave him a nod of understanding and a prompt to continue.

"As I said, the first few shows are important for the future of the show, but I know that the future of the show is important *for you*. That said, so is maintaining a professional environment. Especially on a show that walks such a thin line with subject matter like this one does. That's why when Larry approached me about the viewership statistics and Ryder's unfavorable perception in our own viewer survey, I agreed wholeheartedly that it was time to give the asshole the boot."

I couldn't stop a small grateful smile from creeping onto my face. I'd been in this business for seven years now, and I'd *never* met someone this honest and ethical. Howie really was like a Hollywood version of dear old dad.

"But I'll be honest," he whispered conspiratorially, "I was kind of enjoying listening to you put him in his place." He paused and smirked just slightly. "*Creatively.*"

The sound of wood splintering rang out like a gunshot as the door to Ryder's dressing room swung open and slammed into the wall no more than a foot from my body.

Instinctively, I jumped away, bumping into Howie and nearly knocking him down. I bent to help him recover, but didn't get the chance for long. Before I knew it, Ryder had me pinned to the wall behind me with a fierce, bruising grip on both of my arms. His fingertips pulled at my skin and crushed painfully into the muscle and bone underneath.

"What'd you say to them, you fucking bitch?!" he spat in my face, his own features contorted into a sincerely ugly, rage-driven version of themselves.

Thankfully, I didn't have enough time to really panic—to understand what was actually happening to me or the very real danger I was in.

"Fuck!" Larry swore from behind him, jumping into the fray and pulling Ryder off of me. "Call security!" he yelled, pinning Ryder to the opposite wall with some assistance from Howie. Howie may have looked inconspicuous, but watching him and Larry subdue Ryder together, it was clear neither of them were lacking in brute strength.

I noticed Ashley for the first time, her face stricken with fear as she pulled her cell phone out of her pocket and dialed the number for help at the opposite end of the hall.

We didn't have to wait long for security to arrive, but there was no doubt in my mind they were coming from the studio next door. There was no way in *hell* our fledgling show was paying for security.

Ryder's eyes scorched me, cutting through the people between us and spewing all of the world's hate.

Okay, maybe not the *entire* world's hate, but trust me, it was a lot.

I tried to look away, but couldn't seem to physically manage it until Howie got directly in my face and forced my eyes to him.

"Do you want to press charges?"

"No."

"*Easie.*"

Look, I know. I should have pressed charges, but honestly, I was over it. I wanted Ryder to be gone, and I wanted to figure out if there was a way to salvage the show. Charges meant hours of questions and disruption.

A glance down the hall had me finding Ashley in Larry's arms, but for once, I wasn't weirded out. I was just happy she had the comfort.

"No, Howie. Thanks, but there aren't even visible bruises on my arms," I told him, flashing them in front of his face as evidence. I had always been a delayed bruiser. "I'm fine."

"Alright." He didn't like it, but *alright*. As much as I liked Howie, he wasn't anything more to me than a director. Maybe, if I really pushed it, a friend. So he didn't have the proprietary clout needed to change my mind.

"What are we going to do?" Ashley asked Larry as security hustled an embarrassed looking Ryder past them.

"We're gonna dig out the old casting resumes, and we're gonna get someone else in here. This episode's a wrap, so it will air as planned. Any future episodes will feature someone else."

"Were there any other guys you seriously considered casting?" I asked in an effort to be helpful.

Larry speared me with a look conveying he didn't want any of my help. Hard eyes, hunched shoulders, laser beams scorching through an imaginary bullet hole right between my eyes. You know the one.

Right.

Widening my eyes comically at Howie, I opted for the road much less traveled. You know, *not* poking the bear. Apparently getting slammed against a wall by a psychopath had me off of my game.

"Your dressing room. Now," Larry commanded, addressing me directly but meaning everyone.

"Whoa. Hold on there, compadre," I said with the palm of my right hand up and out toward him. "I understand your desire for expediency here, but I've got a deeper need for nicotine. I'll be in my dressing room in ten minutes."

Rattled by violence and rare work-related physical activity, Larry conceded to my needs quickly and without too much attitude. "Fine. You have ten minutes to char the inside of some of your most vital organs."

A smile formed on my face, cloaked in a cloud of laughter. I couldn't help it. For one of the first times on record, I'd actually found something Larry said funny rather than annoying. Go figure.

"I'll come with you," Ashley offered, and it was at that point I knew just how shaken up she was. She never offered to come with me when I smoked. Something about wanting to live to be one hundred and fifteen years old just so she could be on the news.

I'd told her it'd be much easier, and you know, efficient if she'd just go into acting now. She was bound to make it on TV at some point prior to aging a million years.

She'd laughed in my face. I'd given her the finger.

That was how things usually went down.

I didn't need her to come with me, but I also wasn't about to deny her whatever relaxation she was seeking.

"Well come on then," I called, ducking into my dressing room to grab my smokes out of my purse and heading straight down the narrow hall toward the outside.

Bright sunshine sank deep into my skin, cutting through the chill of the indoors and warming me from the inside out. I loved the reliability of Southern California weather. As much as I complained about the people and traffic, I could never find it in me to complain about the weather.

The flint of my lighter struck true at the first flick of my thumb, and the heat ate the paper back at the end of my cigarette instantly. Sounds of traffic bleated in the distance as I touched the tip to my lips and inhaled, but it didn't last long. My lungs surrendered to the weight of the ingested smoke immediately, and my brain turned off.

Nothing mattered but that moment, that hit of nicotine, and the ease of knowing my sister was safely at my side after one hell of an encounter.

"So . . ." she ventured slowly, wrecking all of that hard-earned calm with one, useless word. "What the hell was that about?"

"You know how it is. Larry fired Ryder, and he didn't take it well. Most men have mastered the skills it takes to cover their Neanderthal with makeup, but not all of them."

"That's not what I meant."

"Oh?" I asked, studying the flecks of orange and ash as the end of my cigarette dwindled to nothing.

"Easie. What the hell happened between the two of you that he thought his being fired was your fault?"

"Ash—"

"No, E. Answer me."

"God, you're a demanding little bitch these days."

"Yeah," she quipped, "You must be rubbing off on me."

"Ah, fuck, Ash. You know it's nothing," I avoided. "You know I can't get along with anyone."

"No," she disagreed strongly. "I don't know that. That's just what I tell you when I'm in the mood to throat punch you but I can't."

"Hah," I huffed in a chuckle. "Well, that's a creative way to torture me."

"Stop avoiding the subject, and tell me what the fuck is going on."

"Look. I'm telling you, it's nothing. Ryder was giving me a little bit of a hard time, and I was giving him one back. Honestly, it's nothing more than normal."

She shook her head. "This was obviously the right career choice for you. It's just a matter of time before you make it big."

"What? Why?"

She laughed cynically. "Because of that bullshit you just spewed. I've known you my entire life, and I still almost believe you."

"You believe me because it's the truth."

"No. I believe you because you're so good at lying that you believe that shit yourself."

Using it as a crutch, I clenched the damp paper of distraction between my lips and sucked hard.

Looking at the ground, Ashley shook her head again. But this time it was resigned. "Right. Well. Whatever." Turning abruptly, she pulled the door open and mumbled over the tight line of her frustrated shoulder. "I'll meet you inside." Ever the manager of my life, she checked her watch before instructing, "Two minutes," and disappearing into the darkness of inside.

My head lolled back, smacking into the brick of the building with the thud and punishing me the way I deserved. Sometimes I didn't know if my attempts to shelter Ashley from my problems actually protected her or just subjected her to a different torturous fate.

I took two final long drags before tossing my dirty habit to the ground and snuffing it with the toe of my shoe. Sunlight burned through the darkness my eyelids provided even before I opened my blue eyes.

One glance down confirmed what I already knew.

Purple and blue and positively mottled with lies and deceit, the skin of my arms told the story I was too scared to tell. The problems between Ryder and I had been more major than minor, and I'd carry the marks of his final encounter for days to come.

Larry rubbed at his forehead with the flat of his palm and glared at the resumes strewn across the table with disgust. "Nothing about this is working." After one quick pinch of his nose, his hand jumped to his neck, trying to vanquish his anger from the back as well as the front. " This is my ass on the line—"

"Like mine isn't?" I cut in on a protest, pulling at the sleeves of my strategically placed sweater. Ashley's eyes sliced to me on a hard glare.

"I'm not looking for commentary. Jesus Christ, Easie, for once, just *once,* stop giving me fucking heart palpitations and actually help me. You need this show's success, and, lucky me, so do I."

Obviously, the candidates presented so far weren't living up to snuff. I knew he hated it, but given the circumstances of the last dismissal, Larry was giving me an actual say in who I'd be working beside day in and day out.

At least, he had been. Something told me his patience was wearing thin.

"I can't take much more of this!"

Or maybe that something was just him. Voicing it over and over and over again. It was actually kind of starting to feel like listening to a broken record.

"What about that waiter from the other night?" Ashley ventured, breaking through our tension with a simple suggestion.

"The one at El Loco?"

She just looked at me. We both knew I knew who she was talking about. No other guy had made any kind of lasting impression, annoying or not.

"Are you fucking crazy? All that guy did was bust my balls all night."

And shake me up enough that my organs were still settling back into place two days later.

Larry's response was immediate. "He's hired."

Turning to Ashley with metaphorical murder in my eyes, mine wasn't much slower. "Disowned. Forever. Pack your bags."

"Technically," she pointed out, a smirk just starting to take shape on her annoyingly pretty face, "*You* live with *me*. My name is on the lease." At the narrowing of my eyes, she finished, "Good try, though."

Larry's laugh cut straight to my ears.

Ignoring him, I told my sister the truth. "I hate that you're the smart one."

"I know. I'd hate to be you too."

Somebody was pushing their luck today. Little bitch.

Good thing she was my favorite person in the world or I'd have really had to hurt her.

Hopeful faces stared at me from all around, a large group of people weary from the day and counting on me to end their pain hanging on my every word.

"Fine," I conceded against my will. "But you're going to ask him yourself."

"We'll ask him together."

Fucking fuck. I didn't like this. I didn't like this one bit.

The way he'd challenged me inside had been scary. But what I hadn't admitted was that the way he *hadn't* challenged me outside—the way he handled me gently, admitting to his shortcomings so easily—had been downright terrifying.

Chapter 7

I WAS GOING TO HAVE to start calling my sister Assley, or Rash-ley . . . or something equal parts demeaning and creative.

Sneaky little thing that she was had pulled a fast one on me, promising a team effort and then bailing at the last minute.

"I'll meet you there," she said. "I'll take the bus," she said. "I have an errand to run," *she said.*

Lies. Everything she said had been nothing but a giant lie until her call five minutes ago, when she'd finally told the truth. *"Yeah, I'm not gonna make it, but he liked you. You'll do fine all on your own. Let me know how it goes!"*

The demonic little voice in my head promised swift retribution.

But there was no turning back now.

I was already here. In the parking lot of El Loco. And the longer I sat out here, the more I feared being the victim of a carjacking.

It was now or never.

My door squealed loudly as I kicked it open, climbed up and out, and straightened my jean skirt down the line of my thighs.

Locking the door manually, I checked to make sure I had my key in hand, and then gave it a shove with my hip to slam it shut.

The idea of locking my car made me laugh, but it was all I had.

Unless I won the lottery—which wasn't likely since I didn't play—or got invited to star in the next Fifty Shades of Grey, I was pretty sure holding onto my piece of junk was my only current option.

A slapping rhythm took shape as I walked, courtesy of my flip flops, and an already heavy door felt downright immobile in my hand as my nerves swelled and swooped from the top of my head all the way to the soles of my feet.

It took a solid thirty seconds before my eyes adjusted to the lack of light, and by the time they finally did, a tall brunette woman stood waiting for my attention.

"Hey, you're finally looking at me," she noted. "That's cool."

"Yeah, sorry," I apologized, feeling less combative than normal. "It takes my eyes a while to adjust after being shocked by the light. Something about photophobia and light eyes."

She smiled.

"I'm not actually sure," I continued to bumble. "I kind of tuned out the doctor when he told me what the hell it meant."

Amusement lit the chocolate brown of her eyes as she asked, "Table for one?"

Coughing through my discomfort, I couldn't help but blush a little. "Uh, actually, I'm looking for someone."

She raised a mocking brow. I tried my best to ignore it.

"I'm not really sure about his schedule, but is, um, Anderson working by any chance?"

Her attitude changed from teasing to knowing.

"I see."

But she didn't see. She *really* didn't.

I floundered a little trying to convey just how much she didn't know.

"No, no, no . . . I mean, no."

"Right."

"No, I'm looking for him about work."

"Waitressing? Because he's not in charge of hiring—"

"No, no. Not waitressing. Um, acting. An acting opportunity."

"What's your name? I can tell him you were here," she offered, pulling a pen from her apron.

Fuuuuck. This had to be one of the most awkward experiences of my life.

"No. I mean, thanks. But I really need to speak to him now. Like, soon. The job is kind of time sensitive."

"Sure it is. A time sensitive, life or death acting job. I hear about those all the time."

Were those new bruises forming on my arms? Christ, this girl was beating the hell out of me.

Truth was, we probably would have been great friends under other circumstances. Ones where I had the luxury of time, and I didn't want to stab her in the eye.

"Do you know where he is or not?" I asked, done jumping through hoops.

"Manhattan Beach. Twenty-sixth street. Surfing."

Glancing down and pulling my watch from underneath the edge of my long sleeve, I cringed. Four o'clock on a weekday. "Manhattan Beach? It's gonna take me twenty years to get there."

She smirked and clicked the pen in her hand gleefully. "Yep."

Fuuuuck.

"Thanks." I guess.

"Yep," she said again with a gleam in her eye.

Backtracking swiftly, I shoved open the door and dug around in my bag for a cigarette on the way to my car. Clenching it and my lighter in one hand, I used the other to shove the key into the hole in the door and turn, yank the handle, and throw myself down into the seat.

My left hand turned circles, the crank of the window giving me my only exercise for the day, and my right fired the ignition. Foot on the brake, I lit my cigarette and placed it between my lips before shifting into reverse and backing out of my spot.

Just as I was flooring it out of the parking lot a thought occurred to me.

People have the ability to tell you things that aren't factual.

That fucking bitch better not have lied to me about his where-abouts. If she had, and I spent years of my precious life driving down to Manhattan Beach for nothing, I'd be coming up with the slowest, most painful way to murder her.

I mean, probably not.

I didn't think I'd do good in prison. But I'd imagine it a whole hell of a lot. It'd be like the film reel for *The Purge* up in this bitch.

Two hours and several road rage incidents on the 405 later, I finally arrived at the end of Twenty-Sixth Street in Manhattan Beach.

After I'd calmed down and driven for an hour, I realized that even if Miss Brunette Leggy Boobs-a-lot hadn't lied to me, there was still a distinct possibility that he would already be gone. I mean, how long did people stay and surf? I had absolutely no breadth of knowledge on the length of a session in this sport. Or any sport, for that matter.

Still, I knew that my reason for coming here was important, so I went through the motions, driving the rest of the way, climbing out of my car, and walking down onto the soft creamy sand to scan the water for someone I'd only met once.

Once.

One single encounter in a dark Mexican restaurant.

And yet, I spotted him in an instant.

Carrying his surfboard with his wetsuit half off and hanging from his naked hips, he took several sure steps away from the water, eyes focused intently on the sand.

The line of his jaw was strong and smooth, lending itself perfectly to the lingering salt and water that clung there, and the sight of him top-less was enough to break all of my focus. I couldn't tell you what the lines of his chest looked like, or how many hairs lived there. All I could tell you was that everything he was, everything he had, was enough to make my heart speed up and my brain function slow.

Slightly desperate and several hours into my journey at this point, I didn't hold back or think for even a second. Instead, I let my baser instincts take over and screamed like a madwoman.

"Anderson!"

Highly attuned to the the sound of his name, Anderson's wet hair swished up and over the top of his head, and his eyes met mine as his head jerked up.

My insecurities built as he studied me for several seconds, the fear that he didn't recognize or remember me taking hold for the first time all day.

I'd just *assumed* he would.

Wow. Note to self: Lower expectations to the bottom of the barrel.

That way, when someone pokes a hole in the bottom and drains the water out from under you, you won't have far to fall. And you'll have a supply of water until the very end.

All of this is assuming you're a fish, of course. Prolonged water submersion is presumably bad for humans.

So, basically, my philosophical wisdom is a little sketchy on this one. Do your own research.

Finally, his feet moved with his eyes, in the direction of me, and he broke his torturous vow of silence.

"Easie?"

"Oh, cool," I murmured aloud by accident. "You do remember me."

His toes stopped two feet shy of mine and one corner of his mouth rose into the meat of his cheek. "Of course I remember you. Surprised to see you though. I guess that whole *I'll never run into you randomly* thing isn't holding much water."

Oops. He didn't realize I was stalking him.

Yikes. Things were about to get awkward.

"Yeah, about that. This isn't randomly. I came here looking for you."

"You came here looking for me?"

"Uh, yeah. That's what I just said."

"Why in the hell were you looking for me?"

Before I could answer, another question formed in his head and spewed out. "How are you looking for me here? I mean, *how* did you know to look for me *here?*"

Suddenly, I was regretting not getting Miss Brunette Leggy Boobs-a-lot's real name. It probably would have been helpful in the next two minutes of my life.

I decided on being vaguely evasive.

"I went to the restaurant."

"El Loco?"

My look clearly said *really?*

"Jesus. Sorry. You're throwing me off being here. I feel like I can barely speak English."

"Qué?"

"What?"

"Exactly."

"Easie."

"Sorry." I shrugged. "It was fun while you allowed it though."

"So . . . how did you find me?"

Ah, shit.

"A girl . . . woman . . . whatever . . . at the restaurant."

"Tammy?"

"Brown hair. Long legs."

He nodded in understanding, confirming, "Tammy." Apparently, he'd noticed Tammy's legs.

Great. Now that we'd officially confirmed the completely inconsequential girl's name, we could move on.

Oh yuck.

What a gross taste in my mouth. Tangy. Green. A little earthy, like lettuce.

Hmm. I guess jealousy is considered roughage.

"Easie?"

"Yeah?"

"What did you want?" he asked, reminding me of the entire hodge-podge of drama that had brought me here.

Man, today was a long fucking day. Filming, firing, physical abuse, verbal berating from Larry as he caved to the pressure of finding a new lead, getting shanghaied by Ashley, verbal volleyball with Tammy, driving millions of miles to Manhattan Beach, and finally, now, putting my emotional boundaries through the paces by talking to the one guy to make any kind of lasting impression on me in the last four plus years.

Yeah. Long day.

"Oh, I'm here about a part."

"A part?"

"My, my, we're big on repeating things today."

Ignoring my smart aleck remark, he moved on. "For me?"

"Yeah. On a show I just started."

"Quirks and Kinks?"

Agog, my head lurched forward and my neck stretched out like an ostrich. A really fucking surprised ostrich. "Excuse me?"

He shrugged, nonplussed. "I caught the first episode."

"Only one episode has aired."

"Okay," he conceded. "So I caught the only episode."

"So you saw—" I started, thinking about the ridiculous getup I'd donned for most of the show.

"Sure did," he confirmed with a cute wag of his brows and rock up onto the balls of his feet.

"Greeaattt."

"Stop. You were great."

I scoffed.

"No, seriously. It takes serious talent to depict something so far out of your comfort zone."

My head tilted to one side in question. "How do you know clown-sex is outside of my comfort zone?"

I said it as joke thinking that clown-sex was outside of most peo-ple's comfort zones, but he took it seriously, never taking his eyes off of mine as he spoke. "By the way you reacted when I told you I saw it."

Breaking the intensity of his eye contact, I rummaged in my bag and pulled out the one thing guaranteed to make him like me less.

His eyes flared as I lit it up, but he didn't say anything.

When neither of us had broken the silence for a full minute, I took the initiative to bring things back on point.

"So . . . the show?"

He looked from my cigarette to me and back again, and then huffed out one big breath. "I'll take a meeting."

"You'll do it?" I asked, trying to speed up his decision process. Or just trick him into agreeing. One way or the other.

"No," he chuckled. "That's not what I said. I'll come talk to the producer, and you, if you want, and if I like what everyone has to say, then I'll do it."

"Fine," I conceded. "That's better than nothing."

"When?"

I knew Larry would want me to say right now, this minute, there's no time to spare, blah, blah, blah. But I was tired. I didn't have it in me. So I answered the way I wanted to.

"First thing tomorrow morning."

Okay, if I had *really* conceded to my wants, I probably would have said never. But this was the best I was going to get.

Staring contests had nothing on us as we sat there, soaking in our awkwardness for all of Manhattan Beach's onlookers to see. The urge to leave battled with the pull to stay, but in the end only an uncomfort-able handshake won.

"So, um, I'll text you directions and stuff," I babbled, turning quickly and stumbling in the sand as I tried to make a quick getaway.

Change is always hard, but if the transition from skilled speaker to mumbling idiot was a permanent one, I was going to have to commit myself. It had only been a few days of living like this, and I was already beyond sick of it.

"What's your number?" he called after me. "I'll text you mine."

Right. A number. That'd be helpful.

As I walked back toward him to avoid yelling my number across the beach, I moaned. Giving into my desire to be close to him felt too satisfying, and I didn't like not being in control of it. Something about him sucked me in. I hadn't figured out which part it was, but I was pretty sure he was hiding magnets in those bumps he was pretending were abs. When I launched my formal investigation, I planned to start there.

"Sorry," I mumbled when I got back within range. "I forgot."

He smiled and shrugged, but neither one of us said anything.

Of course, I was the one who was *supposed* to be saying something.

"And?" he prompted when I didn't snap out of it fast enough.

Fuck. Stop thinking about abs, Easie. Like, for real.

"It's 213–418–8487."

"Eight, four, eight, seven?" he asked, reciting the last four digits to confirm.

"Yep."

"Was it by any chance a guy who assigned your number to you when you got it?"

"Assigned my number?"

"Yeah. When you first got the phone, did a guy help you?"

Thinking back more than five years into the past was seriously not my strong suit. "Um, yeah. I mean, I think. It was a while ago. Why?"

"Because the last four digits of your number spell tits."

Flicking my cigarette to the sand below, I stepped back again, turning to leave and refusing to look back. Knowing his mind had picked something like that up on the fly had too many conflicting thoughts fighting for supremacy in my brain, and the chaos that ensued had it threatening to explode. The only logical thing to do was ignore him.

He chuckled behind me, calling out, "I'll see you tomorrow," and at the sound of his voice, my resolve to avoid looking back crumbled.

Leaning casually into his board stuck standing in the sand, a smirk lit his face and my discarded butt graced his hand. Twirling it mindlessly, he watched as I walked away.

By the time I climbed into my Honda and slumped into the seat with fatigue, the screen of my phone lit up with a message from an unknown number.

Don't worry, Litterbug. I'll clean up after you . . . this time. See you tomorrow.

Chapter 8

B Y THE TIME ASHLEY and I walked into the studio the next morning, my system was experiencing caffeine and nicotine overload. Fidgeting, rolling bouts of nausea, and the occasional stench permeation from the pores of my saturated skin.

Sleep had proven elusive, the threat of the day to come shining like a spotlight directly into my brain.

For the first two hours, I tossed and turned and worried about how I would get along with Anderson. Namely, if I would get along with him *too* well.

But when two hours of lying awake turned into three, I realized that the previous two hours of nerves had been wasted. Anderson hadn't even agreed to do the fucking show yet. So, for an entire hour, I nagged myself about my needless nagging.

By the time I'd been awake for a full three hours, I gave up on the prospect of bed and channeled all of my energy into smoking. The night air of my balcony had a chill, but instead of taking that as a sign that I should ease up on my lungs, I strapped on a coat and slippers and lit up again.

Chain smoking, for as bad as it was for my health and odor, did its job as intended and allowed my brain to rest from three o'clock to four.

Four o'clock seemed too late for sleeping. So, I didn't.

I did manage a lingering, hot shower and about fifty cups of coffee though. So there was that.

"Good morning," Larry greeted cheerfully as he busted into my dressing room without a knock.

"Good morning," Ashley recited back at the same time that I complained, "Thanks for the warning. What if I had been naked?"

"I guess I would have lost my eyesight," Larry quipped, smiling at Ashley instead of looking at me.

A small laugh bubbled in my throat, but I forced it back down with a rough swallow.

What was happening? Was I actually starting to *like* Larry?

Not *like him,* like him. Tolerate him. Find amusement in his arrogance.

His phone chirped in his hand and he dragged his eyes away from my sister so he could look at it. "Excellent." Ashley and I looked on in question until he filled us in. "That was Bill out at the gate. Anderson Evans has arrived and should be on scene shortly."

Evans. His last name was Evans.

Butterfly wings skimmed the inside of my stomach as Larry focused on me.

"Quick, Easie! Cover your horns."

This time the humor hit me harder, and a laugh escaped before I could stop it.

Shit! I was. I was starting to like Larry.

God. This was the beginning of the end.

"Come on, we'll meet in the empty dressing room," Larry instructed, waving me out of my chair from a distance and helping my sister up from hers with a hand.

Instinctually, I wanted to argue and tell him I needed a smoke break first, but after last night, even I couldn't stomach it.

The three of us filed across the hall, with Ashley in front and Larry bringing up the rear. While I slumped down into a chair at the table and

Ashley found a seat on the couch, Larry stood sentry in the open door and waited. His toe tapped in opposition to the calm line of his body.

We were all on edge and would be a lot better off when all of this was over. With a shooting schedule of one episode a week, and only the same amount of downtime before it aired, that didn't leave us much room for problems.

And we were already swimming in them.

I'd imagine other shows shot a bunch of episodes at a time, but we didn't have the budget nor the guarantee. We lived or died by each episode, and wasting time on something that would never see the light of day wasn't in the network's plan.

With the second and final episode starring Ryder scheduled to air tomorrow night, we needed to be filming for next week today. Editing would have to be done, and it was always ideal to leave time for re-shoots. If the cutting room floor was left empty and uncluttered, some-times a second attempt or additional shot was necessary.

When Larry straightened to full height from leaning, I knew An-derson had entered the hall and was making what was surely an attrac-tive approach.

I thanked the attraction gods for the fact that I couldn't see him. All that would bring was a meltdown, and as far as I knew, a pile of goo didn't really do well in a conference type of situation.

"Anderson," I heard as a tan hand came into view. Larry reached out and clasped it, giving it a professional yet welcoming shake.

I'd gotten no shake at my meeting. I'd gotten dissed.

Maybe I didn't like Larry.

"Come in, come in," Larry cooed. "Have a seat."

Green eyes caught mine and smiled, the lush, dark lashes around them plumping with the slight squeezing of each corner.

"You know—" Larry started in an attempt to perform some sort of formal reintroduction.

Anderson didn't let him finish.

"Easie." The sound of my name on his tongue seemed sensual,

and as soon as the second and final syllable rolled off of his tongue, his smiling eyes seeped all the way down to his lips.

Scooting the chair out beside me and settling into it gracefully, Anderson pulled a stylish black ball cap off of his head and a pair of gold-rimmed aviator sunglasses out of the front of his shirt and tossed them gently to the worn surface of the old kitchen table.

I mentioned that the show was low budget. Accordingly, furniture in our dressing rooms was the thrift store variety.

"Ashley," he said in greeting, squishing his nose in a way I feared would ruin me forever. It was honestly the most endearingly adorable thing I'd ever seen. Not necessarily the most masculine of descriptions, my words did the unique, intensely male action no justice. But I didn't mind. Anderson's nose scrunch was the kind of trait that God purposely made indescribable, because if I couldn't describe it to anyone else, that made it easier to keep it all my own.

Shutting the door softly, Larry made his way over to us and took a seat on the other side of the table while I signaled Ashley to join us. I had kind of thought that Howie would be attending the meeting as well, but so far there hadn't been any sign of him.

As if she was reading everyone's minds, Ashley waved me off with a shake of her head and flipped a hand out to indicate I should turn my attention to the now closed door.

Almost immediately it opened, revealing a t-shirt wearing Howie carrying a doughnut in his teeth, a bag in one hand, and a folder in the other.

Okay, I was officially impressed.

And frightened. Really and truly frightened.

"How did you do that?" I mouthed to Ashley, curious as to exactly when she'd become clairvoyant.

She shook her head and giggled, a soft tinkly noise that had Larry turning into the back of his chair to witness it. Oh yeah, there was definitely something going on there.

When I brought my attention back to the table, weighty eyes bored holes into the side of my face. Unable to resist the call of his scrutiny, I flicked my eyes to the side and brought Anderson into view.

Warm and watchful, the features of his face transformed into a mere venue for his eyes. I could see everything there, but an intense sense of longing shined the brightest. Open as they were, they lacked the whole story, thus I was at loss for the cause of such a desperate emotion.

"Sorry I'm late," Howie apologized as soon as he set his belongings on the table and freed the doughnut from his mouth.

I shrugged and smiled, earning a wink from Howie that had Anderson looking curiously between us. I could see how a wink from a guy who looked like Howie, in a power position like Howie, might look weird. But it wasn't. After what had happened yesterday, it was just his way of telling me that he'd look out for me with Anderson.

I sighed to myself.

If only my problems with Anderson could be solved by protective intervention.

Wiping glaze crumbs off of his hand with the leg of his pants, Howie outstretched his hand to Anderson and shook. "Nice to meet you, Anderson. Howie Plenson."

"Plenson?" Anderson asked with interest, doing a good job of ignoring the fact that his director had just given him the crumb hand. "Any relation to Ansel Plenson?"

Howie smiled proudly. "He's my father."

"Wow!" Anderson breathed excitedly. "He's one of the greatest directors who's ever lived."

"I'm sure he'd appreciate your opinion," Howie chuckled good-naturedly.

I had no idea who Ansel Plenson was. Obviously, I was slacking in my research.

Read: I hadn't done any.

I wondered if I could pull up Google on my phone under the table without anyone noticing.

Probably not.

Anderson's eyes slid to me momentarily, took in my face, and then snapped back over to Howie.

"*Gypsy's Myth. The Promise of Paxton.* They're pop culture classics. I'm sure I'm not the only one with a favorable opinion," he prompted, intentionally feeding me not only the titles of Ansel's better known films, but an opportunity to contribute.

My brain immediately jumped into a fantasy reel of ways to pay him back, but due to their extremely sexual nature, I was forced to rate them all NS-WT. Not safe—wishful thinking. My very own version of NC-17.

"Definitely not. Everybody knows he's the best," I chirped, smiling slightly when Howie's amused look told me he knew I was full of shit—and didn't care.

Larry didn't coddle me quite as much, rolling his eyes at my obvious ignorance.

"Okay, Anderson. Let's get down the facts. None of us are here to bullshit you. We need to cast this role, and we need to do it quick. *But,*" he emphasized, "after an incident involving Easie yesterday, we need to make sure to do it right."

Halfway through his speech, I started threatening to slit his throat. Or gave him the universal sign for shut the hell up. One or the other.

Maybe both.

But he didn't listen, and as soon as my name and the word incident came together, all hope of moving forward was delayed once again.

"What incident?" Anderson asked, his face a stony mask, completely devoid of all traces of happy. I just knew he would be the type of guy to go all crazy in the face of any sign of female mistreatment.

Not that this was a bad thing, obviously. I just didn't have the normal time or energy to deal with it.

"Seriously, it was no big deal."

Howie, Larry, and Ashley all piped up with some version of, "Um, yeah it was."

"Gahhh," I whined, losing all pretense of propriety and timing and blurting it all out. "Ryder was an asshole, okay? From the moment I met him until the time he got dragged out of here yesterday, he was all over me. Saying fucked up shit and touching me without my permission. After he got fired, he pretty much assumed I'd ratted him out."

"You fucking should have," Larry barked, enormously angry now that he had all of indelicately delivered facts.

"Yeah, well, whatever. It's over now."

"Damn right it is," Anderson declared.

"Oh come on. Stop. All of you stop. Put away all of your protective penises before you start a party." Three surprised faces jumped away from me slightly as their chins jerked back, and Ashley laughed in the background. "It's done because he's gone. Let's leave it at that and move the hell on. We have a show to shoot. Am I the only one who seems to remember that?"

"Anderson, did you have questions—" Howie started to ask as soon as he recovered from my one woman show.

"I did. I don't anymore."

My eyes narrowed, but I didn't get a chance to say anything.

"Great! I've got your contract right here," Larry offered, practically pulling the paper out of thin air and sliding it across the table for Anderson to sign.

Mysterious green eyes flicked to mine once, ever so briefly, before grabbing Larry's pen and signing his life away to a messed up show and endless hours at my side.

He'd seemed like he needed to be wooed on the beach, and the change of tune and easy concession of this morning was completely disconcerting.

"That was fast," I accused, pulling his eyes from the paper and over to mine once more.

"Sometimes . . . you just know."

Powerful and foreboding, his words swirled and swooped through my chest, squeezing my heart when they got to it and forcing it to pump faster.

"I'll go rally the troops," Howie offered, scooting his chair back from the table quickly and shoving the entire last half of his doughnut in his mouth.

I tried not to smile at how ridiculous he was, but for all my effort, I still failed. He was just so lovable.

Anderson watched me watch him, a smile of his own lengthening the line of his nose and enlarging the volume of his cheeks.

"He seems like a good guy," he noted as Ashley and Larry quietly followed him.

Apparently, nobody was actually that protective of me. They'd all left me alone in a room with a strange man.

I shrugged, answering honestly. "I wouldn't know. Not really anyway. But I do know that he's been good to me, and he's taken an otherwise mockery of a show pretty seriously."

Intrigued, his head tilted to the side in question. "What do you mean 'mockery of a show'?"

Sensitive to his tone, I tried to defend myself and my meaning. "It's a show about people's fetishes and idiosyncrasies. It exploits people's quirks as a means to entertain the masses."

"Huh," Anderson hummed thoughtfully, pursing his lips and nodding to himself.

"Huh? What are you huh-ing?"

"Nothing."

"No, not nothing, that huh meant something," I demanded, poking a finger in the direction of his chest.

"Fine," he chuckled, raising his hands in surrender. "I was just surprised to hear you harboring such a judgmental point of view is all."

"Judgmental?" I shrieked, alerting all of the stray cats in the neighborhood that a party was about to commence. "How on earth is what I said judgmental?"

A smirk settled onto his face as he spoke, but I couldn't see it. All I could hear were his words. "It's not what you said, it's how you said it."

Christ.

Unable to resist mocking him, I patted my crotch explicitly, rooting around and searching for something I knew I wouldn't actually find.

"What are you doing?" he asked, his eyes drawn unavoidably to my hands.

"Checking to see if I have a penis," I explained.

His eyes squinted with amusement and his chin jerked back. "What?"

"I thought we'd pulled a Freaky Friday moment back there with your extreme chick logic. If you were so obviously inhabiting a female body, I figured I must have become a man."

Rolling his eyes, he stepped toward me dramatically, grabbing my hand and squeezing.

And officially touching me for the very first time.

Okayyy, holy shit. There was a moment happening, people. Sparks were definitely involved.

"We should hug," he blurted out, completely changing the subject and staring at me in a way that scrambled my mind.

No, no we shouldn't. My mind was an absolute minefield of muck, but I knew one thing with absolute certainty. Hugging was one of the last things we should be doing.

Of course, I didn't tell him that. Instead, I asked, "We should?" and mentally slapped myself as I felt my eyes going all doe-like with female stupidity.

He gave me a self-assured nod, hypnotizing me even further with his eyes and good looks and gentle voice and generally comforting disposition. Damn him. "Definitely."

"Okay."

He stepped toward me even closer, imposing chest and arms closing in on me steadily, ready to commence, when my anxiety spoke up again. "Um, just as a, like, reminder and stuff, why is it that we should hug again?"

He smiled a sexy smile, the edge of his top teeth cutting minutely into his plump bottom lip, and tucked a loose strand of hair behind my ear.

"We're going to be in a lot of intimate situations today. Don't you think it'd be better to get acquainted with touching one another now rather than on camera in front of hundreds of thousands of people?"

Were that many people actually watching this show?

"Right, right, good idea," I pretended. "I remember now."

Logical as his reasoning was, it meant nothing to me. Right then, in that moment, with his minty, sweet, musky smell enveloping me and threatening to never let go—and influence potentially stupid actions—I thought hugging was a monumentally *bad* idea.

But I'd built most of my life on bad ideas, and I wasn't about to stop now.

Lifting up onto my toes and raising my arms in time, I wrapped myself up around his shoulders, settling my nose into his neck like it was meant to go there. He was tall to my short, but his strong arms wrapped comfortably around the low line of my waist and lifted, pulling my already straining toes off the ground and seating the front of my body firmly against his.

It wasn't vulgar or explicit in any of the usual ways, but I felt every inch of his body that lined mine as if it were a piece of snug, knit clothing. It didn't smother or suffocate, but instead supported and hugged all of the places that most desired it.

I wasn't sure how much time had elapsed or how many gulps of Anderson filled air I'd sucked into my lungs when he finally set me on my own feet and untwined his limbs from around me.

Refusing to believe that a bereft longing in his absence was the cause of my resulting shiver, I focused on the temperature.

There was a fucking draft in this room. Surely that was the reason I now felt all cold and trembly.

"Right. Yes. Okay. Good hugging," he stuttered as he backed slowly toward the door. "See you out there."

I managed only a nod and awkward salute before slumping down and free-falling into the chair behind me.

Orrrr . . . sprawling ass over face on the floor.

Fuck! *Ow.* I could have sworn there was a chair behind me.

This was not good. One hug and I was in serious danger of injuring myself.

Shallowly, I prayed, asking God to give Anderson some kind of abnormality or imperfection. I'd take anything, but for some reason, all I could picture was a third nipple.

Chapter 9

GETTING DRESSED DIDN'T TAKE long and makeup didn't take much longer. Which was good. I had enough anxiety in my body to fill an entire day's worth of time. That didn't leave much time for anything else.

The script sat unread in my lap, words blurring together from one into the other, none of it actually registering in my hormone addled brain. Honestly, I was a little mad at myself for reacting so strongly to a stupid hug, but I hadn't had sex in years. Apparently, all that deprivation had heightened my sensitivity.

Deprivation *and* sexy, green-eyed men.

"Hah!" I laughed out loud, scaring the people around me with the transition of my one woman conversation from internal to external. "Well, that makes perfect sense. Kryptonite is fucking green."

And on that note, it was cigarette time.

Jumping from my chair in the makeup room, I jogged toward my dressing room until I got tired and then succumbed to a slow walk. It was an agonizing twenty step journey.

One, lonely cigarette sat waiting in my pack when I found it in my purse, but it was all I needed for the time being.

Grabbing my lighter, I headed back in the direction I had just come, out the door, back down the hall past the makeup room and toward the exit. Ashley turned the corner from the set, opened her mouth to ask me where I was going, and then noticed the contents of my hand.

"Don't be long," she instructed instead of questioning me. "Howie wants everyone on set in fifteen minutes."

"No problem," I agreed, lengthening my stride to avoid running into anyone else before I found the solace of the outdoors.

Sunlight poured into my brain with the snap of a door handle, and my free hand came up palm out to shield my extra-sensitive eyes.

Not expecting to run into anyone out there, I didn't check my surroundings before turning to the building to look away from the sun and lighting up my waiting cigarette.

"Ahh!" I screamed at the feel of a foreign hand on my shoulder, jumping and turning and very nearly dropping my one and only smoke on the dirty ass ground.

"Jesus Christopher!" I screamed at the sun-shadowed figure in front of me. "I almost fucking dropped it!"

"Good!" Anderson snapped, turning me around so that he was facing the sun. Now that the sun wasn't in my eyes I could see every single one of his angry features. Aviator sunglasses sat perched atop his cute nose, and a single bead of sweat was starting to form at the apex of his hairline.

"What's your deal? If you don't like my smoking, go somewhere else!"

Aggravation tightened the circumference of my veins, forcing my muscles to tense in reaction. Jesus. Maybe swooning over him wasn't going to be a problem. I couldn't take it if he tried to nag me every day of my life.

Clenching his eyes tight, he seemed to reboot.

"You're right. God, I'm sorry. You just caught me out here . . ." he started to apologize, fading out inexplicably mid-sentence.

I tried to figure out the answer on my own, but no matter how hard I looked, I couldn't seem to find him sporting any contraband.

"I caught you out here what?" I asked, but he waved me off with a shake of his head.

When he didn't answer, I started guessing. "I caught you out here . . . playing with barbie dolls?"

He smiled. "No."

"Jerking off?"

"Hah!" he laughed. "No."

"Torturing kittens?"

With a shake of his head, he rejected that too.

"Well, you're gonna have to help me out here. I've plum run out of guesses."

He bit into his bottom lip, let his head roll back on his shoulders. Roughed up his perfectly styled hair enough to piss off the hair people. "Thinking. I was thinking . . . God," he struggled to admit. "I was remembering."

"Remembering what?" I dug, tilting my head to the side.

"College," he answered with a self-deprecating snort. "I was remembering what it was like to be in college."

"Okayyyy," I replied, drawing out my word for a lack of anything else to say. College didn't seem like some excruciatingly painful experience, but I wouldn't really know.

Backing up against the building with my cigarette at my side to keep the smoke out of his eyes, I admitted, "I never went to college."

"No?" Anderson asked with relief, turning and leaning against the building next to me.

"Nope," I confirmed with a shake of my head, looking down at the ground to hide my slight blush of embarrassment.

"Hey," he called, bringing my eyes from the ground to his with one word. "College isn't for everyone, you know?"

"Ha," I laughed without humor. "Try telling that to my parents."

"They wanted you to go I guess."

"Oh yeah."

"Seems like they *really* wanted you to go."

"They did. They *do,*" I corrected myself.

"They still want you to go?"

"Yeah," I nodded, too busy talking to smoke. Instead, I watched as the paper slowly turned to ash, embers and heat eating it away. "They keep telling me it's never too late."

"It isn't."

"Yeah, I know. Except I don't *want* to go. This is it for me, you know?" I lifted my eyes and turned my head to the side to look directly at him. "I know I don't have a lot of fame, or even a lot of success, but doing this, even struggling like I am, it feels right. Do you know what I mean?"

Slowly, he nodded, the line of his throat seeming to bob with emotion. "Even if all you do is this right here, it'll be worth the effort."

"Exactly," I agreed, feeling an indescribable warmth claw its way up my throat with the knowledge that he got it.

"This . . . difference of opinion. Has it hurt your relationship with your parents?"

"I don't know. I mean, it hasn't changed my opinion of them or their opinion of me, if that's what you mean. But they're disappointed. I guess they didn't really see it coming."

He pitched his head to the side in question, studied me closer. I buckled pretty easily under the pressure.

"They had me really young. There was a lot of pressure to raise me right, give me all of the opportunities they never had. That kind of thing. I worked pretty hard to be everything they wanted me to be."

"Until," he surmised with a raise of his brows.

"Yep," I nodded. "Until. Total dirty word in the Reynolds family. Everything was great *until* they got pregnant with me at sixteen. I was the perfect daughter *until* I told them I didn't want to go to college. They still had one chance to raise one kid right *until* Ashley told them she wanted to come work for me."

"That's a lot of 'untils'."

"It sure is," I agreed, looking down again and catching a glimpse of the time on his watch. "Oh shit."

I dropped my unsmoked cigarette to the ground and stubbed it out. "What?"

"We've gotta go now if we don't want to hear an earful. We're supposed to be on set in two minutes."

Putting both of his palms to the bricks he pushed to stand up, only to snap right back.

"What the hell?"

Trying again, he was served the same result.

"Hold on," I instructed, leaning around him to look at the wall. *Aha.*

"Your shirt is stuck to the bricks."

Back and forth, back and forth, his head went from side to side trying to find a way to see his back. It wasn't happening.

"We're just going to have to take it off. It'll be a hell of a lot easier to get it detached."

Not thinking, and certainly not protecting myself, I reached for his buttons, working them out of their holes until I'd gotten all six of them. Sliding my hands inside, I officially lost my mind.

I was undressing him.

When I opened his shirt, all my twisted dreams came true, the tight peak of a misplaced nipple winking slyly at me from the center of his chest.

I rubbed my eye with the heal of my hand and blinked rapidly, trying to bring my wandering imagination back to reality.

No matter what I did, it wouldn't disappear.

Reaching out as though of a mind of its own, my thumb tweaked it, just barely scraping over the top edge. "You really have a third nipple," I murmured more to myself than to him.

"Uh, yeah," he confirmed matter-of-factly. Blasé. La di da. Like people had third nipples every day.

God, what did I know? Maybe they did.

Studying me more closely as I continued to fondle him, he asked,

"Do you not read the script at all?"

"Huh?" I was distracted.

"The script," he repeated, knocking my hand away, sliding the sleeves from his arms, and turning to the wall to work on untangling the fabric.

Bye, bye, you strange glimpse of heaven, I mentally told his disfigured chest.

"It's all about how Miranda likes to do all kinds of interesting shit to Gary's nipple." My eyes shot from the phantom image of his naked chest up to his eyes. He'd obviously gotten his shirt free and slid it back on while I was busy fantasizing. "His *third* nipple."

Right. *Gary's* third nipple. Not Anderson's.

Fuck, I was losing my mind.

"Actually," he amended, "It's about people with minor physical deformities finding comfort and relief from persecution in their lovemaking with similarly unconventional people. Miranda's passion for Gary's third nipple is only one of the scenarios."

I just stared. Dumbfounded. Fucking *impressed.* I certainly hadn't gleaned that interpretation from the damn thing. Of course, as he'd pointed out, I hadn't actually read it.

"Come on," I reminded him. "*We're* going to be persecuted if we don't get our asses inside!"

Chuckling, he held open the door and gestured for me to proceed him inside. If I'd had time, I might have stopped to swoon over the existence of chivalry.

But I didn't.

So, instead, I ran down the hall, ducked quickly into my dressing room to grab my script, and ran the rest of the way to the set to find Anderson already there like an overachiever.

I bet he already knew his lines too.

"Alright, kids," Howie called, just as I made it to their huddle. "We're going to start with the physical stuff today and come back to the intro. Gary and Miranda have to leave early, and I want to be able to consult with them during their scene if we need to." Turning to Anderson, he asked, "You ready?"

When he replied with a respectful, "Yes, sir," Howie and I both smiled.

Talk about a noticeable difference.

"What about you?" he asked me, ruining my happy bubble.

"Um—"

Anderson saw me struggling, and tried to step in.

"Sir, you see, she was outside . . . um . . . rescuing a bird?"

It was sweet.

And really fucking unbelievable.

I shook my head in shame.

"What?" Howie asked, understandably confused.

"Torturing kittens?" Anderson offered, making me laugh at one of the worst possible times.

Howie's eyes studied me, and I broke down. "I'm not *completely* ready. But I will be."

Amused by something I couldn't figure out, he winked and let me off of the hook. "Good enough for me."

"We'll start with the lovemaking," he offered. "All you have to do is lay there and react to him."

I raised my brows and laughed. "I'm pretty sure he expects more effort than that."

Anderson's mouth turned up at the ends and the black of his eyes ate away at the green. His body promised me things—things I wasn't ready to know; that the extra effort would be worth it.

Man, I was in trouble.

Hot, raspy breaths bathed the line of my spine all the way to the dented dimples seated just above my butt. Anderson blew soft puffs of air into the hollow between them, and then shocked my system with a touch of his lips.

I knew it was fake, and I knew all of this action was meant to culminate at my very imaginary tail. I *knew* it shouldn't be turning me on, but sweet baby Jesus it was. It really fucking was.

I couldn't discriminate properly between real and make believe, and my sluggish, aroused mind struggled to remember that the man behind me was no more enjoying his actions than I should be. He was acting. Doing our *job*. He was just really freaking good at it.

"Love this part of you," he murmured into my skin, further igniting my senses and making me push my ass toward his face. If I had an elongated tailbone, and needed it serviced, Gary would be the man for the fucking job. At least, Anderson's interpretation of him would be.

Stretching for it, yearning for it, I clenched my hands in the sheets and threw my head back in—

"Cut!"

Fuck.

Eyes shut tight, my forehead dropped to the surface of the bed below me, and if I wasn't mistaken, Anderson's forehead briefly did the same on my back.

"Okay. We got that, guys. Change positions so we can do the take of Miranda's attention to Gary," Howie instructed like my world wasn't tilting even further on its axis. Becoming one with my character was part of the process, but my body was taking it an entire step further.

Anderson moved gently, careful to manage his weight as he picked his body up off of my legs and shifted to laying on his back next to me. Crawling into position straddling him, I avoided his eyes, afraid of seeing something I didn't like.

The rational part of my brain claimed that signs of real arousal were what I didn't want to see, but I knew deep inside of myself that the absence of it was what I actually feared.

"Great. Yep," Howie interrupted my thoughts. "Positioning looks great, Easie. Just start with the kiss and work your way down slowly, okay? We'd rather have more material than less, so take your time."

"Can I get a lighting adjustment?!" he yelled off to the side, causing a couple of guys to scurry into action from the wings and me to have to sit straddling Anderson in awkwardness.

"So . . ." I offered, finally trailing my eyes up to his. Warmth bathed my skin from the affection I found waiting there as he studied me. His eyes didn't meet mine, but rather, moved from one of my features to the next, starting at the line of my neck, working their way up my throat, and settling at the middle of my mouth.

"So . . ." he echoed, scrunching his nose in that adorable way before focusing his eyes on mine.

With the conversational ball back in my court, I struggled to make something witty out of the nexus of chaotic thoughts running laps around my brain. Howie and the set gods took pity on me.

"Okay, guys. We're ready again." After allowing a few seconds for the set to go silent—and giving me time to take a deep, cleansing breath—he gave us the green light.

"And action!"

Reaching up before I could lean forward, Anderson fingered the ends of my long, fake brown hair. I'd seen him notice the obvious change when we were outside, but we'd gotten too involved in other things to have time to mention it.

He looked at me longingly, the way Gary needed to look at Miranda and the way she would want it. But for me, it got me dangerously lost in the moment.

My eyes held his as I leaned forward, hovering just above his mouth momentarily. Something happened in those fleeting seconds, as our attention focused on one another. Electricity surged through my chest forcing a deeper, darker breath, and his free hand tightened noticeably on my waist.

Too overwhelmed by the power of the sight of him, I clenched my eyes tight and touched my mouth to his. Partially conscious of the rules of a stage kiss, I moved thoughtfully, tasting every inch of his exposed lips, but being careful not to delve inside. Until his hips shifted upward and brushed meaningfully into mine. Hard and unyielding, his arousal was unavoidable, and the surprise of it all elicited a gasp.

Suddenly his tongue touched mine, abandoning the professional boundaries and our characters in the blink of an eye.

Lost in him and the moment, my tongue danced back, twisting and caressing the inside of his mouth with the fervor of someone who feared they'd never get another chance.

His chest and the call of the script beckoned in the back of my mind, but one moment turned into two and before I knew it, we'd both lost all sense of time and spacial reasoning.

We didn't have all the time in the world to explore, and we sure as hell weren't alone on an island of lust. People were waiting. People were *watching*. But neither of us managed to put a stop to it before it landed us in an uncomfortable place.

"Cut!" came Howie's loud and startling call, breaking us apart quickly and without an ending that did justice to the beginning and middle of our first kiss.

"Well, I know I said to take your time, Easie, but maybe not that much," he teased, bringing a rare rosy blush to the center of my cheeks.

Glancing to the man between my legs, I found something completely unexpected. Because for as repentant and embarrassed as I looked and felt, Anderson *didn't*.

His eyes were hot and completely—intently—focused on me.

Luckily, Howie didn't push it, nor did he let it linger, announcing, "Let's go again!" before any of us had a chance to do anything else.

"And action!"

I kept my mouth closed this time, breathing shallowly through my nose as little as possible. He smelled so damn good, but each hit of his scent seemed to significantly affect my decision making skills.

Hell, it was exactly like a drug.

His throat was smooth and long, its thickness thinning a little as he stretched to give me better access. A small nip of his collarbone transitioned into an exploration of his chest, but I didn't give myself long before zeroing in on the extra nipple.

I told myself that if I focused on the part that wasn't *actually* attached to Anderson, I could get back into the right frame of mind. The *Miranda* frame of mind.

Purposely shutting out Anderson's motion and response, I treated him like a mannequin, praying for a swift end to the take.

Howie, evidently with a direct line to God, chose that moment to tell us we were done.

"Cut!"

Sitting up quickly, I separated myself, compartmentalizing the lower half of my body into a box labeled "Open This Later."

"I think we got everything we need for this. You guys go into wardrobe and get ready for the intro."

Following Howie's instruction immediately, I swung my leg over Anderson's body as though dismounting a horse and scurried free until our bodies no longer touched at all.

I could feel his eyes on me, their weight dimpling the skin like a physical touch, but I studiously avoided them.

I may not have a college degree, but I'd just earned an honorary one in avoidance.

Wardrobe was waiting, and as far as I was concerned, it was screaming my name.

❧ ✦ ❧

Trudging through a cloud of awkward fog that I'd largely created with my impression of Speedy Gonzalez, Anderson and I managed to finish shooting the intro after an agonizing twenty-four takes.

I wasn't proud of the number, but I was content to live with it. Howie wasn't mad, and the show got done. In the face of everything that had happened in the last couple of days, professionally, I really couldn't ask for more.

But there *was* something that bothered me, so after getting changed back into street clothes and removing all of my TV makeup, I hiked up my panties and went in search of Anderson.

When I found him, he was gathering his stuff in his dressing room, just pulling the bottom of his t-shirt down to cover his exposed abdomen.

Focus.

Stay fucking focused.

"Hey," I greeted softly, alerting him to my presence for the first time.

"Hey, Easie," he murmured back, slapping his hat back on his messy-haired head and tucking his sunglasses back into the front collar of his shirt. The day had truly come full circle.

"So, um . . ." I stuttered to a start. "The second episode airs tomorrow. I know it's not you, you know, yet. But, um. Did you . . . Do you maybe want to come over and watch it?"

"Oh," he said, surprised, scratching at his chest with long, tan fingers. I couldn't blame him. I'd totally blackballed him since the moment his tongue left mine. He probably wouldn't be expecting me to invite him over.

"I can't."

I tried not to let my face fall too noticeably.

"I'm sorry, Easie. I wish I could."

I waved it off like it was no big deal. *Because it wasn't.*

No, really. "That's cool if you don't want to. I get it," I offered with a smile, internally cringing when I realized it probably looked faker than Pamela Anderson's boobs.

"No," he disagreed vehemently. "You don't."

"Huh?"

"I *want* to come," he said with a chuckle before explaining further. "I *can't.* I have to go train, and then I'm covering Tammy's shift at El Loco."

Instead of focusing on the part of his statement that made me imagine stabbing people, I honed in on the other part.

"Train?"

"Yeah. I'm running the 100 mile Rio Del Lago Endurance Run

later this year."

"100 miles?" I coughed. "People miles?"

"What other kinds of miles are there?" he asked with a smirk that just barely rumpled up his nose.

"I don't know. Hamster ones?" I asked hopefully.

"Nope," he replied, the shape and intensity of his grin growing into a smile. "Definitely the people ones then."

"And by running you mean?"

"Running."

"Like, with your legs?"

One raspy laugh coughed sharply from his throat. "That's the plan."

"All at once?"

"Yep."

"Holy shitballs. That makes me weep inside."

Finally, he let go, laughing the kind of rolling hilarity that started deep in his gut and ended at my ears.

Yeah, at my ears. Definitely not by forming a floral wreath around my swelling heart. Definitely.

"I'll pretend to be impressed by you doing it though."

"I'd appreciate it. It seems like it'd be a waste if you weren't impressed," he teased.

"Okay, well . . ." I mumbled, "I guess I'll see you—"

"If you aren't intent on watching the show," he cut in, "You could come hang out in my section at El Loco."

"Yeah?"

"Yeah," he confirmed, offering, "I'll buy you a drink."

"Oh, thanks. I don't really drink, but thanks."

"Addictive history?" he asked compassionately, being so understanding that it made my real answer seem even funnier.

I shook my head and shrugged. "Poor."

His Adam's apple bobbed as he burst out laughing. "You're one interesting woman, Easie Reynolds."

With a knock to the table, he walked toward me and the door, pausing in its opening just inches from me. The dark metal of his chunky ring glinted as his hand came up and tucked my hair behind my ear. His nose twitched and his face turned cautiously hopeful. "Text me if you're coming tomorrow night?"

I nodded my acquiescence.

His half smile turned full. "Later, Litterbug."

Chapter 10

"**W**HAT'S WRONG WITH YOU?" Ashley asked as I paced from the kitchen to the living room and back again for the sixty-second time.

What was wrong with me? That was a good question. I'd venture it had something to with the all out war going on inside of my chest as I tried to decide whether I should give in to the urge to go the restaurant or not.

Explosions. Bullet spray from an army of AK-47s. A grenade launcher in the distance. It was fucking bedlam in there.

I'd managed to put it out of my mind until now, but with the time until the show aired dwindling down, my entire body had become overwhelmed with the possibility of going.

"Are you anxious about watching the show?" she asked, tuning into my angst but misjudging the cause. "You know, with Ryder and everything?"

Truthfully, I hadn't given even one thought to Ryder. But, apparently, I *was* just shamelessly desperate enough to see Anderson to use it as an excuse.

"Yeah," I lied. "I guess that's it. Maybe we should go out."

Oh, you dirty, dirty liar.

"Okay, we can do that," she agreed easily. "You wanna just run down to the pub?"

Shit. The pub was just up the street, so it was no surprise that she'd suggested it. It just made it a lot harder to explain why I had a different idea.

Now, I know I should have just told her I wanted to go see Anderson.

But it's called denial for a fucking reason.

If you're not admitting the truth to yourself, you certainly don't admit it to other people.

"I'm not sure I'm in the mood for the pub," I evaded.

"Chinese food?" she suggested.

Fuck.

"Ehh," I murmured with a shake of my head. Hoping to slide it in innocently, I mentioned, "I'm not sure. Maybe tacos or something?"

Wow. Major failure on the innocent thing. Red flags were fucking waving all over the damn place.

Her blond hair swung dramatically over her slender shoulder as her head came up, and her midnight blue eyes narrowed on me.

"Tacos?" Her tone edged toward suspicious.

"Or something," I avoided. "I'm not sure exactly what I'm craving, but those don't sound bad."

"I don't suppose you want to go to the Mexican place two blocks over, do you?"

"Eh," I breathed, officially giving in to the desperation and digging my grave. "I'm not sure those are exactly—"

"Easie."

"Shit," I muttered before admitting, "I was thinking El Loco."

"Any specific reason?" That fucking voice. She knew there was a reason.

I glared at her.

"Okay," she caved. "We'll go to El Loco. Sans explanation."

Well, damn. She gave in so easily that now *I* was suspicious of *her.*

"That was too easy."

"Do you want me to argue? Press you for answers? I totally can if that'd make you feel better."

Ugh.

"Let's just go."

"Yeah," she agreed, nodding like the winner she was. "Let's just go."

Bawk Bawk Bawkkkk.

Something tasted like chicken, and I was guessing it was me.

I must have taken my phone out no less than thirty times on the drive to El Loco, and yet, not during a single one of those times had I actually texted Anderson.

For some completely bogus reason, texting him to let him know I was on my way felt intimate on a level I wasn't ready for. Like, *I'll see you soon, honey.*

He'd know I was there soon enough.

There was at least some comfort in the fact that I knew I wouldn't have to run into Tammy since he was covering her shift. And in the lingering tobacco of the two cigarettes I'd smoked on the way there.

"Table for two?" the hostess asked when we stepped inside and approached the podium.

Succumbing to the pressure now that we'd come all this way, I spoke up before Ashley could. "Yeah, but, um, could we sit in Anderson's section please?"

Ashley was annoyingly unsurprised, nodding and murmuring, "Uh huh," under her breath.

"He's pretty busy, but I'll see what he's got."

"Uh, um," I called as she turned away, catching her attention and making one of the bravest decisions I'd ever made. The truth was, I was terrified. Terrified that I'd commit to someone who couldn't see beyond the bitch.

Terrified that he wouldn't like what he found when he did.

"You can tell him it's Easie asking."

"Mmhmm," Ashley hummed.

"Shut up."

The hostess came back fairly quickly, waving us forward with a smirk curving her lips and a twinkle lighting her eye.

"Right this way."

Following her silently, I ignored the holes I felt Ashley's eyes drilling in my back and focused instead on preparing myself for my hello with Anderson.

I wasn't sure if we would wave, or shake, or maybe even hug. I wasn't thinking he'd stick his tongue in my mouth again, but that didn't mean my body got that very important memo.

Anticipation churned like a stormy ocean in my gut, sloshing at the edges and making me dance on uncomfortable feet.

But as soon as Anderson turned the corner and came into view, a huge smile highlighting the light of his eyes and a piece of dark, wild hair curling down onto the line of his forehead, it all settled. The waves abated, the skies cleared, and the sight of him happy and at ease seeped into me and made me feel much the same.

"Here you go," the hostess said, settling us into our table and handing us each a menu.

"Thanks," I murmured as my eyes followed Anderson across the room—watched him laugh at something another table said.

He walked away and his eyes scanned the tables, and I had absolutely no doubts whatsoever that he was looking for us.

When he finally found us—found me—his smile deepened, his long legs eating up the space twice as fast as I ever could.

"Easie," he murmured, pulling me out of the booth, into his arms, and inhaling the skin at the side of my throat.

I got lost in it for a minute, reveling in the feel and soaking every last bit of his warmth inside me.

And then Ashley called my name.

"Easie!" She waved a hand dramatically in front of my face. "Are you okay? You've been staring at the same spot across the room for a long-ass time. Like, without blinking."

Um . . . what?

Scanning my surroundings, I found no Anderson, no body of any kind. The only thing in my arms was a cold dose of reality.

Great. So I'd completely made up the hugging and throat sniffing. This did not bode well.

"Oh. Yeah. Swell."

"You're weird tonight."

I'd say that was a completely fair assessment on her part. In fact, just saying *tonight* rather than *lately* was unflaggingly generous.

"Yeah," I admitted, "It's probably going to stay that way."

Her face scrunched, but after a few seconds, she decided finding out what I meant wouldn't be worth her time or energy.

Instead, she shrugged.

I didn't blame her.

Anderson was nowhere in sight, and the daydream left me feeling like I didn't know my left from my right. I didn't know when he'd disappeared, or where he'd gone, or if I'd ever even seen him in the first place.

Sinking my face into my hands, I did my best to regroup through a series of deep breaths and rough facial scrubs. Unfortunately, all it probably got me was wrinkles.

"What's she doing?" I heard whispered in an achingly familiar voice. I peeked just one eye open.

Anderson sat crouched at the end of our table with his chin resting on his folded arms. Afraid it was an illusion, I didn't trust it, waiting instead to see if Ashley would answer him. If she didn't, I was driving straight to the nearest hospital.

"I'm pretty sure she's on the verge of a mental breakdown, but I'm hoping the real hysteria holds off until I've had my tacos."

Slowly, I opened the other eye, dragging my fingers roughly down my face as I pulled my hands away. The skin drooped and pulled appropriately, leaving Ashley's face a mask of disbelief and Anderson's smile beaming.

"Long day, Easie?" he asked, a lighthearted lilt making my heart sprout wings for the sole purpose of fluttering.

"Something like that," I responded, feeling the pieces of my scattered self put themselves back together courtesy of a little Anderson flavored glue. "How were the fifty million miles?"

He chuckled, shifting from his squat back to standing and forcing my eyes to follow the line of his lean body all the way up. "It was just slightly less than that actually. But the old legs are feeling it. If I didn't get up just now, I never would have."

"Yeah, you're a real Grandpa," I remarked sarcastically. "How old are you these days, eighteen?"

Luckily, I already had my tackle box and pole all packed as I headed off on my fishing expedition.

"I'm twenty-seven."

"Right, right. So basically a hundred."

"If we're using the same scale you use for miles, then yeah."

"Boom!" Ashley offered, entering the conversation uninvited.

Both of our heads swung to her, surprised, having pretty much forgotten that she was there. At least, I had.

"Oh, sorry," she apologized sarcastically. "Don't mind me. By all means, continue volleying your ball of explosive sexual tension. I'll just wait here."

"Don't you have someone named Larry you could be texting?" I fired back, satisfied when a sharp blush stole across her cheeks.

"Reallllly?" Anderson cooed, turning his attention fully to her. "Larry, huh?"

Looking her up and down, he slid right into the role of a protective big brother. "Isn't he a little old for you?"

Naturally, she blamed me.

Shooting poison-laced daggers through my head, she denied, "I'm not with Larry."

I raised a skeptical brow, and she got a defiantly challenging look in her eye.

"I'm not with Larry, just like you and Anderson aren't together."

"We *aren't* together," I reiterated, glancing at the man in question as he looked on, intrigued.

Her smile only grew. "Exactly."

"You guys are incredible," Anderson murmured in awe. "I'd stay here all night to watch the show if I didn't have other people to serve."

"The show's over," I assured him.

He bit his bottom lip and leaned closer to me, smiling in a way that made my womb contract.

"Shame."

My restless hands clenched into fists under the table while my eyes sought out his features as a balm to the absence of his physical touch.

"You guys know what you want to eat, or do you need me to come back?"

"Tacos," we both said in unison, finding common ground for the first time that evening.

All three of us smiled. Anderson because he was amused, and Ashley and I because we were remembering why we spent so much time together.

As much as we teased and prodded at one another, there truly wasn't any other person I'd rather be around. After all, there had to be reason we both chose to live and work together in our adulthood, barely scraping by, making just enough to survive.

We *liked* each other. And neither one of us would ever find a bigger supporter.

"And to drink?" Anderson asked, crossing his arms across his chest.

"Lemonade," we answered as one again.

"Okay," he laughed. "This is getting a little freaky."

Tiny wrinkles formed around his eyes, pointing to their minty green flecks and making it nearly impossible to look anywhere else. He wired my emotions at the same time that he settled them. Nothing other than smoking had ever been able to focus my self-acceptance so well before.

As we sat there in silence, awareness bounced between us like a spider, weaving and webbing our feelings into a delicate, untouched connection.

I hated my growing need to touch him, the way it pulled at my brain and threatened to make me do it without my permission.

Apparently, Ashley hated it more.

"Okay, seriously, guys. I want some freaking tacos."

Anderson looked away first, laughing and knocking just one knuckle on the hard surface of our table. "Okay, Ash. Tacos coming up."

He looked back at me once but turned to leave before I could make eye contact again.

His back swayed with his steps, the muscles bunching and pulling under his perfectly tight shirt.

"Chips wouldn't go unappreciated either!" Ashley called before he got too far away, eliciting an acknowledging wave over his shoulder.

Studiously avoiding her eyes, I waited patiently until Anderson brought our lemonades over and set them on the table in front of us. Treating unnecessary eye contact like an eclipse, neither of us looked directly at one another.

When he walked away again, Ashley piped up.

"We're not coming here again until you guys bang."

Fresh lemonade just beginning to quench my dry mouth, I spewed, spraying her with its fruity contents and making her laugh uncontrollably.

"What?!"

"I just want to eat my damn tacos in peace, and I'm pretty sure that's not going to happen until you guys bump uglies a few thousand times to take the edge off," she said as she wiped at her sticky face with a napkin.

"What are you talking about? He's getting your tacos right now! We aren't impeding your ability to eat them."

"Yeah, see, no. He's getting my tacos, but there's this . . ." She paused and twirled her finger in the air, searching for the explanation she wanted. " . . . *Cloud* of pent up sexual frustration enveloping this entire area, and the freaking smell is pungent. Pretty sure it's gonna affect the taste."

"We need to stop spending so much time together. You're becoming too much of a smart-ass."

"I've always been a smart-ass. It was just overshadowed by you being *more* of a smart-ass."

"Yeah, well, I need you to be the yang to my ying. That's what makes us dynamic."

"No," she denied. "That's what gives you the freedom to be a bitch. I'm there to smooth it over." She said the word 'freedom,' but I heard the word 'security.' I could hide behind the mean mask because my sister was there to weight the other, nicer side of the scale.

The realization of her feelings felt like a sharp knife in my gut, and the sudden intrusion of it made me sit up straighter.

"Ashley . . . do you . . . is that how you really—"

"No, Easie." Her voice was soft. Gentle. *Wise.* "I don't really feel like that. You have always given me the freedom to be who I want. I'm just pointing out, that no matter *how* we act, you and I will always be dynamic. Because we're sisters, and I love you."

"I'm sorry."

"Don't be," she stressed. "Just be who you want. Don't worry about what people expect from you and what they don't. They'll adjust." She smiled. "You're too funny for someone to really hate you."

I wiggled my head with fake laughter and scrunched up my face. "Gee, thanks."

"Anytime," she offered with a wink, taking a swig of her lemonade and leaning further back in the booth.

I looked up just in time to see Anderson take his last few steps on his approach to our table.

"Chips," he said with a flourish, setting down the basket and waving his hand gallantly.

"Why, thank you, kind sir," Ashley teased, inclining her head in turn.

"It was my utmost pleasure, fair lady."

Enthralled, I watched as they interacted with rapt attention. It was fun and honest and surprisingly *not* flirtatious. He saved all of those looks for me.

Jesus. Did he really save all of those looks for me?

"Earth to Easie," Anderson said, leaning down to smile right in my face.

"You were right," Ashley remarked to herself. "The weirdness remains."

"Hey," Anderson said with a smile when my eyes met his, one gentle hand reaching out to tuck my hair behind my ear.

He was always doing that.

"You're always doing that."

"What?" he asked, surprised by the sudden intrusion of my foot into my mouth.

It was too late to take it back though. "Tucking my hair behind my ear. Why?"

Squatting down beside me, he shrugged. "I guess I want to see your face."

Arching my brows and scrunching my nose, I stuck my tongue between my teeth and attempted an ugly smile.

He laughed, shook his head, and then winked. "Well, maybe not that one."

My chest swelled and heaved, the feel of his smile getting sucked straight into the depths of my body. I was two seconds from getting swept completely away when a swift kick landed on my shin.

"Ow!"

My startled, accusatory eyes jumped to my sister. "We're not coming back," she mouthed, pretending to swim through her imaginary cloud of sexual tension.

Anderson was understandably confused, standing up again and stepping back from the table just in time to see another patron trying to grab his attention.

"Oops," he muttered. "Gotta go." His eyes met mine once more. "It probably wasn't a good idea to invite you here while I'm working. Too much of a distraction." Grabbing my hand laying on the table, he gave it a squeeze and then left.

Ashley clucked over her victory.

Meanwhile, I was still trying to pick my jaw up off of the table. It'd probably help if I could get my hand to stop tingling.

"Better make it an even ten thousand."

"What?"

"The amount of sexual encounters it's going to take to burn off the fog of this cloud."

Half of me hoped she was right while the other hoped she wasn't. The whole damn thing hoped I got the chance to find out.

Chapter 11

"IS THIS A JOKE?" I asked Larry as Anderson looked on from the doorway. "Tell me it's a joke."

Five whole days had passed since I'd left El Loco that night, and Anderson and I hadn't spoken to each other on even one of them.

I'd worried a little that it would be awkward when I got to work today, but by all accounts, everything seemed to be normal. From the list of things he'd told me he'd done since I'd last seen him, I was really starting to believe that he had, in fact, just been busy.

"It's not a joke," Larry replied.

"It has to be a joke," I repeated, turning to face Anderson again.

"It's not a joke," he confirmed. "I met Devon and Shavon."

"How are you so calm about this?!" I questioned, throwing my panicked hands in the air.

"What do you want me to be?" His head tilted inquisitively to the side.

"I don't know! Freaked out, like me."

"And why are you freaked out?" he asked, using an annoying therapist-like voice.

"Because this is sick!" I nearly shrieked. "It's some sick, weird-ass fucking shit!"

"It's not sick. It's just different," he argued calmly, walking into the room to stand directly in front of me. Larry traded positions, slipping out the door and away from the psychopath (me) while he had the chance.

"And sick!"

"It's only sick to you because it's not your kink. To them—those super nice, normal people out there—it's what feels right. Can you honestly tell me you want someone telling you not to do what makes you feel right?"

"No," I admitted begrudgingly.

"Exactly."

I narrowed my eyes at the know-it-all. When he was schooling me like this, I couldn't remember why he made me feel all mushy the rest of the time.

"What Devon and Shavon find acceptable is up to the two of them. They're both consenting. That's all that matters."

"But it's icky."

"To *you*," he emphasized.

"Why on earth would this show be the one Larry chose?" I whined as I leaned my head back to look at the ceiling.

"Because," he called, reaching up and tipping my chin back down with his thumb and forefinger. "Believe it or not, the statistics on the number of people who feel persecuted or disassociated because of sexual preferences they have no control over—that bring harm to no other people—are unbelievably vast. That's why. This show, whether you realized it or not, is going to help people."

"A show about menstrual sex on Quirks and Kinks is going to help people?" I scoffed.

His answering nod was crisp. Resolute. "Yep."

"Alright. Alright," I repeated, trying to wrap my head around it. All the focus in the world couldn't have stopped me from struggling.

"I just . . . I'm not judging."

He raised a thick brow.

"No, really," I promised, my nose only growing minimally with the small fib. "I'm just having a hard time figuring out the appeal."

"Devon likes the taste and feel of it, and Shavon is secure enough in herself to enjoy the heightened sensitivity," he explained easily, not even blinking an eye at the abnormality of it all.

"I'm not secure enough," I admitted.

"No," he laughed. "I think I got that. And menstrual sex might never be your thing. But something is, and if you're with someone who's open to helping you embrace it, you'll find it."

Good God. This guy was so . . . *accepting.*

Was menstrual sex *his* thing? Oh, chicken biscuits. *Was he a Blood Hound?*

Ew. What a horrible thought.

I spent a lot of time fantasizing about Anderson, and I really didn't want to have to take my daydreaming in this direction. I mean, it wasn't so much the actual intercourse I really struggled with as it was the idea of him not only going down on me during my period but downright craving it. According to the script, Devon literally had to fight the urge to sniff Shavon's used pads and tampons. He enjoyed it *that* much. I mean . . . *no* . . . I couldn't even think about it anymore.

"Alright. I'm obviously going to give it my best effort here. I'm just not sure—"

"I'll help you however I can."

"You better," I threatened and poked him roughly in the chest.

"Come on. Let's go get our makeup done."

"Great idea, *Andrea.*"

"Hey now! You know I don't have a choice about the makeup."

"Yeah, sure, that's what they all say."

"Come on," he said, grabbing my shoulder and pulling me in and out of his side. "I think you should have a talk with Shavon before we start shooting too."

Normally, I didn't have a problem talking to the real people behind the show. But, this time, I was afraid I'd say something that sounded disparaging. "Are you sure that's a good—"

"Oh yeah. Definitely. You might learn something." He waggled his eyebrows.

Shit. I knew it. He was into period sex. He had to be.

Sliding his hand from my shoulder down my arm, he grabbed my hand and clasped it, linking our fingers as we made our way down the hall.

Sweet baby purple unicorns.

He was holding my hand. And apparently I was in third grade again, making that a big deal.

Feelings of excited contentment bloomed in my belly, mushrooming and building on themselves until they ran out of room.

The closer we got to the makeup room (and other people), the closer the excitement got to the top of my esophagus—and started to feel a little less like excitement and more like vomit.

"Ergmaged," I squealed, dragging my feet enough that Anderson started to laugh.

"What's the matter with you? This is no big deal. I can assure you that you don't need to worry about having a conversation with Shavon. She's one of the most sexually open people I've ever met."

"Um, hello?" I called, pointing to my own chest. "Sexually closed. Right here."

His eyes positively danced. Stopping in front of the guest dressing room door, he knocked.

It was only a few seconds before a seriously attractive blond guy answered.

"Hey, Devon," Anderson greeted.

Oh Jesus.

"Hey, Anderson." He held out his hand to me.

"Oh, hi. Easie," I stumbled to introduce myself.

They both smiled.

Speaking for myself like a big girl, I explained, "I was hoping I could talk to Shavon . . . and maybe you . . . about the show."

"Oh, yeah. Cool."

Before he could even call her over, she was there, peeking her absolutely gorgeous head around the doorjamb. Smooth, mocha skin and lush lashes surrounded a stunning set of amber brown eyes, but both of them acted primarily as servants, born to a life of highlighting her welcoming, bright smile.

"Easie!" She pulled me in for a hug, officially separating my hand from Anderson's.

Huh. I hadn't even realized it was still there.

"It's so nice to meet you!"

She was bubbly in the cutest possible way. "You too, Shavon."

"Come in, come in," she invited easily. "Let's talk."

A gleam danced in her eye as she dragged me inside. Involuntarily, my eyes sought Anderson one last time in desperation.

But he was already gone.

Anderson's eager hands formed a trail down my body, laying out a path for his lips that led to my sex. Each inch of skin felt like it was wired with extra nerves, just the way Shavon had described it.

My role and her pleasure-clouded words acted as a placebo, making my body feel like it did at the height of shark week—only . . . *good.* Aching, hypersensitive, and unbelievably turned on.

If my period got the wrong idea and tried to sync up with my role, Anderson would have hell to pay.

Responsive and eager, my womb seemed to pulse with extra fervor, a second heartbeat setting up at the apex of my thighs and bringing a new supply of blood to the layer of tissue just under my skin. His dark head looked criminally good against my skin, and when his light green eyes flicked up to meet mine, my timer popped. This turkey was done.

My inner thighs ached in anticipation, and for the first time in my entire life, being involved in a blood bath sounded like a good thing.

No. The *best* thing.

"Cut!" Howie called, bringing me down from my high on a cruelly steep downslope.

Sexual frustration was ripe, the tease of having Anderson's hands and mouth all over me day in and day out becoming the absolute worst form of torture. Forget the waterboarding, America. Strap people down and blue ball 'em to death.

It'd be sure to turn confessions almost immediately.

"You okay?" Anderson asked right away, obviously feeling the tremor run through me.

This guy. Jesus.

Fuck him for making something so gross seem sexy. My ability to frivolously make fun of unknown, seemingly depraved things would seriously decrease now that he'd opened my eyes. I was ruined for life.

"Yeah. I just . . ." I shook my head, moved him off of me. "I need a cigarette."

Understatement.

Scurrying off of the bed, I signaled to Howie, and he gave me a nod. I didn't look back as I made my way down the hall, got my stuff from my dressing room, and then sought comfort and normalcy in the warm sunshine of outside.

More solace waited at the tips of my fingers, and I didn't waste any time before lighting it up and bringing it to my eager lips. Two quick pulls gave me the hit of nicotine I needed desperately.

When Anderson came out of the door looking for me fifteen seconds later, I was glad I had gotten it already.

"Are you okay?"

"Yeah. I just needed to smoke," I replied, conveniently leaving out the fact that my needing to smoke *stemmed* from being slightly less than okay.

He rolled his eyes and scoffed.

Wrong move.

"Why are you so closed-minded about the smoking when you preach open-mindedness like gospel for everything else? I don't fucking get it!"

He took a deep breath, closed his eyes, and retreated into a place deep within himself—a place that definitely didn't include me. Quiet lilts sounded from swooping birds, and wayward leaves tinkled and scraped on the concrete as they blew by.

I watched his face, tight and tense and lost in a whirlwind of emotion. The muscles of his cheeks twitched, and the wrinkles at the corners of his eyes deepened and flexed perfectly in time with his breathing.

Whatever he was thinking about, he was living it. Each breath moved raggedly, and every flit of a memory was enough to make his eyes flinch.

I watched him battle, and after several moments, his face calmed with the evolution of his victory.

When he finally came back from his place of introspection, opened his eyes and met mine, his attitude had completely changed.

"You're right." He nodded. Adamant. "This is my issue, not yours. I won't say anything anymore."

I wanted to understand, to delve deeper. I wanted an invitation to the place he'd gone so I could know *why* this was his issue, *what* made him this way. His intentions behind coming out here had been so pure, so kind-hearted, but with the help of one bad habit, it had all rolled straight into the gutter.

Before I could ask, he was gone, the sound of the door clicking closed behind him the only sign that he had ever been.

So complicated were his ups and downs, I was starting to fear that Anderson was *too good* an actor. All of his defining lines blurred and curved, completely disguising the shape of his personality and turning it into one, huge, soul-sucking mystery. I could lose myself in him for hours trying to figure out the differences in real and fake, and somehow, at the end of my exploration, all I found were more questions.

Chapter 12

B Y THE TIME WE wrapped filming for the day, Anderson and I were back in a routine of pithy comments and reactions. Ironically, we'd both been nominated for Oscars for our performance in *Let's Pretend That Didn't Happen*.

Small film. Limited circulation.

Hah.

"So . . . our first episode airs tonight," I said, hoping to take our olive branch and turn it into a real relationship. Bouncing around one another was exhausting, and when I'd come back inside from our tête-à-tête, just the sight of him made me realize enough was enough.

Our dance wasn't satisfying me anymore. Our relationship was either going to orgasm or it wasn't, but whatever the outcome, it'd be better to find out now.

"So . . . I know," he teased, tilting his head and settling his thumbs into his front pockets.

"Do you think it's cute to mock me?"

"Yes."

"It's not."

"Maybe the mocking isn't cute," he conceded, "but your reaction is."

"My reaction?" I shook my head and scrunched my face. "You mean me being annoyed?"

He smiled and popped his eyebrows.

"You like that, huh?" I asked. "Well, then you should love this!" I yelled, reaching out to swat him on the arm.

He ducked and weaved, laughing as his feet shuffled back a couple of steps.

"Alright, alright. Relax."

"Me relax? You fucking relax!"

His laughter only loudened, echoing off the walls and concealing the sound of Larry's entry.

"Guys," Larry called, startling me into a running trip. My toe caught on the carpet, pealing the front of my flip flop away from my toes and sending me into a head first journey to the ground.

Anderson stepped forward just in time, scooping me up with two hands in the divots of my armpits.

"Easy there, Easie," Larry teased, practically choking on his self-induced laughter.

"Fucking hilarious," I grumbled as Anderson placed me safely on my feet.

"First episode airs tonight," Larry said as I moved to stand on my own. Anderson's hands loitered.

"Yeah, you're about two minutes too late," I replied, just before Anderson explained, "We already had this conversation."

"Great. Then you won't be surprised when I tell you that we're having a meeting tomorrow, just as soon as the rating statistics come in."

I elbowed Anderson in the ribs playfully before asking Larry, "Planning on firing us?"

"Not if viewers like you," he deadpanned, looking each of us in the eye individually.

I knew the public could turn on me in an instant, but at least they'd liked me before. There was some comfort in that knowledge. As for

Anderson . . . yeah, I was pretty sure he was impossible not to like.

Larry headed for the door, scooting out it with one final nod in our direction.

As soon as he cleared it, Anderson whispered conspiratorially in my ear. "I don't think Larry likes you very much."

"Thank you!" I nearly screamed, excited that someone else could finally fucking see it.

Laughter shook my shoulders, but it wasn't my own, as Anderson's jovial arms came around me, wrapping me up in a vibrating hug and squeezing. Everything started to tingle, and after only a few seconds, the pleasure overwhelmed me, forcing my eyes to close.

"Don't invite me over tonight," he whispered into the curve of my neck, the soft silk of his lips skimming my skin as he did.

My eyes popped open, and my body went stiff.

"I know that's where you were going before, the direction our conversation was headed, but I'm begging you, *don't* ask me."

Tightening throat threatening to completely choke my only connection to air, I tried to pull away, but he wouldn't let me.

"Easie," he murmured into my skin, squeezing me even tighter as he did. "I don't want you to ask because I don't want to tell you no." He chuckled softly to himself, groaned, and then whispered nearly silently. I wasn't even sure I actually heard the words I thought I did, but it sounded like, "I'm not sure that I could."

"Okay," I agreed, dumbfounded and completely vulnerable, promising, "I won't ask," as my head tried to talk louder than my wildly beating heart.

His arms tightened just slightly, lingering and making me long for things I shouldn't. Just as I started to settle into it again, he pulled away, leaving me swaying in the breeze of his exit and floundering in the wake of his embrace.

For us, a pattern had started to form.

The more he pushed, the more I pulled, nearly guaranteeing myself an ending that could only be agony.

"Anderson looks good, huh?" Ashley asked as the intro of the show played on our TV. She was in charge of getting the show turned on. I was in charge of getting snacks.

Looking across the expanse of our apartment, I could see that he did. His thin green tie pointed to his eyes like an arrow and proved that the wardrobe people knew what they were doing.

But I had more on my mind than his looks, and most of it fell on the ugly side of angry.

"He looks like an indecisive, confusing psychopath is what he looks like," I grumbled to myself as I poured a bag of baby carrots onto a paper plate. Ranch bottle: decimated.

I was still confused about how we'd parted that afternoon, frustrated by the fact that the more I saw him, the less I seemed to understand about him.

He was flirty with me. That much I knew. But every time I tried to turn the corner from flirtation to fornication—or, you know, *something real*—he pulled back, swearing other engagements and promises.

I mean, Jesus. I wasn't a masochist. Eventually it would be time to stop trying. Smart money said that time was now.

Too bad I was a poor idiot.

"Stupid, irresistible jerk," I muttered to myself, ripping a couple of paper towels off the roll with far more vigor than necessary.

"What was that?" Ashley asked.

"Nothing."

"Okay," she shrugged, glancing at me briefly as I approached before focusing back on the din of the television.

Settling onto the sofa, I let my eyes wander all over Anderson's presence and tried not to get all mumbly again as I did.

"It's crazy how busy he is, isn't it?"

"Huh?"

"Anderson," she clarified. "I was talking to him earlier, and today alone he had to go run, like, ten miles, work a partial shift at El Loco, and then go play some gig at a bar in Santa Monica."

"A gig?"

"Yeah. Apparently, he plays guitar and sings at this place every Wednesday night."

He played a *gig*. Every Wednesday night.

"Wait . . . what?" This was the first I was hearing about it.

"He didn't tell you?"

Ragged breaths racked my airway and threatened me with tears. *Fucking shit.* I was not going to get worked up over some guy. Especially not some guy who I so obviously knew nothing about.

"No. He didn't."

"Huh." She popped her eyebrows. "That's surprising."

"Why?" I snapped, losing my tenuous hold on my last thread of control and throwing my arms in the air. "It's not like we're together or something. He doesn't have to tell me everything about his life. Jesus!"

It didn't take a rocket scientist to realize I wasn't angry with her. I was mad at myself for wanting and fantasizing about all of those very things.

"Uh, no," she muttered looking shellshocked. "I, um, meant it's surprising because he literally *told* me he was going to tell you about it."

My chin jerked back into my chest. "Wait . . . what?!"

"Yeah," she nodded nonchalantly, ignoring the fact that I was slowly losing my shit with a champion poker face. "I talked to him right after we wrapped for the day. He said he was going to talk to you before he left or something."

"But he didn't . . ."

Oh. I'd talked to him after we wrapped alright. And I'd immediately tried to invite him over to watch the show. Which he was, very fucking obviously, too busy to do.

But still. Why wouldn't he have just told me that?

I'm not sure that I could.

Maybe he just had to leave before he could tell me? Before he could back out of a weekly obligation.

Hmm.

"Maybe we should—"

"Go see the show?" Ashley finished my sentence, mocking my attempt at innocence with the look of a knowing woman.

I narrowed my eyes at her.

"Yeah. I figured you were going to say that. Good thing I know the name of the bar and the time he's playing, huh?"

"Well you don't have to be a gloat-y twaintasaurus about it."

"Twaintasaurus?"

"Twaint, the mix of twat, taint, and cunt means you're a ho. The dinosaur part means you're vicious."

"So . . . you're calling me a vicious ho?"

"A gloat-y one."

"Do you want to go or not?"

Closing my eyes, dropping my head back, and stomping my foot, I complained, "Why do you have to hold so much power over me?"

"Are you talking to me . . . or Anderson?"

My head rolled forward, and my eyes popped open.

"You're not cute."

"I disagree," she teased, smiling and speaking with a song-like lilt. "I'm the cutest of all of the cute people everywhere."

Okay. I could admit it. She was starting to get cute.

"Let me just put on a bra," I said instead of adding to the swell of her head.

She wagged her eyebrows and jumped up from her spot on the couch. "Maybe you shouldn't."

"Shut up." The only thing that would come of me not wearing a bra would be accidental strangulation. I was still young, but they were heavy, and when left to their own devices—especially in a scenario that might include dancing—everyone was in danger.

Speed walking down the hall and into my room, I dug through

the pile of not-that-dirty clothes on my bed until I found what I was looking for, pulled my shirt up to a comfortable resting place around my neck, and then strapped into the flesh colored, man-made torture device.

While my shirt was up, I reached for the deodorant on the top of my dresser and swiped it around a few times per armpit. I wasn't sure if I smelled, but freshening up was never a terrible idea.

A lot of women would have primped harder, but I was in a race with my mind, trying to get out of the apartment and on our way before I talked myself out of it.

Pushing my arms back through the sleeves of my bright pink t-shirt, I headed back down the hall and into the living room to find Ashley with the TV already off and my keys in her hand.

"I guess you're ready?"

"Yep. I'm not trying to impress anyone."

I scoffed. The urge to argue was alive and well, but with a well placed fist in my throat, I managed to squash it down.

Instead, I prompted, "Let's go," walking toward the door with efficiency and speed and snagging my purse on the way.

I hated carrying a purse, but the purse was all important.

It wasn't money or lip gloss I was worried about.

No.

My purse was the holder of my cigarettes, and with the prospect of a guitar playing, smooth singing Anderson hanging over my head, I had a feeling I was going to need a couple.

Words swept and flowed into a melody as soon as we entered the bar aptly named Hunger Spot, magically managing to sound husky and smooth at the same time. One moved into the next with ease, but the bite of each note assured not one word would slip by without notice.

The lighting was low, appropriate for a late night spot, and the crowd was thick. My only line to Anderson was his voice, and the microphone-amplified volume of it vibrated in perfect timing with the waves of sound from his guitar.

I had apparently entered the zone, and I didn't mean twilight. No, this was the perfect storm of seduction, and I feared that upon actual sight of him, I might pull a Wicked Witch and turn into a full-blown puddle.

What's the melting temperature for jeans, a t-shirt, and human flesh anyway? The same for all three?

I fanned myself at the thought.

"Come on," Ashley called from up ahead, waving me forward with urgency.

Shaking my head, I snapped out of the mental picture my brain had rendered and followed her prompt.

When I stepped forward, the sea of people parted, letting in the light from the tiny stage and illuminating the man of my literal dreams. I thought of his haunted green eyes and easy smile when I slept as much as when I woke, and solving the mystery of his personality had become my priority goal.

His fingers flew expertly along the strings of his guitar, and when the final note hung from his lips, his eyes closed. It didn't look like concentration. Instead, it looked like he was living in that moment as if it were his last, experiencing every facet of the song and his performance like it mattered to so much more than him.

It was the kind of gut-wrenching connection that moved you. Immersed you in the music and moment in a way that a cynic like me never thought possible.

"Multitalented," Ashley murmured under her breath, the cadence and timing of it offbeat from Anderson's by just enough that I noticed it.

She was right. How *did* one person manage to master so many things?

Applause and catcalls broke out around us and made me jump as Anderson stood from his stool behind the mic stand and gave several cool-guy-nods of gratitude.

He looked slightly uncomfortable with the attention, but not enough to avoid it completely. He stayed there on the six by six foot stage and accepted the audience's praise until they were finished before hopping down with his guitar in one hand and heading for the opposite back corner of the room.

I followed him with my eyes as one step faded into two and the muscles in his back bunched his white button down shirt with the effort.

Stuck in the land of perusal, I was surprised once again when Ashley grabbed my hand and tugged, pulling me from my spot in the middle of the room and guiding me toward the Anderson-occupied corner.

I wanted to thank her for doing what I so obviously couldn't do myself, but after careful consideration, decided to keep it in my head. She would know by the look on my face, and I wouldn't have to deal with the uncomfortably sentimental moment that would follow. The murmur of the crowd made it hard to hear anyway.

Right.

"Anderson!" my sister called loudly, bringing his dark-haired head up with a jerk.

"Ashley," he greeted as we got to him, his eyebrows rising to a height worthy of the mixture of surprised delight and equal panic marring the normally smooth lines of his masculine face.

And that was all just at the sight of her. It didn't even look like he had noticed the Easie shaped human attached to her arm yet.

"We had to come check you out!" she explained exuberantly, chucking him on the shoulder like a guy pal. "You were great, by the way!"

Stuck back on her first words, he ignored her praise and instead questioned, "We?" as though I was actually invisible.

Had I somehow figured out how to pull that off some time in the last few weeks?

I looked down to check, but my glaringly pink shirt stood out like a neon sign.

Not invisible.

His eyes walked the line of her arm like a tightrope, skating its length and, at the same time, struggling to keep his emotional balance. His face was a slideshow, changing from one thing to the next as he first noticed my nails, then my arm, and eventually wandered through a zigzag pattern all the way up to my nervous face.

I pasted on a smile and hoped it portrayed some kind of excitement.

In the end, I think it was just a mirror image of his.

"Easie."

"Anderson."

"Ashley," Ashley chimed in cheekily before smiling coyly, shaking her head, and walking away without another word.

"So I guess—"

"Ashley told me you were—"

"Sorry," we said in unison.

Awkward.

Expelling one deep breath, he chuckled to himself and started over. And I let him. "I meant to tell you about it this afternoon, but well . . . you know."

"Yeah," I confirmed, smiling a genuine smile for the first time since we'd arrived. "Is there anything you don't do? Every time I see you, you're involved in another hobby."

His smile faltered slightly, but he caught it before I could really investigate.

What he didn't do was actually give me an answer.

Sensing the growing need for a change of subject, I moved on. "You were really good. Did you write the song?"

"Nah. It's just a cover of an old Hunter Holston song."

"Oh. Then I take it back. I'm absolutely not impressed with you at all."

The corner of his mouth curved and his hand shot out to squeeze my hip playfully.

"Thanks," he said through a laugh, confirming that I'd finally broken all of our carefully crafted tension and found a way to span the gap an unexpected evening and secrets had created.

We were back to Easie and Anderson.

"You do this every Wednesday night?"

"I do."

"And there aren't swarms of women hanging on your every word? Waiting with bated breath, hoping you'll sign their heaving boobs?"

"Hah!" he barked, a startled laugh nearly choking him as it surged out of his throat. "No swarms. No hoards."

Just one at a time then.

Inclining my head, I studied his eyes as they studied me, moving from one feature to the next as itchy fingers stroked at the skin of my hip.

I started to tingle from their constant rubbing, living in the comfort of their silence as we stared at one another.

We still had so much to learn about the other, but to a certain extent, Ashley was right. All of our untapped sexual tension was interfering with our conversation.

"When did you learn to play guitar?" I asked.

"A few years ago," he answered, leaning into the stool behind him and finally pulling his hand away from me.

Sap that I was, I missed it.

Looking down to my bare toes, I scuffed the wood floor with my flip flop once before looking back to his face.

"Wow. You really are good for just a few years of playing."

"So I *did* impress you," he teased, leaning in and bumping my ankle carefully with the toe of his boot.

I shook my head with a smile. "Some advice?"

"Sure."

I leaned in closer and dropped my voice to a seductive whisper. "Don't call a woman a liar." He chuckled, and I leaned closer. "*Ever.*"

"Noted," he agreed just before reaching up and tucking my hair behind my ear softly.

"Good," I said, clearing my throat and taking a small step back.

Fuck, Easie. You are an idiot. When you look back on tonight and remember this ruined moment, you'll have no one to blame but yourself.

"Can I assume that a place called Hunger Spot has food? Or do I need to go shake down some employees and cause an all out riot?"

"I'm pretty sure they've got food," he comforted, his eyes lighting with mirth and life.

"Good. I'll be back then. I'm going to go order some before I die of starvation."

"My, my, we're dramatically hungry tonight, aren't we?"

"I had carrots and ranch dressing while I watched the episode tonight. That's it."

Actually, I hadn't eaten any of them courtesy of my Anderson meltdown. He didn't need to know.

"How *was* the show?"

"You were good."

"That's it?"

"Okay. You were *really* good."

He laughed and shook his head before standing up. "Go order food. Maybe some sustenance will improve your vocabulary."

I narrowed my eyes.

"I'll be here when you get back."

Giving him attitude by turning on my heel and heading directly for the bar, I put an extra sway into my walk and listened to him chuckle as I did.

The bartender made ordering easy, pointing out the quickest, most filling items on the menu at the prompting of my growling stomach. His smile was genuine and a little bit flirty, but the blond of his hair and the hazel of his eyes did nothing to elicit an extra beat of my heart or a calming flip of my stomach.

All of that waited for me in the far corner of the room.

Eager to get back to it, I thanked the bartender with an easy wave, and he promised to let me know when my order was up.

Pushing my way past a few crowded clumps of friends, I finally emerged into a chasm of empty space and cleared my view of Anderson.

His eyes were as happy as his smiling lips, and the low, glowing light of the bar made his eyes seem like they were lit from within.

But he wasn't looking at me.

I followed his eyes all the way to Tammy's long, dark hair and exposed, silky legs and locked on just in time to see her glance my way.

Her eyes never met mine, but a chill ran up my spine as she smiled a cat-like smile and fell into a strut on a path that could only lead to Anderson.

His smile never faded as she walked right into his arms, wrapping him in a familiar hug that made my heart squeeze with a similar fervor.

Anderson laughed a little, blowing her hair out of his mouth and pushing her back with a gentle grip on her upper arms. He didn't set her away though, but instead, seemed to hold her there, watching her closely as she spoke and tucking his chin into his chest with mirth as she teased.

He looked at ease with her in a way that I had only thought he was with me, their conversation steady and their touch commonplace.

The two of them embraced with the knowledge and security of a couple. There was no denying they had some deep-seated relationship that I could only dream of superseding.

My feet felt like they were encased in concrete as I watched, unable to look away and powerless to stop it.

He watched her face closely as she moved into him and touched her lips to his, the meeting of the two coinciding perfectly with the stab of a big, sharp knife right through my heart.

Air was moving in and out of my lungs, but I could scarcely breathe, and I knew something with absolute certainty.

One moment had caused what years of smoking had yet to. Catastrophic lung failure.

Finally able to move, I scrambled for the door, leaving behind the bartender and my food, my sister, and the guy I thought would change everything—and shoving people carelessly out of the way to do it.

Gravel crunched under my feet as I ran, and an unrealized sob kicked and scratched its way up my throat with reckless abandon.

I fought for myself, keeping it together long enough to get my keys out of my purse and let myself into the passenger side of my car.

Gathering all of my strength I texted Ashley that it was time to go, leaned back into my seat, and finally let it all go.

The frustration of my self-doubt and insecurities, my want for a meaningful relationship that no one knew I wanted, and the reality of the heartbreak of my want's destruction.

They all left me in a series of soul-wracking sobs, the power of their meaning shaking my entire body and draining every tear in my reserve.

I was done being this vulnerable woman.

I'd given the dream a test drive, and Anderson had crashed the fucking car.

Easy Easie was gone.

The bitch was back.

Part 2

Anderson

"Sometimes the strongest thing you will ever do will be to let go of someone. It will be painful, you will suffer guilt, and you will second-guess yourself, but for your own sanity and quality of life, there will come a time where you hand them to God, with your love, and trust Him to be who and what He is. May our Lord comfort you."

— Lee Goff

Chapter 13

THE STARK WHITE WALLS of my apartment screamed at my foggy brain as I poured my second cup of coffee of the morning.

I normally tried to limit my caffeine intake to one cup a day, focusing on replenishing water and electrolytes through both water and sports drinks throughout the day. Nutrition was an important part of my training for the 100 mile run I planned to do in the early fall, but after last night, my resolve was close to zero.

"Are you alright?" Tammy asked as she walked into the kitchen. Apparently, she noticed how shitty I looked and felt.

"Yeah, I'm just . . ." I scrubbed my face. Shook my head. "I don't know. Everything was good last night until . . . well, until it wasn't."

I didn't understand what had happened. Easie had gone to get food and never come back. I looked everywhere for her and Ashley, but I never found either of them.

Worried, I sent her several text messages, all without a response.

"Easie left without saying goodbye, so I guess I'm just hoping everything's alright."

Tammy puffed out an uncomfortable laugh. Looked at the ground and back up again. "Don't hold your breath."

"What do you mean?" I asked, turning to face her completely.

"I mean, everything *isn't* okay."

"What? How do you know that?"

"She thinks we're dating."

"She thinks we're dating who?"

I took a sip of my coffee.

"You and I. Each other. She thinks *you're* dating *me.*"

Brown liquid spewed everywhere, coating the counter and the front of my white t-shirt. "WHAT? Why in the fucking hell would she think that?"

Silence.

Tammy cocked a perfectly groomed brow, and that was all it took for everything to make sense. I was completely guilty of still seeing just my best friend when I looked at her. The example of feminine beauty she was today was no more than background noise.

And then . . . I remembered it was even worse.

"Jesus Christ, you have *got* to stop kissing me in public!"

"Okay," she agreed, laughing and grabbing a paper towel from the rack to clean up my mess. "I'll just do in private. No problem."

"Tammy!" I snapped, slamming my cup onto the counter so hard she winced.

"Okay, okay. Chill." My eyes closed as I took a deep breath. "Only on weekends."

Not opening my eyes, I let my head roll back. "Is this what a stroke feels like?"

"Relax, Romeo," she laughed. "I'll stop cockblocking you."

"I'd say thank you if you deserved it. You caused this whole fucking mess."

"I was just looking out for you."

"Looking out for me?"

"I guess I just wanted to see how much you mean to her."

"Jesus. This is all because of some protective bullshit? Thanks, but no thanks." I rubbed a rough hand down my face.

Tammy had been around for everything. Before, during, and after.

She knew everything about every version of myself, and I knew she had my health and happiness in mind when she stepped in.

But fuck that. I was an adult man. I could make my own decisions. Of course, there was a ripe irony in that statement alone. But I could make any declaration about my life that I wanted because it was just that.

My life.

Sensing my mood and wanting to avoid a fight as much as I did, she moved on.

"Seriously though, you're in for a world of pain when you see her again."

"Why? We aren't together," I reasoned immediately out of reflex. I almost rolled my eyes at myself. We'd both been saying that a lot, but it never sounded true.

"Riiight. You guys are the most couple-y non-couple on record." My head dropped backward on my shoulders in exasperation. "And that chick has got a wicked streak inside her. You better wear a cup."

I knew Easie had a hard facade she used as an excuse not to go deeper, but I didn't think she was actually malicious.

"She's not that bad."

"Fuck, it's gonna hurt when she knees you in the unprotected balls, Bro. Maybe you don't know her as well as I thought."

"Well, I guess we'll find out soon. I have a meeting with her and Larry in an hour. The ratings are in."

"Good luck," she sing-songed, turning with a feminine swish and waltzing toward her room.

It was going to be fine.

I didn't need luck. Right?

I mean, how bad could she be?

God, this was fucking bad.

I thought I'd seen an ice stare before, but at the realization of Easie's, I could confidently say I never had.

Her normally vibrant blue eyes sharpened like shards of glass, reaching out to stab me with each look. Any interaction between us was a forced cordiality at best, and to make matters worse, Larry had just given us the news of a lifetime—under any other circumstances.

"So what you're saying—" Easie started, trying to confirm all of the uncomfortable details Larry had already announced.

"Is that you guys are it? Yes. Ratings are in, projections are good, and the network has just confirmed a full season of guaranteed episodes starring the two of you. What else do you need me to repeat?"

She shook her head, and then put her hand to her mouth, looking as though she might be sick. While she tried not to puke on Larry, all I could do was look at her. Beg her with telepathy to look back at me.

"Why do you both look like I just killed your puppies? This should be the best news you've heard in at least a year. There should be jumping and whooping and a generally cheery disposition."

When neither one of us said anything, his face grew even more concerned. "Seriously? What the hell, guys?"

"I think we're just taking it in," I answered for the both of us, trying to play the part of an adversary, but all it earned me was another dirty look.

So noted. I would be able to do absolutely no right today.

"Take it in better," Larry commanded, standing from his chair with a frown marring the normally smooth line of his brow.

I stood to shake his hand, offering, "No worries. We at least have a week to get out of this funk before we have to shoot."

"No," he refuted immediately, looking from Easie to me and back again. "Didn't I mention we secured a full season deal?"

"Well, yeah—"

"That means we can speed up the shooting schedule. You guys are shooting an episode today."

"Today?" I asked with a resigned quiet at the same time that Easie shrieked it.

I'm pretty sure I heard a dog or two yelp from somewhere outside.

"Fucking today," Larry confirmed for both of us, mocking, "Take the word 'to' and the word 'day' and fucking smash them together. *Today*."

Shit.

"You can have forty-five minutes for lunch, or chain smoking, or whatever it is the two of you do, but at the end of that time, I expect you to be in makeup and ready to roll." He moved to round the table, shoving his chair dramatically and dropping two identical packets to the surface of the table below.

"Your scripts."

I waited for Easie to go first.

"Fine," she gritted out through clenched teeth, folding her small body into itself and practically radiating rage.

"Yeah," I agreed, as Larry made for the exit of the room, obviously not really caring if I was okay with it or not.

Easie stood up quickly, rushing to follow Larry out rather than risk being left in the room with me alone, but I pinched closed her route to the door and put my hands up in a placating gesture.

"Easie, please, hear me out."

"No."

"Come on," I pleaded, "Give me a chance to—"

"Fuck that shit and your fucking face, Anderson Evans!" she yelled, pointing a more than irritated finger directly at my offending mug.

I reached out to grab her hand, hoping that touching her would go over slightly better than all of my attempts at verbal reasoning.

It didn't.

Her other arm swung wildly, taking a twisted path but intending to end right where Tammy predicted it would.

I shifted to the side to protect myself, but took my hand off of hers for fear I would hurt her.

She took the change in my position as an invitation to slide right by me and out of the room.

"*Easie.*"

Hope bloomed when she actually turned to look at me one last time.

Knowing she wouldn't let me go into a full explanation, I offered the only thing I could. "I'm sorry."

And then crashed and burned when I saw the look on her face. It was closed and hard and unwilling to look back.

"Yeah," she laughed without humor. "Me too. You have no fucking idea how much."

With one last sweep of her hair, she gave me her back, exiting the room and effectively shutting me out for good.

I might not have known before I got here, but I sure as hell knew now.

I needed luck. And lots of it.

Chapter 14

A T FIRST, I'D THOUGHT Easie's overall hatred of all things me would make for an awkward day of shooting. Especially since the script called for even more intimacy than we'd been asked for before.

Blindfolded, she was required to fully trust me, follow my actions, and wait for her only cues through our bodies. I knew it would be hard for her, and it was pretty fucking hard for me. The amount of pressure I felt to handle her respectfully was nearly crippling.

But I had underestimated her completely, and her sheer talent— both raw and cultivated—mesmerized me more and more as the day went on.

She completely left herself and surrendered to the character, drawing me in and challenging me to resist her charms.

I'd been failing miserably all day, but this scene was the worst.

With her hands on me and her smell in my nose, she consumed me. Transported me out of my role and into myself and erased all signs of rational thinking.

When my lips touched hers, it felt real and right and free. I couldn't stop myself, giving into the temptation was too easy and resisting was too hard, so I let my tongue control my mind instead of the other way around, slipping it inside her mouth when a tiny gasp created the opening.

Lost in the feel and taste of her, I didn't measure myself but rather got lost in her all over again, squeezing her body tightly against mine and allowing my tongue a probing caress.

She gave back to me equally at first, caving to my body's will and following along wherever I might take her.

And then her signature dirty word became mine.

Until.

My worst nightmares took shape as she went cold. Both in reception and action, she broke free from herself and the character and punished me despite the ramifications.

Metal and regret flooded my mouth when she bit down on my unwelcome tongue. I yelped in both surprise and pain, and Howie immediately put an end to a scene that had already been broken.

"Cut!"

"Fuck," I muttered bringing a hand to my mouth and sampling the blood. She'd gone gentle, biting only hard enough to break the surface. I'd have to thank her for that.

Unfortunately, she didn't stick around to let me do anything, emotion and duress ripe on her face in a way that I'd never seen before as she ran off of the set with speed and purpose.

Howie's accusing eyes shot to mine, but I didn't have time to pay a debt of explanations to him. The only one I owed anything to right now was Easie.

Taking off to follow her at a jog, I didn't look back, knowing that there was only one place I'd find her.

The sun was bright when I broke through the door to outside, but the immediate sting of her hand across my face was hotter. Knowing what she thought she knew, I didn't blame her. If it weren't for the refusal of my aching cheek, I would have admitted that it made me like her more.

I didn't want a girl who would eat shit she didn't deserve.

"Easie," I coaxed, trying to get her to look at me as her shaking hands struggled to light her stupid cigarette.

"Fuck, Anderson!" she yelled, pulling the offending stick out of her mouth when she couldn't make her hands cooperate.

Her eyes were vividly beautiful out in the light, but I'd flooded them with tears I had to make right.

Doing something I never thought I'd do, something that went against everything I'd ever known or fought for, I gave in for her, reaching to take the cigarette and lighter out of her hand and lighting it for her.

"Here," I said, offering the cigarette like a peace gesture.

Skeptical and assessing, the petite features of her face wrinkled and rolled, trying to resist but finally giving in.

Taking a deep breath and closing her eyes, she inhaled, harming herself physically but healing her emotional holes all at once. A calm came over her as she finally met my eyes, and I held them, selfish and unwilling to lose them any time soon.

"What's your problem?" she asked, throwing her hands out to her sides in desperation.

"I—" I started to explain, only to be cut off by her unwillingness to wait me out.

"You're spoken for!" she accused, the harsh line of her body breaking my heart and telling me I had a chance all at once. People who didn't care didn't look like that.

"I'm not," I disagreed with acute precision.

She didn't want to hear it, and, as inopportune as it was for me, I admired her ability to resist naivety. "Don't give me that shit! I may have the face of a fucking angel, but I wasn't born yesterday!"

Part of me marveled at her ability to be mean and funny all at once. "Easie—"

"I saw you with her!"

"It's not what you think with Tammy. I can promise you that." If I didn't think she would hit me even harder, I would have laughed.

"I know I saw her kissing you."

"You did. I know. But Tammy and I live together—"

"You *live* together?!" she shrieked violently, taking a swing at my balls but thankfully missing.

"Christ!" I screamed as I executed defensive maneuvers. "No! No! Jesus, that came out wrong. Tammy was my roommate in college—"

She started to interrupt, so in a panicked rush to stop her I spoke quickly and without tact.

"But she wasn't a *Tammy* then, she was a *Tommy*."

Eyes blinking in surprise, her half-burned cigarette dropped to her side.

"You . . ." she choked out, empty hand climbing her throat. "You . . . like men?"

"*No!*"

"I . . . I don't understand," she admitted with a thankfully renewed sense of calm. It was eerie and a little Stepford, but I'd take it.

"She's my best friend. And she has been since she was a he."

"God," she blinked rapidly. "I don't . . . I don't even know what to . . ." Her eyes snapped to mine sharply. "She makes a *really* pretty girl."

I've never smiled so hard. "I'll tell her you said that."

She shook her head in shock, trying to make sense of a myriad of racing thoughts. I understood. Really. It wasn't everyday that someone told you their best friend was transgender.

"Wait . . . why was she kissing you?"

I rolled my eyes. "Tammy gets a kick out of messing with people, and that night she picked you. And I don't know, she claims it was something of a test."

"Girl sabotage," she murmured thoughtfully before bringing her reflective eyes back to mine. "Don't tell her how pretty I said she is. If she's that good at mind games, she's already a diva. Compliments will only make it worse."

"You're right," I laughed, taking the opportunity to take several steps closer to her. "She is a diva. But I think it's only because I'm one of the only people she can get away with it around. Most of her life is spent watching her step and fighting for acceptance. All of our other friends abandoned her when she transitioned."

"Well, then all of your other friends were pricks."

I tucked her loose hair behind her ear and nodded, my face two inches from hers.

"Yeah."

"Sorry I bit your tongue," she whispered, her inquisitive eyes watching mine intensely.

I used them to smile, and then brought my lips gently to hers. Slowly, I teased the line of her lips with mine, taking my time and avoiding putting my tongue anywhere near her mouth. Each corner tasted better than the other, and the middles of her lips cushioned mine like perfectly erotic pillows. Eventually, she grew frustrated with my withholding, challenging it by sliding *her* tongue into *my* mouth . . . and her heart right into my trap.

I smiled as her tongue touched mine, bringing my palm up to cup the line of her jaw softly. Side to side, I tilted my head and went deeper, welcoming her melting body into my ever-hardening one.

Breaking the kiss was one of the single hardest things I'd ever done, but getting to live the moments after it made it worth it.

"I'm not," I finally responded, surprising her enough to cause a rolling giggle.

The sound was soft and innocent in the face of her hard facade, and I welcomed it, breathing it in until I couldn't take anymore.

Bringing our foreheads together and eyes to the ground, we both noticed her abandoned cigarette at the same time.

"I'll get you another," I offered easily, knowing that I'd do anything she wanted me to right then.

Her eyes lit up with wonder as she shook her gorgeous head. "I don't need it right this second."

Her lips met mine again, this time of her own volition, and my accompanying surge of satisfaction fortified my shaking legs enough to prevent their buckle.

I worked hard to go slow, but I didn't go easy, pillaging the line of her tongue from front to back and pushing her gently against the wall.

She went easily, wrapping her arms around my shoulders and stretching to the very top of her tippy toes to ease my slump. I appreciated the gesture, but I didn't intend to let her work at all. Lifting from her firm thighs, I wrapped her smooth legs around my waist and let my fingers linger a little longer than necessary on their exit.

I would have left them there forever, such was the temptation of their satiny texture, but her hair brushed the line of my neck and called to my hands with a louder, more insistent need. There would be plenty of time to explore her legs, I would make sure of that.

A soft moan ached sweetly in her chest as my palm cupped her jaw and the tips of my fingers slid back into her hair.

I'd touched her before. I'd tasted her skin and her lips and even sampled the minty heaven of her tongue, but I hadn't done any of it like this—with nothing between us, with no one there but Easie and Anderson.

I needed inside of her. Pronto.

"Inventor of pants," Easie panted between kisses, breaking her mouth from mine occasionally but offering her neck when she did. "Bad . . . Evil . . . Murder."

I wholeheartedly agreed, groaning pathetically when she rolled her hot hips desperately into mine.

Fast fingers trailed the front of her body, eager, shameless, and unthinking as I zoned in on the siren warmth between her legs. I didn't quite make it there, but I did find the bare skin above it with a quick shift of her billowy shorts.

Easie's breath left her in a rush, and her head flew back so hard I feared it would hit the wall. My body shifted backward out of instinct though, pulling her with it and protecting her skull.

Neither of us could see or hear anything but each other, the heat of the afternoon sun only fueling the tingle that ran through our skin and the whoosh of blood in our ears.

"Ahem." A throat cleared from an uncomfortably close distance.

Right. All that whooshing blood is probably why we didn't hear the door open.

My first concern was Easie, but she made me realize pretty quickly that I needn't have bothered.

"Whoops," she muttered, peeking just slightly around the curve of my head before bringing her delighted eyes back to mine. "I guess we forgot to lock the door. Isn't that what most people say in these situations?" And then she winked.

I rolled my head to hers, breathing her in and letting all of that air come back out as a chuckle. "I'm pretty sure there's an *actual* locking door in those situations."

"I suppose you guys still aren't together?" Ashley asked with a cute tap of her toe.

Easie opened her mouth to speak, but, not sure what she would say, I beat her to the punch.

"We're together," I declared, setting my clinging monkey down on her feet gently as I did.

"That's funny," Ashley remarked, as I adjusted myself surreptitiously and turned to face her head on. Certain parts of me didn't get the memo to stop saying hello.

I kept an arm around Easie and pulled her into my side. "Just last night I'm pretty sure you were the one who had her crying in her cheerios."

Wincing, I didn't even want to think about it. So I didn't.

"We're together," I repeated firmly, giving Easie a squeeze as I did.

"We're together?" she questioned.

"We're together," I affirmed, looking down to meet her eyes directly.

Did she not think we were together?

Ashley had enough. "Okay, seriously? I know Larry mentioned a budget increase, but it wasn't a lot. Do the two of you realize there's an entire crew in there waiting for you, clamoring about why you ran out after a showing of unscripted mutilation?"

"How do you know about the mutilation?" Easie asked embarrassedly, knowing her sister hadn't even been on set when she bit me.

"Did I not mention the clamoring?" Ashley asked, growing impatient. "Back inside. Both of you. Before Larry himself comes and gives you shit about it."

Easie jumped forward to comply, but I pulled her back, squeezing her against my body once more.

"We'll be in in two minutes and ready to work," I compromised sternly.

Ashley's eyes narrowed, but with one last huff and an attitude-ridden toss of her honey blond hair, she pulled open the door and disappeared.

"Come on," Easie said, trying to pull away from me. "We have to go back in there." She gasped low. "Oh God. I have to explain things to Howie. That was so unprofessional."

"Easie," I called, pulling her in like an accordion and turning her to face me before she went into a complete tailspin.

"Just relax. Howie doesn't give one shit about the professional nature of your biting me. He cares what I did to you to make you do it and wants an opportunity to exact his own revenge."

"He said something to you?" She looked mildly horrified.

I remembered the promise of a long, painful death I'd gotten before I left. "It was less about words and more of a look."

"Oh God." Her face sought solace in her hands.

"As long as you're okay when we go back in there, we'll both be okay," I assured, stroking her back and fighting the beginning of a smile.

She really was too cute.

"I'm okay," she said, promising both me and herself and bolstering her nerves. "I may have a small beef with Tammy, but that's for another time."

"You have a problem with Tammy?"

"She kissed you on the lips!" she yelled. "Transgender best friend or not, that bitch did it on purpose."

The ends of my lips edged upward again.

"So you don't want other people kissing me on the lips?" I fished, reaching out to stroke her tiny hip.

She glared. "I think we've pretty much established that we're together, don't you?"

"You were the one questioning it!" I accused.

"That was a test."

I rolled my eyes in exasperation. "What the hell is it with women and tests?"

"Don't fight it," she teased, patting me on the cheek with exaggerated compassion. "You're in a relationship. This is your life now."

She turned to the door again, and this time I followed, ducking into the cool air of the studio behind her and reaching out to take her hand. Now that I could touch her without the threat of a knee or well placed elbow to the balls, I was taking advantage.

"Come on," she hurried me with a tug, letting go of my hand just before we got to set and pretty clearly painting a boundary I could live with. When we were on set, there would be lots of touching, but it would be the mostly fake kind, staged in a professional manner and purposed for the entertainment value of our show.

Like I said, pretty understandable. But, considering the state of my balls, it would probably just be a little harder to live with today.

I smiled on the inside as Howie's eyes carefully assessed the two of us, narrowing noticeably when they moved from Easie to me. I liked that he was looking out for her, and under the amiable circumstances, it was easy to find amusement in his disdain for me. If Easie still felt the same way, I doubted I'd be feeling this cheery about it.

"Easie?" Howie prompted, assessing her state of mind but attempting to do it without embarrassing her further.

"Ready," she responded with a firm nod, meeting his eyes and obviously communicating everything that needed to be.

"Right then. Let's try it again," he instructed before teasing, "Maybe without the bloodshed this time."

I looked from him to her expecting to find a tinge of pink or a shifty-eyed glance, but all I found was the distinct raise of one manicured brow and a smart-ass smirk. "Yes, sir."

She was so complex, layering a quiet smile under the sass of a thousand women and topping it all with a occasional blush of innocence. I couldn't wait to explore every facet of her character and the many inches of skin that housed it.

God, I couldn't wait for tonight.

And then I remembered everything I had to do.

I had to run no less than ten miles, play the basketball game with the adult league I was in, put in the obligatory phone call to my parents, and make up my pre-made meals for the rest of the week.

Maybe *not* tonight.

Fuck.

"Action!" Howie called loudly, snapping me out of my reverie and reminding me to do my job. I'd have to figure out everything else later.

Right now I had to focus on running my hands all over Easie's body without getting too noticeably hard.

It looked like I was going to be failing at a lot today.

Chapter 15

"SO YOU'RE OFFICIALLY TOGETHER?" Tammy asked, making air quotes around the word officially.

I had just finished telling her about the whole day; the tongue biting, the arguing, and the making up. Though, I'd left the details of the last part out of it.

"We're together," I confirmed, choosing to avoid her carefully placed taunting. "You're not in really good standing either."

"What? She's mad? Didn't you tell her everything about me?"

"I told her the basics. She's still pissed you kissed me."

Tammy smiled slightly. "Ah," she breathed. "A woman with balls. That's my kind of people."

"You scare me sometimes," I muttered teasingly.

"You scare me!" she shot back seriously, giving me and the letters in my hand a long once over. "Finally together, finally allowed to act on all of that sexual tension you've built up at the show by pretending to fuck, and now you're here, on the first night, alone, looking at those fucking letters again. What the hell is wrong with you?"

Glancing down at the paper in my hands, I fingered the frayed edge, smoothed out the wrinkle of each fold. "You know. You *know* how important this is to me. And she knows how busy I am."

"She doesn't know why," Tammy countered. "And it must have fucking stung to hear you tell her you couldn't cancel any of your other stupid plans to be with her tonight. If *she's* important to you, you might want to think on that."

It had stung. For both of us. I could still picture the surprised disappointment as it tainted her eyes after the show. I'd almost caved, but at the thought of abandoning all of my responsibilities, I'd felt nauseous with guilt.

"It's not that simple!" I yelled hoarsely. A throb in my chest set up camp, making me rub at it with the heel of my hand and take several deep breaths. "It's not that simple," I whispered.

"I know this is tough for you," Tammy responded softly. "But I'm telling you, as your best friend . . . you better get your ass on your phone and call that girl. At the very least, take her with you to one of your activities tonight."

She was right. I knew she was right.

"Don't let the first thing you've wanted in a long time slip through your fingers, Anderson. It might do you some good to take that fucking ring off and read it every once in a while."

The metal felt cold and heavy against my heated skin. Flexing my fingers, I tried to work away the sting.

"It says the same thing as the letters," I muttered petulantly, staring down at the words as they ran together.

"Then fucking listen." She lowered her voice, gentled it. "This is not *living free,* my friend. You're so trapped in this cycle, it's not even funny."

Tammy didn't understand. No one did.

I *wanted* to be trapped. It was the only place I could still feel *him.*

"Call her."

The second hand ticked loudly under the glass of my watch, calling my eyes directly to it.

Seven fifteen.

I had forty-five minutes until my basketball game. That would be just enough time to pick her up and get there.

Not ready to break my routine fully, I carefully folded my brother's letters, tucked them safely into the large padded envelope, and secured the clasp on the fold. Feeling their weight in my hands, I tucked them to my side as I walked into the living room, opened my tall, oak cabinet, and slid them safely into their spot on the right hand side. With one last glance, I closed the doors, took a deep breath, and dug my phone out the pocket of my shorts.

There weren't many contacts in my phone, so she was easy to find, and I pushed send before I could back out.

I shook my head at myself as it rang in my ear.

I didn't *want* to back out. I fucking wanted to see her. Change is apparently just hard.

Even if it's a good thing.

"Hello?" she finally greeted in my ear, settling my stomach and making me smile.

When I glanced up, Tammy was shaking her head and smirking.

"Hi, Easie."

"Anderson," she said with bite. She was mad at me for not making plans with her tonight. My smile deepened.

"Listen," I said through my grin, hoping she could hear it, "I've just finished my run for the night—"

"A gazillion miles?"

"Yes," I laughed, turning around to face away from Tammy when her knowing stare became too much. "I used my legs and everything."

A soft giggle rumbled in my ear, pulling the tiny strings of my heart and nearly making my tired legs give out.

"Better than mine."

An ache started in the deepest part of my cheeks, that much mass unaccustomed to sitting so high on my cheekbones.

"I'm getting ready to go to my basketball game here in a few minutes, but the more time I spend without you tonight the more I realize—"

"What a prick you are?"

I barked a laugh. "I wasn't quite thinking of that exact wordage, but that's pretty much the gist of it."

"I can meet you there," she offered hopefully, the end of her offer wavering slightly like a question.

"No—"

"Oh."

"No—"

"Okay."

"No—"

"I get it! You don't have to keep saying no. Jesus."

"*Easie.*"

"What?" she asked snottily. I couldn't help but laugh again and shake my head in exasperation.

"If you'd stop talking for a minute, I might have time to finish explaining that no, I don't want you to meet me there *because* I want to pick you up."

"Oh."

"What did I sign on for here?" I teased, scrubbing a hand down my face as I did.

"Another one of those universally female things. It won't be any better with another woman."

I bit into my lip as she added tentatively, "You know, just in case you were considering that someone else would be different."

I was beginning to think someone else would be *totally* different. And a lot less entertaining.

"How do I get to your apartment?"

"Here. Ashley is better at directions than I am," I heard her say, followed by a sound of shuffling, a muffled argument . . . hair pulling?

"Ashley here," her sister greeted, slightly out of breath but covering it well.

"What the hell just happened?" I asked through yet another laugh.

"She doesn't really suck at directions. She needed time to make herself look human again."

"Ashley!" Easie screeched in the background loud enough for me to hear.

"Human?" I guffawed. "What does she do? Take off her skin when she gets home?"

"Just trust me on this. There's a reason people don't live together right away."

"Ashley!" Easie hissed this time.

"I can't imagine Easie looking bad. Ever."

"How sweet," Ashley murmured. "And naive. I'll pray for you."

A loud scrape of wood against wood rang out in my ear, followed pretty closely by an "Ooof!"

"Ashley?"

"Directions," she wheezed. "Do you know where South Street Pub is on Forty-Eighth Street?"

I turned to my window. Looked out it and zeroed in on the neon green sign that read South Street in flashing bold letters.

"Uh, yeah. At the corner of Eight Avenue."

"Yes, exactly! We're one block up from that at the corner of Seventh. 667. Third floor."

I nearly dropped my phone, but squeezed it unbearably tight to stop myself.

Rubbing my neck and shaking my head at the same time, I laughed softly. "Tell Easie I'll be there in five minutes."

"Five? Like, as in five?"

"Five."

"But that's impossible in L.A. unless you—"

"Live one block away. Across from the pub."

Tammy's glass hit the kitchen counter loud enough to make me turn toward her.

"That is some freaky shit," Ashley muttered in my ear, prompting Easie to plead 'what' over and over again in the background.

"Nothing," Ashley said. "He'll be here in about a half hour. You have plenty of time."

"Now that's evil."

I could almost picture her rolling her eyes. "Fine. Anderson says I shouldn't lie. It's very bad of me, and he plans to spank you for my behavior when he gets here."

"Ashley!" Easie and I both chastised at the same time.

"Which will be in five minutes. Assuming he gets off the phone."

I took that as my leave, murmuring a polite, "See you soon," and hanging up the phone before I could hear any more of Easie's yelling. This early on in the relationship, she was allowed to have those kinds of reactions in private and pretend like everything was perfectly fine to my face. My being able to hear her was kind of ruining it for her.

Phone tucked back in my pocket, Tammy had commentary of her own. "A block away?"

I nodded.

"It's like kismet."

"Seriously? You know I respect you completely, but is my old friend Tommy in there anywhere?"

"What did you want me to say?" She let her voice deepen. "Whoa, dude. Easy access. Get laid every night."

"Don't be an asshole."

"Just following by example."

"Fuck." I ran both of my hands backward through my hair and blew out a breath. "You're right. Sorry for the Tommy remark."

"It's fine."

"It's not. You shouldn't have to put up with that shit from me."

"Why?" she asked, inclining her head slightly.

"Because I'm your best friend, and I accept you completely."

"I'm not an idiot, Anderson. While my transition was for *me,* and about *me,* it affects other people. It affects you greatly."

"Yeah, but—"

"Stop. Being accepting does not mean hiding your reactions and feelings. You're allowed to miss Tommy. You're allowed to tell me that." She smiled. "As much as I'd like the world to revolve around me, it *doesn't.*"

"You realize that?"

I expected her to tease back, but she just smiled. Lifted a hand and pointed to the glowing time on the microwave. "How many minutes did you say you would be?"

"Shit!"

Grabbing my keys and my wallet, I slammed my bare feet into my socks and shoes and barely looked back on my way out the door.

I was already three minutes late.

Chapter 16

BOISTEROUS CHEERS AND CATCALLS. Whoops, whistles, and hollers. Heckling and profanity.

And that was just Easie's contribution to our team.

It was without a doubt the absolute best time I'd ever had playing a game in this league, and if the smiles on the other players' faces were anything to go by, I wasn't the only one that felt that way.

Easie had no trouble finding a rhythm—something I'd worried about on the ride over. I knew she didn't need to be babysat every second of the day, but I felt bad bringing her along only to abandon her while I played and she watched.

But, as was often the case with her, I shouldn't have bothered.

"That was exciting!" she cheered, jumping into my sweaty arms and wrapping her equally sticky arms and legs around me. I think she might have jumped around even more than I did.

"We lost," I noted with a smile, holding on to both of her hips and staring at her sparkling blue eyes.

"I know. That's because you guys really sucked."

"Gee, thanks."

"Not you," she comforted, adding with a wink, "You only kind of sucked."

I laughed. "Thanks. I think."

"Don't worry. You have real potential. If you hadn't already run a million miles today, you probably would have been above average."

"Ouch."

"Sugarcoating won't get you victories," she said with a smirk. "Now tell me how flawlessly pretty I am."

God, she was fantastic. Funny and fun and relaxed in my presence. I couldn't get enough of her.

"You *are* flawlessly pretty."

"Hmm," she pondered. "That seemed a little forced. It was probably the word for word repetition. We'll work on that too."

"Come back to my place with me," I whispered through a groan as I squeezed her tighter. This wasn't enough. I needed more.

"Okay," she breathed back, lifting her body slightly and then letting it fall again, rubbing herself against my cock just teasingly.

Fucking hell.

Startling her, I never put her down, instead jogging all the way to my Toyota Tacoma with her in my arms and her legs around my waist.

She snickered as we bumped and rubbed, but I couldn't manage anything other than the task at hand. My blood supply had already made the official migration.

Rational thinking and reasoning were a thing of the past, and my sense of humor was on vacation until after I'd had the chance to be inside of her.

Dumping her into the passenger side quickly, I rounded the hood and jumped in, firing the ignition amid the sound of more of her giggles. I was fairly certain she tried to get my attention further, but my vision had completely tunneled.

Good thing that court was only ten blocks away from my apartment. I normally wouldn't have even driven, but I knew how Easie felt about extraneous physical activity. And now that I was faced with this urgency, I was glad for her faux laziness.

Reaching over the console, she put her hand on my thigh and

rubbed maddeningly teasing strokes through the fabric of my shorts.

I completely zoned out, flying the ten blocks and staying conscious of only things that could affect our safety.

Thankfully, the mental block seemed to work, and the magically empty parking spot in front of my building beckoned.

Screeching the tires to a stop, I barely shifted into neural and pulled on the emergency brake before flicking off the key and jumping out of my side.

Easie took pity on me for once, climbing out of her side on her own and waiting on the sidewalk while I rounded the hood.

She giggled as I grabbed her hand and pulled her behind me, jogging into the building and through the door to the stairwell. She yelped as I scooped her into my arms and took the stairs two at a time.

Setting her on her feet at the top as gently as I could manage, she grabbed my hand and wagged her brows as I took off at a jog again, eating up the too long distance between the entrance to the stairwell and the door to our apartment as quickly as possible.

The key slid directly into my fingers as I reached into my pocket, and Easie pressed tightly up to my back as I stuck it into the lock and turned. We stumbled in, getting tangled in each other as we fought to turn so that we could taste each other finally.

My lips took control of hers, and she gave into it, turning her head to give me better access and allowing me to lead the way on an exploration of her mouth. I tuned my ears to the apartment though, listening for Tammy and, thankfully, hearing nothing.

The rough edge of Easie's pant reeled my ears right back into the moment, daring me to listen to anything but her. I could feel the heat of her excitement against the hardness of mine, and with fumbling precision, I backed us toward the open door of my bedroom.

Tripping and bumping into walls along the way, we eventually made it, the loud crack of the door slamming coming slightly after her well placed kick.

Her skin was everywhere—a line of it exposed at the bottom of her tank, the hollow of her breasts, the line of her neck, and her arms all begging to be tasted and touched.

I planned to sample every inch, not leaving any of it untouched, but I needed to take the edge off if I didn't want to make a complete fool of myself. It had been several years since I'd—

"Oh, *shit.*"

"What?" she gasped and leaned forward, having just pulled her shirt over her head and eased onto the bed.

"I don't . . . *Fuck!*" I rubbed the back of my neck and sank to my knees. "I don't have any condoms."

"How in the fuck is it possible you don't have condoms?" she demanded loudly, making her exposed breasts bounce and distracting my eyes.

I shrugged, smiled a little at the insanity of the situation.

My dick wasn't smiling though. Not at all.

"I haven't dated since college."

"No, I don't believe that."

"Yes."

"Dated or *dated?*"

"Either."

"No, no, I don't believe that."

"Why not?"

"I just don't. I mean, how is that even possible?"

"I've been . . . well, I've been busy," I answered truthfully. I hadn't thought about doing even one thing for myself since Evan died. It had all been for him. The harsh realization that stemmed from that admission was truly startling. Until that very moment, I'd never even considered it.

"Don't even suggest that we do it with no protection!"

Did she really think I would do that? I would never disrespect her like that.

"I didn't suggest it."

"I couldn't be in a more fertile part of my cycle if I tried!"

"Easie, I was *not* going to suggest it. I wouldn't."

"It's not going to happen!"

"Who are you talking to right now?" It obviously wasn't me.

Her eyes focused on me again. "Oops. Sorry. Personal pep talk."

"You do that often?"

"Normally, I do it silently."

"Probably smart."

"Don't you dare mock me right now. This is your fault. Don't you know that you never, ever invite a girl to your place without knowing you have condoms?"

"I was too busy thinking about you to think about anything else."

"Oh. Well now I can't be a bitch."

"Lie back," I instructed with a smirk, picking myself up and towering over her.

"Why?"

I dropped my voice to a serious whisper. "Easie."

She looked up at me longingly, the line of her lashes fluttering with each heave of her chest.

"Lie back."

She complied immediately, scooting up the bed and making her hair fan out all over my pillow.

Crawling over her, I reached between my shoulders and pulled my shirt off, murmuring, "Fair's fair," directly into the soft skin of her stretched neck.

A shuttering breath shook the damp hair at my ear as she breathed out and arched into me, running her nails along the newly naked line of my side.

Eager lips and trailing hands worked together as a team as I started at her neck, nibbling and sucking the soft skin away from the muscle and licking the edge when it entered my mouth. She moaned, opening her legs to let me fall in between, and I used a free hand to stroke the exposed skin of her hip in rhythm with my lips.

Her hips fell in line with the song, moving at the same pace and brushing against me with fervor.

Arousal rumbled in my throat, clotting and clogging at the prohibition of its release, turning into a growl and tingling along the line of her skin with a noticeable vibration.

"Anderson," she whispered, dropping any pretense of inhibition and exposing herself to me physically and emotionally.

Her voice rang with the sincerity of someone who was invested, and the realization of her reciprocation made me harden even further.

I wanted to devour her, spend an hour on each inch, a week on each part.

The beat of her heart stuttered as I moved from her neck to her lips, delving inside and caressing her tongue with mine. She pushed back, moving the dance to my mouth and leading me.

Both of her hands moved from my back to my hair, gripping and pulling and sending a wave of electricity from my roots all the way down my spine to my toes. They stretched in reaction, begging for their own contact, so I worked efficiently to kick my shoes off with the toe to heel method and then used my feet to rid hers of her flip flops.

Tangled together, our legs worked their own dance, touching and exploring and running the line of one another's skin.

The first time together was always an exploratory mission, but this time was different. I'd lived six more lives since the last time I'd done this—and lost one important one.

The connection, the intimacy of it, meant more than I'd ever dreamed it would in the past.

Sitting up and straddling her, I ran both hands along the line of her collarbone, down the center of her chest and along the line underneath her breasts.

"I want to taste you."

I asked for permission and she gave it, moving forward just enough to unclasp the back of her bra and pull it down the line of her arms.

Her breasts were full and heavy, tan, and peaked with the perfect rose red buds.

"You're fucking gorgeous," I growled, taking the weight of her in my hands and molding them together. She watched with wide eyes as I leaned forward and pulled one perfect nipple into my mouth, circling the edge with my tongue and flicking the tip as I finished.

Her eyes closed as I moved to the other one and repeated my movements, finishing by licking and biting the plump skin that surrounded each of them and burying my face in the middle and inhaling.

She smelled like sweet apples and minty gum and mouthwatering juiciness that I couldn't wait to taste fully. And only a hint of cigarette smoke.

I wanted her to coat my mouth, run down the line of my neck and onto my chest when I ate her. I wanted to smell her on me for weeks to come and dream of the chance to consume her again.

Careful to tell my dick to keep his hands to himself, I pulled back enough to kick off my shorts and then pulled hers down to reveal the same.

Naked for the first time, I felt her eyes as they watched me, a question in them making me scoot my hips well away from hers.

"*You*, Easie. I'm going to eat you until you come. And I'm going to dream about the feel of it all on my cock and look forward to next time while I do it."

"Goddamn," she whispered, her eyes dilating noticeably. "That's how you fucking dirty talk someone into submission."

I couldn't stop my smirk as I inched each side of her panties down over the curve of her slender hips and exposed all of the bare skin I'd gotten a teasing touch of earlier that day.

"Bare, baby?"

"It's easier not to have to deal with it. That's the last thing anybody needs to accidentally see on television."

I raised a teasing brow. "It's also sexy as fuck."

"There's that too," she agreed before rocking my world. "Of course, that hasn't mattered in a really long time for me either. You know, in case you were wondering."

Leaning forward immediately, I sucked, pulling her hips off of the bed enough to allow my hands access to her ass. It felt perfect in my hands, and she tasted perfect on my tongue.

Fresh and sweet and really fucking ready for me.

I worked her with the flat of my tongue, watching as her hips writhed with the motion, pushing more of herself into my mouth with each stroke. I gladly accepted it, grinding my hips into the bed with each lick and praying she'd come in my mouth before I had a chance to come all over the comforter.

"Anderson," she breathed suddenly, increasing the tempo of her hips and begging me to get her there quickly. Circling her clit with the tip of my tongue once before flicking it several times fast, I waited, lifting my eyes to watch her face when she finally let go.

A scream echoed throughout the room as it made a strangled escape from her open mouth, and her hips surged forward one last time into my mouth. I moved quickly, taking over at her clit with my thumb to help her ride the wave and moving my mouth to drink the flood of her orgasm.

I'd never tasted anything better.

As soon as I'd finished the thought, I pulled away slowly, licked my lips, and wiped the excess off of my face with the back of my arm.

I barely completed the task before she launched herself at me, tackling me to the ground with enough force to make me grunt.

"Ow. Christ, woman," I complained good-naturedly as she attacked me, licking and biting my neck with urgency and working her way quickly down my chest and abdomen, finishing by running her tongue up the line where my leg met my hip and brushing her cheek along my hard cock in the process.

Sweet baby Jesus.

"Easie, you don't have to—" I started to offer, trying out the gentlemanly thing for our first time.

"Shut. Up," she punctuated between licks, ensuring with the path of her tongue that I did just that.

"Holy hell," I groaned as she moved over, starting her lick at the bottom of my balls and running her tongue up the entire line of my dick.

The head bobbed, just about smacking her in the chin, and weeped a drop of fluid onto the bottom of my stomach.

This was going to go fast.

She didn't though. She worked me slow and easy, making sure to wet the entirety of my cock before wrapping the base with her fist and swallowing the head into the back of her mouth.

Fireworks went off in my spine, warning me with more than a tingle that my release was in the barrel, the gun was cocked, and Easie's finger was poised right at the edge of the trigger.

"Gonna come soon," I warned, doing The Tap and hoping she'd move away if she wanted to, and then settled my hand into the shiny blond strands of her loose hair.

She didn't, opting to keep at me until I broke, circling the head with her tongue and bobbing her head at the same time, and never letting up on the steady stroke of her hand.

Blackness bled through my vision as I came, focusing the sensation to her actions and heightening the experience immeasurably. She hummed as she felt my release hit her mouth, sucking and licking until she'd taken everything and worked me through the entirety of my orgasm.

Panting, I struggled to move, and the bright lights in the ceiling nearly blinded me when I managed to open my eyes again.

Despite the white-wash of the lights, all I could see was her.

Blond hair and blue eyes in the sassiest tiny package I'd ever encountered.

I was ruined.

She had ruined me.

Chapter 17

WHEN EASIE WALKED INTO the kitchen the next morning wearing just my t-shirt, I lost a little bit more of my mind.

All that leg leading straight into a land of pleasure and treats covered only by the fabric of my shirt?

Nothing fucking like it.

So consumed with the sleepy look in her eyes, I didn't even remember that a pajama-wearing Tammy sat drinking coffee at the counter while I cooked all of the meals I'd abandoned last night in favor of sleeping cuddled tightly to Easie's sleek, naked back. As weird as it was, neither of us even considered my taking her home to sleep.

"Well, well, it's the life or death acting job girl."

"Easie," my gorgeous girl said with the raise of a brow. Tammy could stir the shit all she wanted. Easie had no plans of eating it.

"Right. I'm Tammy."

"I know."

They stared at one another for several seconds—assessing—before Easie spoke again.

"Listen, it's nice to meet you and everything. You know, formally." Tammy raised her own brows, waiting for the turn. "But don't ever put your lips on Anderson's again."

And there it was.

"Hasn't he told you, honey?" Tammy asked lightly. "All of my parts are man-made. I don't think he's into it."

"Are you kidding?" Easie scoffed, gesturing up and down the line of Tammy's body dramatically. "Have you seen yourself? Have you seen fucking Caitlyn Jenner? You both have better boobs than I do!"

At that point, I couldn't help but pipe in. I lifted one finger in the air to get her attention. When she looked at me, I only said one, very pointed word. "False."

Tammy scoffed, but with one steely look from me, moved on from what might have turned into an unnecessarily heated debate about gender politics.

Ugh. There was a reason I only liked to deal with one girl at a time.

"What are you to up to today?" Tammy asked, leading the conversation in another overly helpful direction.

"We actually haven't had a chance to talk about it yet," I said tightly, having wanted to talk to Easie about it before I had to deal with Tammy's judgements.

Easie jumped onto a stool at the counter, seemingly oblivious to the tension between me and the other woman.

She shrugged. Reached across the counter and popped a piece of my broccoli into her mouth. "I'd say we're going to a drugstore for sure."

I nearly choked on my tongue, coughing and sputtering into my arm to avoid spitting all over my food.

"You okay, Anderson?" she teased, leaning into her shoulder coyly. The material of my shirt dropped off to reveal it, the neck hole far bigger on her tiny frame than it was on me.

Looking her directly in the eye, I told her the truth. "Better than, Easie."

Her answering smile was dazzling.

"Besides the drugstore," I said, watching as Easie got up off her stool, walked around the counter, and poured herself coffee. She was making herself at home, and I loved it. "I thought I'd see if you wanted to go surfing with me."

Tammy shook her head, got up from her stool, and went back to her bedroom. I did my best to ignore her.

Easie set the pot back on the heater and turned excitedly to me. "Really?!"

I liked her reaction better.

"Yeah," I agreed. "I figured maybe I could teach you a little if you wanted. If not, you can sit in the sand and tan."

"Definitely the learning. I know I don't come across as much of a doer, but trust me, I'm very competitive."

"Well," I laughed. "I can't wait to see you kick my ass then."

"Kicking of the ass today, kissing of the ass tonight," she winked, throwing her unoccupied arm up and around my neck.

"Now that's a deal." Leaning forward slowly, I sealed my lips to hers, getting lost in her and the moment and loving the satisfying feel of it.

Maybe I could have everything after all.

After dropping by her apartment to let her change into a bathing suit, Easie's pragmatic side made an appearance and suggested we go to the drugstore then, while we were both in our right minds.

Not one to argue with a good suggestion (read: demand), I stopped, ran in and got condoms while she bought cigarettes (a fact I worked really hard to ignore), and now we had finally arrived at Manhattan Beach to do some surfing.

Easie's excitement practically poured out of her, but she didn't fidget. Instead she channeled it into the mutilation of her lower lip and the subsequent destruction of my self-control.

Leaning across my shifter, I smoothed my hand up her bare thigh and put my lips to hers, tugging the bottom one free of her teeth with a nip of mine.

"You're driving me crazy," I whispered there, licking the inside perimeter of her lips when she gasped them into a small "o" shape.

"Sorry."

"Don't be. You can't help how sexy you are."

She twisted her face into an ugly smile like she'd done to me once before. And it *was* unattractive, trust me, but it was meant to be.

"How am I now?" she teased, fluffing her hair while her bulging eye twitched.

"Slightly less sexy," I admitted tactfully, feeling my grin all the way in my hair follicles.

"Good. Mood ruined. Let's go surf!" she cheered, jumping out of the truck and leaving me behind with a semi-hard cock and a smile on my face.

I really wasn't sure how she managed to leave me unsatisfied and happy simultaneously, but I *was* sure that she was the only one who could.

Turning from the empty space she left behind to my door, I climbed out and slammed it shut, and then walked the few steps to the back to get my board out. Never having included anyone else in anything that had to do with Evan, I only had the one, but I was kind of looking forward to spending all of my time trying to help her catch a wave.

For as long as she lasted anyway. I had a sneaking suspicion she didn't have a clue what kind of a workout she was in for.

Calling out, I aimed to stop her overly eager romp down the expanse of sand before the ocean. We had one more errand to run, right across the street, before she'd be ready.

"Whoa there, Easie!"

Her head jerked up and her petite feet pattered to a quick stop.

"What?" she asked back, her hands jumping to her hips with a strong show of attitude.

Jogging to get closer to her, I stopped only two feet away. "The water temperature here is about sixty-three degrees."

"Yeah?" she replied with a cute tilt of her defiant head. "And?"

"*And* comfortable water temperature is a good ten plus degrees north of that. You spend thirty minutes in that water with no wetsuit and you'll freeze your very attractive nipples right off."

"Ow." Her arms came up and crossed on her chest in a defensive reflex.

"Yeah. I'm not real fond of that idea either." I chuckled. Stared longingly at her attractively ample chest.

She mocked my chuckle with a fake one of her own. "I'm guessing you have an actual other option for me? A solution to this problem? Because if you don't, I might have to junk punch you. Hard."

"No junk punching necessary," I assured her, surreptitiously placing one hand in front of it, just in case. "Only junk love."

She shook her head, a smirk forming at the corners of her mouth and squishing up the line of her nose. I could feel my smile grow in response.

"Come on," I prompted. "There's a shop right across the street where we can grab you a suit and save your nipples."

"I think you just like saying the word 'nipples'," she accused accurately.

"It's not bad," I admitted through a chuckle, adding a remark that earned me a dainty slap shortly after. "It's not as good as touching them."

The sharp sting of her fingertips on the bare skin of my arm did nothing to deter me. "Of course, that lacks in appeal compared to tasting."

She shook her head. "Are all men this unashamedly lecherous?"

"Yes."

"I'm surprised I don't find every last one of you humping a pillow like those little horny dogs every time I enter a room."

"Ha! Pillows lack a little bit in the warmth and moisture department."

"Gross."

"You brought it up," I pointed out, putting my hand to the small of her back to guide her back across the semi-busy street.

"You're right. I just underestimated your ability to pick up the ball and run with it."

"I'm very athletic," I teased as we stepped onto the curb in front of Rip Curl.

Easie glanced into the window, and in one quick instant, all of her joviality fled. "Anderson, I can't afford—"

"I'm buying it," I cut in.

"No, I can't let you."

The guilt was immediate and very nearly suffocating. If it weren't for me, and my undeniable inability to let go, she wouldn't feel the need to spend money she didn't have.

"Easie," I pleaded with my eyes, hoping we weren't going to have the same old antiquated argument that men and women had been having for years.

She obviously wasn't as keen to avoid it, striking back with a weighty name call of her own. "Anderson."

"I totally respect your attempt to pay. And I promise this isn't the beginning of some misguided alpha attempt to control your life."

She raised her brows.

"But I suggested we do this. I knew you would need one of these. I never considered making you pay for it."

Her mouth opened with the beginning of a word, but I talked on, making her slam it closed like a gulping fish.

"Don't make me waste good time and energy arguing about it."

She cocked a hip to the side, but I ignored it, stepping into her body and bringing my lips directly to her ear.

"If you want to be in control, take it for yourself later, when we're in bed and my head is between your legs."

Her body rolled, her hips sucking to mine like a magnet in time with her small gasp.

Pulling back slightly, her uncharacteristically timid eyes met mine.

"You're willing to give up control *then?*"

I nearly laughed. "When I'm eating you out?"

She nodded, wide-eyed.

Skating my lips from the bottom of her neck upward, I moved them back to the shell of her ear and lowered my voice to a whisper. "I can't think of a better time."

A shiver passed through her body, but as I pulled away, she gathered herself fairly quickly. "Okay, you sex-bargainer, you. Buy me things if you must."

"It's amazing how you managed to make two very good things sound bad just now."

She shrugged adorably. "It's a gift really."

Only when I looked away from her to the store, did I realize just how long we'd been standing out here.

"Jesus."

"What?" she reacted, jumping and turning to look where I was looking.

Two beefy hands formed a cone around a pair of beady eyes, and the set of them all was pressed firmly against the glass window.

"Jimmy," I told Easie, pushing her toward the door and pulling it open.

Jimmy was the owner of Rip Curl, and I'd known him since the first day I came in there, lost and desperate to turn myself into the surfer Evan dreamed of. But even he didn't know the reason behind my desperation, the factor behind my seemingly endless drive and determination.

Nearly no one did.

"Anderson!" Jimmy greeted as the bell rang over the door.

"Hey, Jimmy."

"And who is this lovely lady?" he asked, shuffling his sandaled feet directly over to her and grabbing one of her hands between both of his.

Jimmy's skin was tan and worn with both age and abuse, and his clothes hung shapelessly from his relatively svelte body. An active lifestyle kept him moving better than any other eighty year old man I knew. His hair was completely gray and shaggy with inattention, and the bearded line of his jaw matched it to a T.

And, like *every* other old man I'd ever known, he was a charmer with the young ladies.

"I'm Easie," she introduced herself, smiling at Jimmy's disheveled appearance in a fond way that she never would have if he were twenty years younger.

"Oh," Jimmy cooed. "I don't believe I've ever seen a prettier woman." Leaning in and speaking conspiratorially, he whispered and jerked a hand in my direction. "Are you sure you want to be hanging out with this guy?"

Easie smiled her prettiest, most natural smile at me.

"He seems pretty worthwhile so far."

Fuck if that didn't make me feel good.

"Good, good," Jimmy tutted, still holding her hand. "I've never had a problem with him, but I've also never seen him with a woman before. You can never be too careful."

Easie looked me over as though she was considering the fact that I wasn't a liar.

And I wasn't.

Except by omission.

"In fact, I've never seen him with anyone. Kind of a loner, this one," Jimmy continued, spilling everything he knew about me as quickly as possible all in the name of wooing my woman.

"I think that's enough about me," I cut in. "Easie needs a wetsuit."

"Oh, excellent!" he cheered, the informational dumping a memory now that we were talking about his favorite thing.

Surfing.

Jimmy was a surfer of old, a real lifer. He'd been on a board since he was young and reckless, and then he'd never grown out of it, opening up Rip Curl when a life spent constantly in the ocean became too much for his aging body.

He had a singleminded kind of passion and focus, dumping all of his attention into being a surfer and helping other people become one too. I'd spent my time carefully honing myself into the complete opposite.

Often worn thin and spread just past the point of comfortable, I pushed myself, constantly expecting more and never feeling like it was enough.

I honestly didn't know if I ever would.

"What are we thinking? Full suit? Spring suit?"

"She's going to use it today."

"You spend a lot of time in the Pacific Ocean, pretty lady?" he asked, turning to Easie to survey her face.

Her eyebrows shot up just before her whole face scrunched into a comical showing of shame. "None."

Tilting my chin down toward the ground, I bit into my lower lip to smother a laugh.

"None?" Jimmy questioned, the foreign concept making him reach out to the nearby counter for support.

"None," Easie confirmed and looked to me for help.

"Don't give her a hard time, old man. She's going in today." I lifted my eyebrows in Easie's direction, hoping I'd passed her test. And that's what it was. She'd taught me enough times for me to get it. "Which is why—"

"She needs a wetsuit. Got it, got it," Jimmy muttered. "Full suit it is," he decided, turning to her. "You're gonna freeze your ass off. Pardon my french."

"I get it, I get it," she huffed dramatically. "I'm going to freeze all of my valuable parts off. Consider it noted."

Jimmy looked to me in question, but he did it with a goofy smile on his face.

"You're going to be fine in a full suit," I assured her, realizing for the first time that we were doing a good job of talking her out of something we didn't want to talk her out of.

Pretty fucking brilliant of us.

Jimmy looked at me like I was crazy, so I pulled Easie to my chest and wrapped my arms around her as a distraction.

Over her shoulder I made the universal motion for 'shut the hell up,' slicing a single finger across the line of my throat.

He finally got the hint, making his way to the women's end of the store and pulling a low-temperature-rated suit from the rack.

"Here, Easie," he called, forcing me to slowly let her go. "Why don't you try this one on."

I watched as she swayed her way to the back and slipped into the dressing room and closed the curtain. Jimmy didn't bother walking back to the front of the store, opting instead to lean on the rack from which he'd pulled her suit.

"First timer?" he asked, making small talk for the sake of getting to the bottom of the deeper issue. He'd been trying to get me to spill my beans for years, but I had a lot of practice making sure my nut was tough to crack.

I guess he thought lulling me into his trap with innocent topics first would end in a different result.

It wouldn't.

"How's it going in there?" I asked Easie instead of answering him. He just looked to the ground and shook his head, bemused.

"Fuck me, this thing is like a fucking medieval torture device."

Both Jimmy and I chuckled. "The neoprene can be tricky the first few times."

"Tricky?!" she shrieked. "Spanx aren't even this bad. And the last time I tried to get into those I swore to myself I'd rather jump into a life of prostitution than wear them again!"

"Spanx?" Jimmy muttered, just as clueless as I was.

"Um, what are Spanx?" I ventured, walking over to the dressing room and standing just on the other side of the curtain.

"An invention intended to make fat women feel skinny and skinny women feel even skinnier. Or, one of Satan's best jokes. Depends on how you look at it really."

"And I suppose that means that the fit is too tight?"

"How the hell should I know? I've never worn a wetsuit before."

Sliding the curtain open, I stepped in to find her hair disheveled and her face beet red. She looked like she was about five seconds away from stabbing herself, just to escape having to spend one more minute in that suit. "If it has you contemplating death, I'm going to go out on a limb and say it's too tight."

"Death has definitely been contemplated. Not only that, I've planned it out thoroughly, decided on the method, and found the perfect way to blame it completely on you."

"That's bad." Teeth clenched and eyebrows raised, my lips stretched and pulled back into a grimace.

"I get that you're cute and everything, but if you don't get me out of this thing in the next two seconds, I won't be the only death reported on the news."

I laughed, stepping forward and rubbing my hands down the line of her tightly packaged body. "It should fit snuggly at the wrists and ankles, and just a touch snug at the neck, but you shouldn't feel like an over-swollen tick."

"Then this is definitely too small. Or I'm too big, but I prefer the first option."

I bit into my bottom lip and rubbed my hands up and down her perfect body some more. "It's definitely too small."

"Great," she fake cheered, making fists and shaking them upward quickly. "Now get me out of it. I already made like Gumby to zip the damn thing up, but now my bendy bone is broken."

"We wouldn't want that," I whispered, sliding the zipper at the back of her suit down slowly and letting the knobs of my knuckles drag against her skin. "I have a really strong feeling that I'm going to like your bendy bone."

"Good God," she moaned—and not in the way that I'd hoped.

"You're like a whole different breed of human. No wonder that person wrote that book about us being from different planets."

"Men Are From Mars, Women Are From Venus?"

"More like Women Are From Earth, Men Are From Oh Look, A Vagina!"

Rough chuckles hopped their way up my throat, rattling slightly with the shake of my head. "What? And women aren't into innuendos? Good try, sweetheart, but I don't think so."

"No," she agreed. "Women love the innuendo. We love your big, thick cocks and thinking about you using them."

Andddd I was starting to get hard.

Fuck.

"But we think about dicks when we want to think about dicks. We eat ice cream, we're thinking about the taste, the calories, and how many more servings we can have without wanting to slit our wrists when we pick up a women's magazine. You watch us eat it, and you've got us pictured in a knob gobbler film reel."

"Knob gobbler?"

"Don't even pretend you don't know what I mean."

Busted. I was picturing myself picturing knob gobbling. The male mind was a vicious circle of sex. How we've done it, how we want to do it, and the way she would contribute. Ways to make her want it, what we need to do to make it happen, and after we've had it, how to make it happen again.

Biology at its finest.

I angled my head in concession.

"Now get out." She shoved me playfully to the other side of the curtain. "Thanks for unzipping me, but I need another option and you must be my errand boy. I didn't sign on for wetsuit shopping all day."

Turning to pick out another suit and smiling as I did, I found Jimmy leaning on the rack closest to the room. His elbow was supporting some of his weight by leaning on top, and the fingers of his other hand were laced carelessly with their dangling counterparts.

And his tired blue eyes were positively dancing. "You hooked yourself a feisty one, huh?"

"You have no idea, Jimmy." I shook my head once again and pulled a bigger size off the rack. "You have no idea."

"Hold tight and don't fuck it up."

My eyes shot back to his.

"I won't," I promised even though I wasn't so sure it was true.

"You will," he disagreed, rocking his head back and forth like a man who knew. "We always do."

Chapter 18

"**I**S LEARNING TO BREATHE saltwater one of the skills of surfing I'll acquire over time?" Easie asked as we drove back toward downtown Los Angeles and my apartment.

Her golden hair reflected a sparkle of dwindling sunlight, and her blue eyes rolled back into the comfort of her resting head.

Splaying my hand on the warm skin of her sun-kissed thigh, I answered truthfully. "I don't think so."

Her eyes popped open and pointed their power directly at me. "I don't think I'm ever going to be good at it then."

"Ah, but see. You *will* acquire the skill to not be in a situation where you *need* to breathe water. That's the key."

She'd done well, finally getting up and staying up for a solid ten seconds on a baby wave about halfway through our day. After that, she'd gotten tired, wiping out time after time until her resolve wore thin, scoured away by the sand of the unforgiving sea floor. Settling onto a towel, and sprawling out into one of the most attractive beach bunnies I'd ever seen, she watched me ride wave after wave for the rest of the day.

I'd felt bad keeping her there so long, and yet, I literally couldn't find the strength within me to give in to the temptation to leave.

It might be fucked up, but my sense of loyalty was rooted in Evan so deep I didn't know if I could change it no matter how bad I wanted to. And that scared me more about my relationship with Easie than anything else.

Maybe I wouldn't be able to give her the time and priority she so desperately deserved.

"I'm not sure I believe you," she disagreed. "I'm thinking a few more waves will work me over before I get to that point, and I'm not sure how much more of that I can take."

"You don't like the motion of the ocean?"

"Fuck your cuteness. I hurt."

"Aww," I cooed. "Poor baby. I'll rub you and make it feel better."

"You're going to have to rub it for a long time."

I winked and squeezed her flesh into the palm of my hand. "I'll rub it as long as you want, baby."

Muttering under her breath, she blustered with false disdain. "Sex fiend."

"Sex? Whatever do you mean, sweet Easie?" I asked, obviously faking my innocence. "Who's the dirty minded one now?"

"You're telling me you were referring strictly to a back rub?"

"Of course," I lied. "You mucked that one up all on your own."

"Hah," she scoffed. "Not likely."

I pulled into the first open spot I saw on my block, shifted into neutral and put on the parking brake.

Easie attempted to make a move to climb out, but all that happened was a long-suffering moan.

"Sore, huh?" I asked with a chuckle, kicking open my door, climbing out, slamming it shut, and rounding my hood to help her with the difficult journey from the seat to the sidewalk.

Easing her way by opening her door and lifting most of her weight, I was taken off guard when she looked up at me with unhappy eyes.

"I'll meet you up there."

"Why?" I asked, pretty well aware that she didn't want to tell me.

Like most people, I was a glutton for punishment, demanding to know anyway.

But she wasn't one to bury the lead once the ball was in motion. "I need to smoke a cigarette."

God.

Turns out we'd both accomplished something today. She'd gone this long without smoking, and I'd managed the same amount of time without thinking about it.

Of course, all good things must come to an end.

"Right."

I truly didn't mean to, but even I could hear the colder turn of my voice.

"Fuck," she muttered, reaching into her bag and pulling out a cigarette. The issue of her smoking was stressing her out enough to make her need to smoke that much more. Even I couldn't miss the comedic irony in that.

Pushing her cigarette to the side gently before she could light it, I pulled her body to mine and pressed my lips to the warm, soft skin behind her ear. "I'll meet you upstairs. I know I'm struggling with it now, but I promise I'll find a way to deal with it."

"Why is it so important to you?" she asked, wrapping her tiny arms around me and holding me back.

Panicked melancholy leeched instantly into my veins, clenching my teeth and eyes tight out of reflex. It was on the tip of my tongue to tell her—to open up the ugly box that had shaped me—when my phone rang obnoxiously from the pocket of my shorts.

Pulling back, I apologized with my eyes, but a part of me couldn't help but feel relieved.

Ultimately, there'd come a time when she would expect me to make a choice between her and Evan. And, no matter who I chose, I doubted I would make the right one.

In this hazy, undecided, unacknowledged place, I could hold onto the past and reach for the future at the same time.

"Hello?" I said, putting the phone to my ear without reading the caller ID.

"Hi, honey," my mom said in my ear, her voice the hollow echo of its former self like always.

"Hi, Mom," I greeted back, pointing to the phone and then up to the window of my apartment.

Easie's eyes shuttered with obvious disappointment.

I knew the half-hearted apology in mine was shallow at best, but it was all I could manage. And I hated myself for it. This was why I'd tried so hard to resist her.

She just turned out to be irresistible.

Leaving her behind to go into the building, I tried to put her disappointment out of my mind and focused on the woman in my ear.

Pushing open the stairwell door, my steps echoed and bounced in the largely blank space.

"I haven't heard from you in a while."

"I know."

"A long while," she elaborated, making me stop climbing the stairs to close my eyes with guilt.

"I know, Mom. I'm sorry. I've been busy." The words felt painfully hollow, no matter how true they were.

I could almost feel her shrewd eyes through the phone. "I know you're busy. You've been busy for years now."

"Mom—"

"Losing one son was devastating, Anderson. Losing two is nearly unbearable."

"You haven't lost me." I was still very much breathing—living. I called her every week. She hadn't lost me.

"I have."

"Mom," I cut in, bringing the front of my closed fist to my forehead. "This isn't a good time for this. I'm sorry."

"I know you are." Her words were weighty.

"I'll call you tomorrow."

"Okay," she conceded, her voice sullen.

Gahhh. Bringing my fist forward and back a tapped a slow beat into my pulsing forehead.

"I love you."

"I know that too, Anderson."

The phone clicked in my ear, and I pulled it away to check that the call had fully dropped.

Turning to the wall, I leaned my head into the cool cinderblocks and splayed my hands out at its side.

"Frustrating conversation?" Easie's voice echoed, surprising me enough to make me whip around to face her.

"Uh," I stuttered before giving her an honest answer. I rubbed the back of my neck and then ruffled my hair at the top of it. "It's complicated."

She just nodded, her face serious but not hostile.

For that I was grateful. I didn't want to argue with her. I didn't want to get into a deep conversation that was bound to end in tears and heartbreak.

I just wanted a night with her. Just one night to let my body get to know hers and memorize it for the rest of time without thinking about any of the other stuff.

At least I'd be able to picture her every feature when my stupidity finally caught up with me.

"You ready to go upstairs?"

She looked to me and then back to the door. Indecision contorted the line of her brow and disfigured the normally pleasant line of her pretty face. Maybe living a block away from one another wasn't such a good thing. It gave her a way to run away.

"Are you sure you want me to come up?"

Practically jumping down the five steps that separated us, I grabbed her hips and pulled her body into mine before grabbing her jaw with my palms.

"Yes. God, Easie, I can't think of anything else I want more."

Soft, golden skin and rich minty lips mesmerized me, and the apple of her skin completely camouflaged any smokey stench. She smelled edible and ripe, and I couldn't wait to get my mouth all over her.

"Easie," I groaned, giving into the temptation and sinking my lips deep into the plump flesh of her skin. It gave way to their touch, molding to the shape of my mouth and reddening under the suction it produced. Her nails scratched at my back, and her body finally relaxed and gave way to the moment. All the tension of our differences, the pressure of my sense of obligation, the dispute about her smoking—all of it vanished and morphed, serving as an ignition point for all of our untapped chemistry.

I'd never felt this in tune with a person physically, her bobs timed to my weaves and willing flesh offering itself innately to its searching counterpart.

Her gasps and moans echoed in the stairwell, vibrating through my body like a sixth and extra sense when we got in the way of their percussive travels.

But I couldn't explore the way I wanted, and Easie deserved better than a cold, concrete wall behind her back.

Eager hands ran down the line of her back to her ass, cupping the cheeks and lifting without her permission or preparation.

Her answering gasp invited my tongue into her mouth, and I made use of it, plundering its bounty and exploring each nuance and taste individually. There was something special about her tongue and mine together, like they held the power to conduct a wave of electricity back and forth in a way I'd never experienced.

Each stair felt like a mile as I climbed with her in my arms, the weight of her petite body nothing compared to the heavy load of my anticipation.

I hadn't had sex in years, but my dick remembered the ride as though it was a bicycle, turning to granite and making the rub of friction carrying her created that much more torturous.

Her ankles crossed behind me, and the heels of each of her feet dug deliciously into my ass. I welcomed her enthusiasm, watching my step as I walked but opening my neck up to her ministrations as I did. Each lick of her tongue and bite of her teeth had me moving faster, forcing our way through the stairwell door of my floor with the extension of one, single hand.

She never paused or faltered, sucking at the lobe of my ear and whispering direction into it. "I can't wait to feel you inside me."

I nearly crumbled to my knees right then, but pushed on, knowing that the real relief would come from the inside of my apartment and getting there took a heady mixture of a key, concentration, and luck.

All three came together better than expected, and the freedom of being inside my home was liberating. No longer on the hook for her safety and virtue, I dove in with equal fervor, forcing her head to the side and working my lips down the line of her neck, around the curve of her collarbone, and into the neck of her scooped tank top. Each swell deserved its own attention, and I gave it, working from the base of one, up the peak, down the valley, and up again all before she could even get her hand in my hair and a moan out of her throat.

Walls yielded and braced as we bumped our way down the hall to my room, her legs wrapped around me tighter and tighter like a slowly cinching belt. I would have thought they'd get tired, but instead they worked harder, trying to force our bodies into one despite the barrier of our clothing.

"God, baby," I groaned as my lips left her chest and my knees hit the bed, taking her down and landing on top of her in one, smooth motion.

Her legs fell free and opened immediately, and her scraping hands went to the base of my shirt, pulling it up and over my head with impatience and passion.

"Get this off," she pleaded when it stuck, absorbing the warmth of my skin with a searing press of her palms and following it slowly with a gentle scrape of her nails. I couldn't see even one tiny inkling of a reason to deny her, and reached between my shoulder blades to make her wish a reality.

At the sight of my bare chest, her hands migrated from back to front, working the line of my chest and scraping through the small smattering of hair between my pecs. It was mostly smooth, but the Honduran in me had to represent just a little.

"Easie."

Her hands moved from my chest to my abs, down the line of my torso, and into the edge of my shorts. A surprised gasp choked the flow of air from my lungs and ended in a wheeze.

"Goddamn, baby," I cooed, sitting up enough to get my hands under the edge of her shirt but keeping myself well within touching distance. In no way did I want to discourage her hands from their position in my pants.

It was a good position. Maybe the best of them.

And my big head might be stupid, but the little one knew exactly what it wanted.

"Touch me," I pleaded, unable to resist the proximity and tease. Easie complied immediately, moaning along with me when her dainty fingers wrapped their way around my circumference.

One pump, two, and then three, she tested the efficacy of her grip, nonsensical words pouring their way out of my shaking mouth as she did.

Good God, that felt good. Like her hand was designed to give me pleasure just as sure as my mouth was born to give her hers. I couldn't wait to feel the pleasure of our bodies joined and in motion as one.

With the way this was—with the way everything was—there wasn't even a chance it wouldn't move mountains.

Impatient and unwilling to wait any longer, I dove in, pulling her shirt all the way over her head and freeing her breasts from the triangles of her bikini. Automatically they swayed, forfeiting to the pull of gravity readily and sinking to the sides. Her flesh was heavy, disproportional to her small body in the best possible way. I filled my palms with their weight, pulling them up to the center and sinking my lips into the space between them. She arched into me, pushing them further into my mouth and moving a restless leg up the line of mine.

I pulled back suddenly and shucked my shorts from my body before ridding her of the same.

Her blue eyes looked up at me with a glow, and the peach of her skin turned rosy with arousal.

Starting at her ankles, my hands skated up her skin, digging into the tense muscle of her thighs and eliciting a satisfying sigh. Her muscles felt tight and overused from the hard day, and I worked my fingers slowly in and out, around the line of each thigh, relaxing the taut flesh until her hips flexed upward with well-loosened excitement.

I dug into my shorts and grabbed a condom from my pocket.

She smiled her most mischievous of smiles, and I soaked it in, eager to feel the lash of her witty tongue with my cock deep inside her. It might not seem like the mood of the moment, but it felt real and right and distinctly Easie.

Now I would just have to find the best way to provoke her.

I laughed to myself at the idea, biting my lip to stop it from escaping. My eyes running the line of her sensuous naked body, this wasn't the time to allow an ill-advised laugh to escape the confines of my shaking chest.

I wanted to feel the lash of her attitude, not the maiming of my most eager appendage. I'd have to walk a fine line to make it turn out in my favor.

Apparently unhappy with my speed, or lack there of it, Easie grabbed the condom from my hand, ripped it open, and knocked my hands out of the way, rolling the latex down the line of my cock with speed and efficiency and a gleam in her perfect blue eye.

"Uh," I laughed, before sinking deep to my knees and settling between her legs. "You did that scarily well."

She winked, unwilling to acknowledge me with a verbal response. As much as it irked the compulsive, controlling side of me in the moment, I knew it would be for the best. Nobody needed to get into a discussion about other lovers when we were this close to coming completely together for the first time.

Perfectly positioned, I sunk inside, inch by precious inch. Easie's eyes held mine, unblinking and intent and soul-shatteringly open. She was living this—waiting for the scary bottom to fall out from under us—but in it until the end, breathing me, connecting with me, and hoping I was doing the same.

I'd never seen anything more beautiful.

"Easie," I whispered, my voice appropriately tortured by the feel of her welcoming flesh. She fit me perfectly right, squeezing but accepting as her hips suctioned their way north to meet mine.

The reality was even better than the dream, hours and hours of faked intimacy on the show giving way to a much realer, righter emotion.

I'd thought I'd done a good job of mimicking what this would be like, of the way I would feel seated fully inside her, but I'd actually failed. Miserably.

Because if this was the real deal, everything we'd done on set had been nothing but a very poor man's imitation.

Squeezing the flesh of her hip, I sank deeper, pushed harder, and grunted with the exertion. She gasped with each pulse of my hips, gripping onto the ends of my hair and pulling with an exhalation of sex soaked air.

Sinking deeper into the heaven between her legs, I lifted one, stretching her hip enough to hitch her calf over the bend in my arm. Pressing my upper body down into hers, I brought us even closer together and opened her up at the same time.

Her eyes widened in surprise at the stretch in her limbs, but a rush of excitement slid out of her to coat the inside of her thighs and the skin of my balls at the same time.

Excitement already tingled at the base of my spine, threatening to waste all of our carefully crafted effort, so I pushed her image to the back of my brain and shut my eyes, working the line of her neck, down and across her chest, until I had one perfect nipple in my mouth.

Her hips shot off of the bed as a direct result, and I had to tighten the muscles of my ass to stop the race of my release.

"Come on, baby," I coaxed, working my hand between our bodies and circling the nub above our joining. Her fingers came down to link with mine, mixing in the juices we created and slipping perfectly into a melded mess with mine.

Joined in sex, hand, and heart, we came together, staring into each others' eyes and committing to a level of intimacy that couldn't be taken back.

We weren't just coming at the same time, but instead, *coming together* in every possible sense of the words. Tuning to one another and forming a bond that, no matter what, would never be broken.

"Easie," I called, intending to hunt for some sass, but changing my mind when her tired eyes met mine once again.

"Anderson," she whispered, the most serious I'd ever seen her.

I touched my lips to hers, not moving from the warmth of her body even though I knew I should. Her limbs fell limp to our sides, but her body pressed close to mine, rising up to meet the surface area of my skin instead of sinking into the bed.

"I don't think I'm going to be able to let you go, Litterbug," I whispered against her mouth, admitting the truth to both of us at the same time. I knew I was walking a fine line, that there'd be a time when I couldn't have everything as easily as I had it now. But I was willing to wade in the darkness, bask in the ignorance, until that time came.

Things had changed.

If I couldn't have her, I wasn't sure I wanted anything.

"Hmm," she hummed, the slowing beat of her heart steadying with sleep.

With that, she was done, asleep with me inside of her. And with the trust of the gesture, I may have been awake, but I was gone even more.

I pulled out slowly, careful not to wake her as I did, and extracted my aching legs from hers. She rolled into the bed in my absence, pulling my pillow to her chest and taking a deep inhale of Anderson scented air.

I watched as she snuggled in before tiptoeing into my bathroom to get rid of the condom.

With it in the trash, my hands sank into the hard counter of the vanity and my head descended into the space between them.

Two people lived inside me, begging for different things and making me feel like I was coming apart at the seams.

With one deep breath and a shake of my arms, I ventured back into my room, crawled slowly into the squishy softness of my bed, and placed one tender kiss to the exposed temple of Easie's head.

Her hair spread and dusted the case of my pillow, and her long lashes curled so far they almost doubled back into themselves.

But she was peaceful and resting in a way that I couldn't bring myself to be. Not without doing what I always did.

Scooting carefully back out of the bed, I crept on quiet feet to the door, down the hall, and into the living room, scooting my way through the darkness to the standing cabinet in the corner.

Well oiled hinges opened silently, and the sliver of light from the moon offered just enough guidance for me to find the waiting envelope.

I grabbed it, shutting the door behind me and settling onto the couch in the middle of the room. The light of the night came through the windows just enough that I didn't need to turn on a lamp, and I poured out the contents of the envelope onto the coffee table in front of me.

I scooped up the pile carefully, resting it in my lap and unfolding the well worn pages with ease and precision.

Evan's words bled and blurred, running into one another and making less sense than normal. I struggled to understand the way I normally did, to find the blinding obligation that normally assaulted me.

Live Free and Breathe Easy, he told me over and over again, begging me to do what he couldn't with each healthy breath I took.

I fingered the edge of the letter, picturing his face and trying to feel him talk to me.

Trying to understand what he wanted me to do.

"Did you tell her yet?" Tammy called into the darkness, startling me with her presence. I hadn't even thought to check if she was home when we'd busted our way into the apartment earlier.

I closed my eyes, dropped the letter, and brought my hands to the back of my neck.

"No."

Tammy's head shook softly as she stepped into the only sliver of light. "You'd better do it soon."

"I will. I'm just . . ." Honestly, I didn't know what I was. Maybe I just wasn't ready to admit it all out loud yet. If I did . . . well, I was scared of what would happen. I wanted to do what was right, but I was scared that didn't line up with what I actually wanted anymore. I felt pulled in two different directions, and no matter how obvious the answer seemed, I couldn't seem to merge the solutions.

"You're pretty irresistible, Anderson. She'll be in deep with you soon—if she isn't already. It'll be a shame when she finds out half of the things she knows about you, aren't about you at all."

I started to argue that we hadn't been together but a couple of days, that talking about stuff like this takes time, but I knew it was bullshit. She'd given me her body, connected to me both physically and emotionally in a way that I couldn't deny. It might be true that some things take time, but the viable excuses for continuing to keep such a large part of myself from her were starting to run dry. Certainly none of them considered what was fair to her. They only considered what was easier for me.

I struggled to breathe, feeling the movement of air from outside my body to the inside start to stutter as she walked away. I rubbed mindlessly at the unfinished edges of Evan's paper, touching it the way I thought he would have. On the fourth stroke, my fingers hit gloss, and I realized that I'd brought out more than just his letters from my secret little envelope this time.

Reluctantly, I pulled it forward and settled it in front Evan's words. The regret burned like acid in my mouth, coating my throat with bitterness for the clueless kid I'd been. So ignorant to the ways of the world, I thought not only myself but my loved ones immortal, wasting some of the most important days of my life and *his,* fucking around and disrespecting the blessings I'd been given.

And now I was hypocritically aligning Easie's life with my mistakes. It was hardly fair for someone riddled with so many flaws to expect perfection from someone else.

Tucking the contents back into the envelope, I got up, crossed the room, replaced it into the cabinet, and closed it.

Just one room away a phenomenal woman waited for me, and for once, I decided to set it all aside and give the thinking a rest for the remainder of the night. I wanted Easie in my arms so much I found it hard to care about much else.

And really . . . that was the whole problem.

Chapter 19

"ARE YOU TELLING ME the two of you are dating?" Larry asked a week of tiring days and equally tiring nights later, looking at our joined hands like they were a couple of Nazis in World War II Germany.

Easie and I glanced at one another, and it was clear from the downright threat in her eyes that it was up to me to be our spokesperson. We'd settled into one another fairly well, spending most of our time together, but doing it on my schedule.

I was still a truth-withholding, selfish asshole. But I couldn't help it. I'd grown to like our bubble. I'd even go as far as saying that I'd started to *need* it.

Easie was the only thing that was all mine. But Evan's drive was the only thing giving me purpose. I was afraid to rock the boat.

I know. It was fucked up.

"Yes," I confirmed, turning to Larry and squeezing Easie's hand in support. "We're together."

"Jesus H. Christ," Larry groaned, rolling his head back and slamming his hands on the table at the same time. "Great. Just what we fucking need."

"Um," Easie cut in, leaning forward with a gleam in her eye. "Just what the hell is the big deal about us being together? It's not like we're inviting you in for a threesome."

"Yeah, we're definitely not," I interjected, just in case there was any doubt. I wasn't exactly keen to share, and Larry's connection to Ashley gave the whole avoidance thing an added incestuous incentive.

"The problem isn't in the fact that you're together. It's that with getting together comes the unavoidable breaking apart." He rubbed desperately at his wrinkling forehead. "That's the fucking explosion I'd like to avoid."

"We're not splitting up," Easie argued, starting to really get agitated. "We're not you and Ashley."

I raised my eyebrows and held my breath. I didn't think it was a good idea to poke the bear's most sensitive spot without a loaded gun in our hands.

"No, but the two of you share fucking genes." His eyes came directly to me. "Look out, dude. Shrapnel fucking everywhere."

I sucked into myself, making like I was invisible and trying not to get myself in trouble by taking anyone's side. Agreeing with Larry in this instance could only end badly, but Larry was kind of in charge of paying me. Switzerland looked good this time of year.

"Maybe it's you who's the problem!" Easie yelled, jumping up in a fit of sibling indignation.

"Easie," I coaxed softly, trying to calm her down without putting myself into the line of fire.

Larry just choked on a laugh. "Trust me," he addressed both of us. "The two of you look even more dysfunctional than normal. Ka-BOOM!"

"We're fine!"

"Right. Just don't get your figurative guts all over the set, if you catch my drift."

"I'm a goddamn professional!" Easie yelled, pretty much discrediting her statement instantly.

One choked snort sniffled out of Larry's nose.

With that, he shoved back from his chair, leaving behind our scripts as he stepped out of the room.

"Can you believe him?" Easie railed, spewing fire and looking seriously gorgeous the whole time she did. When I stayed silent, she appealed to me louder. "Well, can you?!"

"Easie," I said softly, gesturing to her wild hair and aggressive stance without making a move from my relaxed sitting position.

She surveyed herself briefly. Untamed hair gave way to flushed cheeks, and the line of her body clearly said she meant to *fuck some people up.* If she wasn't five foot nothing, it probably would have been extremely threatening.

"Shit."

"Easie," I murmured through a chuckle.

She sank her head into her hands and squeezed at her forehead with the tips of her fingers.

"I'm a fucking mess!" she mumble-yelled into her hands. Her head jerked up and her panicked eyes met mine. "He's right. I'm gonna get guts all over everything!"

"Hey," I called softly, chuckling. Standing, I pulled her into my arms and wrapped her up tight, whispering into her tiny ear. "You're not."

"I'm not?"

"We're not gonna explode."

"Okay," she whispered, surrendering to it and trusting me completely.

I closed my eyes tight and inhaled her sweet hair.

And prayed to God and Jesus both that I wasn't lying. Because when she'd gotten upset, this time, she'd turned to me to calm her down.

Not a cigarette.

When I first read that the show today was about a couple with Psychrophilia, or the arousal to being cold and watching others be cold, I couldn't see an outcome where this would be good for me.

When I'm cold I get cranky and all the things that I like to be big tend to get smaller. But, in a nice twist of reenactment fate, we were only pretending to be cold—or doing the exact opposite of what swimsuit models do in beach shoots.

In reality, the heat was cranked to eighty-five, both in room temperature and Easie's hotness factor, and the ice bed we were laying on was plexiglass.

She had managed to trick her lithe body into feeling cold though, and goosebumps had formed up and down the length of her normally smooth arms. Each time the set assistant sprayed her knees and my back with a spritz of water to mimic melting ice, her nipples pebbled further and her body pushed even closer.

She was searching for warmth, and lucky for me, I just happened to be radiating it.

Between her plump lips sat an ice cube, and she moved it from one sensitive spot to the next, getting me colder and colder by the minute.

They'd done her makeup to make her lips look just the slightest bit blue, and I had to fight the urge to be worried. I knew it was fake, but your brain plays tricks on you when it's someone you care about.

Refocusing, I went back to Noah, the man I was portraying, and tried my hardest to slip into the place that came from deep in his mind.

I moved my breath slower, savoring her every touch and watching as my nipples peaked and played their part. She didn't miss it either, working the flesh slower and trying to control the widening of her eyes.

It was a strange kind of beautiful to have this kind of job with your new girlfriend, practically every scene introducing something to our intimate relationship and not at the same time.

We hadn't explored much in our personal encounters, and I was perfectly content not to. Some might describe it as vanilla, but Easie tasted more like any and every other flavor under the rainbow. Salty and sweet, she gave herself in a different and delightful way every time.

When and if she wanted to explore, I'd oblige. But until then, working on this show together was like living a strange double life.

"I give up!" Easie screamed, slamming her butt back onto the heels of her feet and breaking the scene.

Howie looked from her to me and back again, waving off all of the lurking and curious onlookers as he did. Easie, however, didn't look anywhere but at me.

"What are you into?"

Her hair seemed to grow in disarray with each second her pleading question went unanswered. I searched her face for clues, but I couldn't seem to figure out what she was asking me. Her every nuance said that she'd been stewing on this for a while, but for me, it was purely out of the blue.

"What parts of *this* you are real?"

Confusion clouded the link between my vocal chords and my vocabulary, so all that came out was a grunted, "Huh?"

"This version. Of you," she stuttered to explain. "I can't tell where you stop and where your role on this show begins—what's underneath all of these layers."

Howie busied himself with nonexistent tasks, but I knew he was listening—and I was sure he wasn't the only one.

Lowering my voice to barely a whisper, I tried to get to the bottom of her random rant. "Baby, what in the hell are you talking about?"

"This. You. On the show."

"I need more words, Easie."

Her eyes turned mean, and I could practically feel the sting of her phantom fingers on my cheek. She was right on the edge of irritation, just itching to make me feel it with her.

"You just seem so into . . . I don't know . . . *everything.*"

"Everything? That seems like a pretty broad statement."

"Everything we do here. You very clearly enjoy it," she huffed. "But at home, we don't do anything out of the ordinary." She coughed. Cleared her throat. "I'm just . . . I don't know what you're *into*."

Jesus. She was worried she wasn't enough for me. Crazy girl.

"You."

"What?"

I couldn't help but laugh. "I'm into *you*. Slow sex, fast sex, red sex, blue sex. If it's with you, I'm pretty sure I'm going to enjoy it."

"Red sex? Is that period sex? Are you a Blood Hound?" Her words ran together with her speedy delivery, and she looked like she was going to cry. "God, I knew it."

"Um, no," I laughed, shaking my head and looking up to find a smirking Howie not even pretending to work anymore.

Jesus. Nothing was private. I guess I could thank Easie for that one in this instance though.

"I was just kind of Dr. Seuss-ing it. You know, improvising?"

"I don't think Dr. Seuss would approve of the context."

"Hey," I said. "You've got to use what you've got. And all I've got up my sleeve is the Seuss."

"So you don't want me to wear a bear costume and growl through my orgasm?"

Howie laughed out loud, one sharp burst that cut through the air and made Easie notice we weren't alone for the very first time. Her cheeks turned a magenta shade of pink, but she didn't take off running or curl up in the corner.

I shook my head to enforce and validate my verbal answer. "No."

"But you seem so into—"

"I guess I'm a decent actor then," I told her honestly. "If you want to try something, I'm down. I always will be. Otherwise, all the fetishes and kinks you see here are just a part of the job."

"But you're so openminded."

"Being openminded to other people's wants and needs doesn't make them my own. If I have something outside of the box, I've yet to find it." I grabbed her hips and pulled her close, whispering in her ear with a smile on my face. "If you're really set on me being into something weird, I guess you'll just have to help me search."

Chapter 20

"**G**OD, THAT FEELS GOOD."

"Oh yeah?"

Laughter bubbled out of my chest. "Don't get too excited. I don't think this really counts as a fetish."

"It totally does," she argued. "I looked it up on Google."

"Uhhh," I grunted, just barely stopping my eyes from rolling back into the recesses of my head. "You sat and Googled fetishes?"

"Yeah."

"Good Christ, I would have loved to see that."

"Stop talking and enjoy the spoils," she commanded.

"I still can't believe fingernail scratching is the fetish you came up with. You wanted to start easy, huh?" I teased.

It cost me. "Ow!"

"Whoops," she faked. "I must have slipped."

"Is this gonna turn into a good blow job? Or are we just going for a different kind of experimentation in torture?" She was tickling the area with fervor and giving me brief flashes of her neighboring tongue. Too much more of this, and it would have to lead to death. There was just no other option.

"Is there really such a thing as a bad blow job?" she asked, swinging her loose hair over her shoulder and running the tips of her fingers up, down, around, and anywhere she could to make me squirm.

I tried to keep the pitch of my voice even as I answered. "What? You think mouth on penis equals good?"

"That's what I've heard."

I shrugged and tried to push my cock toward her mouth. Some men liked to say there was more to it, that there was such a thing as a bad blow job. But I didn't believe it. As long as a woman was into it, putting in the effort to satisfy you any way she knew how, that was all that mattered. It was pretty hard to find fault in a place that was wet and hot and lent itself to making a woman's eyes look wide and willing and wondrous.

I sure couldn't anyway.

"You're right. Your mouth on my penis equals good no matter how I slice it."

"Too bad that's not part of the plan then."

I might have whimpered.

"Relax," she laughed. "It's not part of the plan because I had something different in mind."

"Oooh, Oh, Oh," I said, sitting up like a dog and pretending to beg. "Tell me it's your ass in the air, knees in the bed, and my cock driving into you from behind."

"Uh," she stuttered, her eyebrows curving with an extra arch. "It wasn't. It is now."

"Ah!" she screamed as I tackled her to the bed and brought my lips to hers, moving slowly down the line of her neck and ending with a nibble on her exposed collarbone and laughing into the skin there.

"Well, we've found at least two things that you're sexually open to. Dirty talking and doggie style."

She pulled my face from her chest and waited for my eyes to meet her surprisingly serious ones before she spoke. Fidgety fingers rubbed at the skin of my bicep. "I think I'm just sexually open to one thing."

Her voice was soft and timid in a way that it never was, and the hold of her body told me it wasn't the time to joke. "Yeah?"

She nodded.

"What's that?"

I wouldn't have thought it possible, but she somehow managed to speak even softer. "You."

My forehead met hers and my eyes closed. "That's the best thing you could have ever said."

"Really?"

I groaned. "Oh yeah."

Rolling to my back, I took her with me, settling her in an enticing straddle at the jut of my hips. She squealed at the suddenness of the ride, but I didn't slow down. One knee up turned into two, and I used the power of my thighs to thrust my hips upward, forcing her weight forward and her body flat against mine.

She tried to push up onto her elbows, but I held tight, forcing her naked skin to stay against mine and her mouth to open in surprise.

I wanted her so completely, that my arousal, unwilling to stay trapped in the confines of my body, formed a cloud around us, thickening the air and making Easie's eyes turn heavy.

"Let me feel you, Easie. From the top of your gorgeous head all the way down to the tip of your cute little toes, make me feel you."

"Anderson—"

"Come on, baby. I'm planning on committing this to memory. You'd better make it good."

With one simple challenge, she came into herself, embraced her every movement, and let go of all her inhibitions.

And sweet baby Jesus, it was good.

Twice.

Ten after eight the next morning, my phone chirped with an obnoxious tweet indicating a text. I tried to ignore it, but unfortunately, I'd brilliantly set my settings so that it wouldn't stop until I made it go away.

On the third little bird noise, I groaned, rolling over to feel the warm skin of Easie's back. She slept soundly through the commotion, and I wasn't surprised.

She almost never woke up before ten, and she never got up before I did. We'd stumbled into a routine over the last week or so, and I couldn't deny that I was sleeping much better than I normally did with her by my side. But I was still a relatively morning person.

Her phone went off then, adding to the cacophony of bird noises with the simulation of a spring thunderstorm.

"Dear God," I mumbled into the smooth skin of her back. "It's like Planet Earth in here. What's next? The sound of rushing waves?"

"Shhh," Easie ordered, snuggling her face even deeper into the plush down of my pillow. "Sleep good. Noise bad."

"Hey, it's not just my phone making noise."

"Fuck the phones, you loud talker. It's your voodoo doll I'm poking with imaginary needles."

I laughed at that, slamming my morning wood against her back. "I'm poking something else."

"No kidding." She begrudgingly rolled over, facing me with sleepy eyes and a slightly swollen, pillow wrinkled face. "Jesus, of all the times for you to be well endowed and ready to rumble, this isn't it. Can't a woman get some sleep?"

Reaching for my phone, I swiped the screen to read the message that had started it all.

Larry: Meeting. Nine AM. Tell your girlfriend.

Though delayed by my curiosity, I finally got around to answering her. "No."

"What?" she whined, lifting her head from the pillow and cocking one eye open. "Last night you said you'd give me anything I wanted."

Shaking my head, I smirked. "Different context, Easie girl."

"Easie girl is not a good nickname. Makes me sound like a whore."

I wagged my eyebrows and took a pillow to the face for my trouble.

"Alright," I laughed. "Sorry." I smoothed a wandering hand over her naked hip, dragging the fabric of the sheets off of her as I did. "But you do have to get up. We've got a meeting with Larry in under an hour. Which means—"

"We're probably already late."

"Righto, baby."

"Ughhhh," she growled. "What's with Larry and the meetings?"

I stood up from the bed with a chuckle, tossed the pillow back at her head softly. "I'm pretty sure that's his job. Keeping us on task."

"We don't need to be fucking micromanaged."

I raised a skeptical brow and looked pointedly at her position— still in the bed despite the tight timeline of our schedule.

She was smart and didn't miss much. This wasn't an exception.

"Okay," she conceded. "We might need to be managed."

"*You* do," I teased, and then yelled like a little girl as she grabbed the flat sheet and MacGyver-ed it into a whip in point two five seconds. "Ahh!"

"Come on," she prodded, standing in the center of the bed and swinging her newly fashioned weapon while her eyes zeroed in on my very bare crotch. "Do the helicopter."

All it took were those three words—and my subsequent serious consideration—to realize that if anyone in this room was being managed . . . it was me.

Engage main rotor.

Ready for liftoff.

Chapter 21

"**Y**OU'RE LATE," LARRY STATED as we stumbled into the studio thirty minutes late.

I knew it was unprofessional, but Easie was irresistible, and the urge to feel her coming all around me one more time before we left won out over propriety.

"Yeah," Easie explained, hooking her elbow through mine and flipping one splayed hand out. "See, there was a . . . helicopter."

"And a cat," I added helpfully, earning myself a well placed, yet surreptitious, elbow to the ribs.

Larry's skin bunched between his eyes as his eyebrows pulled together. Big shoulders hunched, wrinkling the normally smooth line of his charcoal gray suit. "Huh?"

"Traffic," Easie mumbled, fueled by a growing stampede of nerves. All of this meant more to her than it did to me, and this guy held the key to her fate. I lifted my free hand and rubbed soothingly at the skin of her looped arm.

"There was an accident?" Larry asked in an attempt to clarify.

I took the reins, squeezing her arm lightly to let her know, both to help Easie and to ensure we would move on. "Yeah, let's go with that."

Silence crept in as he looked from one of us to the other, trying to make sense of a conversation he had absolutely no chance of decoding.

"Whatever," Larry finally muttered, resigned to the situation for what it was. "Sit. We have big news."

"Big news?" I asked, pulling out two chairs at the table and settling Easie into hers before slumping into mine.

A combination wink and coy head tilt told me I would be rewarded for my chivalry later.

I made a mental note to open all the doors and pull out all the chairs. In fact, I made an addendum on my mental note to add as many doors and chairs to my daily routine as possible.

"Yep. The season finale. As you know we've got two more shows to film before that, but we just got the go ahead."

"The go ahead for what?" Easie asked, gnawing at her lip during the buildup.

Echoing thuds sounded from the converted kitchen table as Larry did his own version of a drumroll. "We're going to Vegas!" His eyes let up, and his hands shot out like horizontal fireworks with a touch of jazz fingers.

Yet, despite Larry's newfound flare for pomp and twinkle, neither of us said anything.

My rapidly closing throat made speaking impossible, and even breathing wasn't a guarantee.

"Jesus. You guys are the worst at reactions. I don't know why I bother."

Easie still had the ability to talk, though, and managed to edge out one distinctly uncreative word. "Vegas?"

"Vegas," he confirmed, happy to have any kind of interaction. "We're doing a huge show. The top 10 most popular kinks. You know, really try to swing it to the common ground, win over the every day crowd." The size of his forehead shrunk with one quick pop of his eyebrows. "And where better to do it than in Sin City?"

I couldn't speak on the reason for Easie's silence, but I knew the reason for mine.

I didn't know how I would keep the rest of my schedule. Vegas didn't fit into my routine.

Vegas didn't have my basketball league or my paddle boarding or access to the ocean to surf. In fact, it was pretty much lacking in every last one of my normal activities.

And in that moment, I had not one idea how to deal with it.

Easie was feeling loose tonight, having let me talk her in to drinking something stronger than lemonade on my dime. I actually felt kind of shitty about it because, as much as I truly did want her to have a good time, I knew part of it was done out of desperation to make her less sensitive to my contemplative mood.

I hadn't quite been able to shake the news of Las Vegas, and with each hour that passed in the depths of that anxiety, I only grew more angry with myself.

I *couldn't* let it go. I kept trying to talk my brain around, but it was like some little part of the train tracks was missing, leaving a gap I could *not* traverse. Through this experience, I could honestly say that *wanting* to change and not *being able to* was one of the most frustrating, self-hate-producing circumstances of my life.

But, right now, tonight—in *this* moment—Easie sure did make it hard to think of anything but her.

I found pleasure in watching her happiness change phases, starting as sound as laughter bubbled out of her mouth and ending as a light in her eyes. The blue pools of her irises sparkled, shooting bolts of midnight to the rim and lining it there and making the surrounding white stand out through the glassy laziness three lemon martinis had produced. Meanwhile, while her long legs stretched out from her stool-perched feet and surrounded me in their cocoon, bouncing along to the music. Her hair was wilder than normal, and a rosy blush stole the show across her high-boned cheeks.

She looked alive from within, and the energy that produced made her seem two feet taller than she was.

"Get up there and sing again!" she pleaded, inclining her head and tweaking her knee so that it settled into my side.

Chuckling, I pushed the falling hair out of her face and settled my palm on her jaw. "Sorry, baby. Gig's done for the night."

There was no fucking way I was getting up there again. I barely got through once every week.

"You're crushing my soul right now, you . . . soul crusher," she drunkenly pouted, leaning her face into my hand, resting her hand on top, and weaving her fingers through mine.

"Easie," I murmured, smiling just before touching my lips to hers.

"How about we go home and I put on a solo performance for a one woman audience?"

"Ooo!" she squealed jerking her head up and settling our linked hands on her thigh. "Tell me it's Magic Mike inspired! Can you gyrate as well as Channing Tatum?"

I barked a laugh. "I seriously doubt it."

"Wait . . . how do you know how well Channing gyrates?"

"His skill level was implied by your question," I covered.

"Yeah, right. You're a secret Tatum Totter aren't you?"

I shook my head in confusion. "A what?"

"A Tatumite. A Channleader."

Perplexed, I just stared. She slapped my thigh with her free hand. "A super fan!"

"Like a Belieber?" I asked and then immediately regretted it. God, did I regret it.

She was incredulous. "Channing you have no idea, but Justin Bieber you're in the know?"

Cue backtracking damage control. "I'm not in the know."

"You so are!" she yelled, jumping up to stand on the bars of the stool. I reached out to steady her, and for the first time in our relationship, had to look up to meet her eyes. "You're a Belieber."

"No," I denied, shaking my head and waving my hand—basically using any body part available to dispute her claim.

"Ah," she breathed. "The gentleman doth protest too much, methinks."

I shook my head in wonder, squeezing her hips and lifting her down from her precarious perch to the safety of the ground. "I'm kind of appalled that you just used Shakespeare to argue a point about Justin Bieber."

"Really?" she laughed, her face absolutely beaming. But beyond that, it was breathtaking. "I kind of think it's awesome."

So did I. *So did I.*

Once Easie fell asleep, I unwrapped my limbs from hers, climbed slowly and carefully out of the bed, pulled on shorts, and crept on silent feet down the hall to the living room.

Taking a deep breath when the cabinet came into view, I didn't waste time getting over to it, opening the door, and pulling out my most familiar envelope.

For the first time ever, I wasn't completely happy with my decision to get out of bed and spend some time with Evan. Warm rather than cold, my sheets were occupied, scented with the rich, welcoming aroma of Easie's sweet skin.

Shaking out the envelope onto the table, the papers scattered. Usually handled with the utmost of care, that had never happened before, and I found myself cursing my hastiness while scooping up my mess and putting it on the table in front of me.

"Shit," I mumbled as I sorted, cringing at the sight of my carefully cared for treasures askew, rumpled, and out of order.

Once I had them back as they should be, arranged correctly and carefully placed, it was easy to find the one I wanted. I'd spent so many years reading them, that I knew exactly how many there were and the precise order in which I'd received them.

Instead of dwelling on the others, I focused on those specific words. Each one talked me off the ledge and prepared me for the trip to Las Vegas. Evan would have wanted me to go, to take a break from all of the other things. He would have loved to have gotten to the point where he had an opportunity for this level of success.

Tracing his signature, I kept telling myself that.

"I hoped so much that I wouldn't find you out here tonight," Tammy said quietly, startling me despite the gentle delivery. I wasn't expecting her, and that was enough.

"Don't start," I warned, but she ignored me.

"She's going to get tired of being with someone who doesn't have any time for her."

I rolled my eyes even though the darkness hid them from her view. "You're starting to sound a lot like a broken record."

"If the song still rings true . . ."

"She's been doing stuff with me," I defended.

"You are completely missing the point." Two steps forward creaked through the old, worn boards of our floor. "I don't mean time with her. I mean time *for* her. For her needs, her wants. There's a difference between letting someone spend time in your life and making them become a part of it."

I wasn't missing the point, but I *was* finding it extremely annoying that Tammy was so good at making it. I just . . ."I'm not ready to let it go."

I wasn't ready to let *him* go. And I didn't know what, if anything, would eventually make it so I could.

She sighed deep and long before walking the few steps that separated us and putting a friendly hand to my shoulder. I thought she would lecture me, but she didn't. Instead, she gave me some of the best advice she'd ever given.

"Go to bed, Andy. Deal with the rest tomorrow."

I clenched my jaw but nodded, and as if her permission held authority, pure air rushed into my lungs as the ever present weight lifted off of my chest.

She gave one quick pat before turning and heading back to her room, and I made sure to work quickly in her leave.

Folding the letters back into themselves, I scraped the contents from the top of the table up and dumped them back into the envelope. Sealing it as I walked, I worked to get back to Easie faster, sliding it into its place in the cabinet and closing the door.

Soft carpet smushed and swirled under the balls of my feet as I walked between the coffee table and the TV, and the hum of the air conditioning blew a steady stream of hair-raising chilled air across my bare skin. I hadn't bothered with a shirt when I'd left the bed, and with the promise of Easie's naked body calling to me from just beyond my door, I wished I hadn't put on anything.

I suddenly couldn't stand the fact that I'd left in the first place, so I moved even faster, shucking my shorts and opening the door at the same time. As soon as I cleared the threshold, my shorts were gone, and two quick jumps and a skip had me diving into the bed and pulling the covers down just enough to climb in.

Easie didn't budge despite my intrusion, and knowing her tendency to sleep deep, I didn't measure my movements.

Wrapping my arms around Easie's tiny body and pulling her close, I absorbed her warmth and scent, feeling for the first time in a long time like everything I needed was right there in within reach.

I knew it might not last, but for then, it was perfect.

She was perfect.

We were perfect.

Part 3

Easie and Anderson

"The most important kind of freedom is to be what you really are. You trade in your reality for a role. You trade in your sense for an act. You give up your ability to feel, and in exchange, put on a mask. There can't be any large-scale revolution until there's a personal revolution, on an individual level. It's got to happen inside first."

—Jim Morrison

Chapter 22

Easie

FLUTTERING EYES PULLED THEIR way out of a deep sleep, taking in my surroundings in beats and flashes. White linens lined the pillow at my ear, and the warm, tan flesh of my huge male counterpart glowed in the early morning sunlight.

Anderson.

His back was to me, and the sheet sat precariously at the very top of his tight, muscled ass. I'd had it in my hands the night before as he sank inside of me repeatedly—something I'd not only gotten used to, but feared I'd no longer be able to live without. He made me feel alive and active, and I was healthier than I'd been in years.

Quitting smoking had taken a ton of will and ambition, and to this day, Anderson still hadn't mentioned it. I saw him watching me though, so I chocked his silence up to an effort to keep the peace. No matter the circumstances, smoking always seemed to turn into a festering sore spot with pus, and infection, and undeniably hurt feelings.

Ultimately, I'd decided he was important enough to me that smoking wasn't anymore. And with how active he had me, I hardly needed it as the main staple of my diet plan.

Stretching and yawning, I tested my sore limbs, lifting myself up to sitting and shaking the bed a little in the process. Anderson was obviously tired, lying there undisturbed despite my motion.

An idea took hold, and I jumped from the bed to take advantage. I wasn't normally awake before Anderson. In fact, I didn't think I ever had been.

But I knew he had food in the refrigerator and a showing of breakfast in bed could never be a bad thing.

Pulling his discarded t-shirt over my head, I walked quietly on careful feet out his door, clicking it shut behind me in order to keep from waking him.

The coffee maker blinked with its automated setting, and a brew started up just as I entered the main living room. I loved a man with a programmable coffee machine.

Wait. I mean, I loved anyone who had a programmable coffee machine. That's what I meant.

Right?

Shaking my head, I put it out of my mind and skated on shuffling feet toward the kitchen. Unfortunately, I missed the transition to the rug, tripping and slipping and just barely stopping myself before falling to my knees.

There on the floor, an upside down picture sat out of place, obviously dropped in transit by Anderson or Tammy.

Too curious to leave it be and not wanting it to get damaged— yeah, right—I picked it up and flipped it over with a burgeoning smile on my face.

Like the fiery meeting of two speeding cars on the freeway, my smile died an instant but painful death.

Glassy green eyes stared deep into mine, a younger, completely different Anderson lazily smiling with an arm around Tommy. They were obviously young and celebrating, the waylay of a college party swirling in the background.

And in the fingers of Anderson's ringless hand sat the straw that would ultimately break the camel's back.

A fucking burning cigarette.

"Morning, Easie," Tammy called, stepping out of her room casually until she saw my face.

And the picture in my hand.

"*Shit.*"

"What the fuck?" I asked, not giving her a chance to prepare or evade. I shook the photo before turning it around and holding it up for her to see.

She didn't even need to look.

She approached me slowly, her hands raised in plea. "Give him a chance to explain, Easie."

This was about so much more than a stupid picture, and Tammy's reaction only solidified that. She wasn't surprised at what was playing out in front of her. She'd more than seen it coming.

"A chance to explain? What the hell do you think our whole fucking relationship has been?" I shrieked, no longer measuring the volume or timbre of my voice. "A chance to goddamn explain!"

I knew everyone had pasts and that people changed. But this wasn't that. The guy I knew—the guy I'd let my heart swallow up nearly whole—would *never* be in a picture like this. And if he had been, he wouldn't have kept it from me.

"I know." She nodded her head, resigned.

"What's going on?" a sleepy and shirtless Anderson asked, stepping out from the mouth of the hallway. The commotion had obviously woken him.

"What the fuck is this?" I yelled, unquestionably handling the whole situation in the most immature way possible.

But come onnnn.

The dude was fucking *smoking*.

Browbeating and nagging me before he even knew me. Condescending looks when he did. Mr. High and Mighty himself was hypercritical at best and a complete fucking liar at worst.

I felt like the sky was shattering above me and falling, and the ground, unforgiving and unyielding as it was, was shoving me higher and serving me up to the spiky shards—when all I wanted was for it to swallow me up.

"Easie—"

"Jesus, Anderson. I feel like I don't know you at all." He stepped toward me, but I threw up a hand, bringing him to an abrupt stop as though I'd encased his feet in cement. "Honestly, I feel like you've ripped the rug right out from under me, stolen the goddamn magic from my carpet."

"Easie—"

"I was fucking falling for you, Anderson!"

He sucked lips into his mouth before reaching for me again. I stepped back out of reach. His speech broke. "Was?"

My voice was no more than a whisper. "You can't fall for someone you don't know."

"You know me," he insisted, stepping forward and grabbing onto my hip before I could stop him. His touch felt like home, sweet and welcoming and cozy in a way that nowhere else was.

My heart sped up, beating at triple its normal pace as I stared into his soft green eyes. They pleaded with me, begging me to see him for what he was, but no matter what I did, I couldn't rationalize the person I thought I knew with the guy in that picture. Everything I knew about him, everything I thought he was, said he would never have been that guy. That he was too good for that life and the mistakes that it brought.

He never treated my smoking like a habit he'd overcome. Never.

And the more my heart broke, the more questions there were that filtered through the cracks.

He'd never done anything I'd invited him to, despite the numerous things I'd done with him. Why was that? What the hell else didn't I know?

Going against everything I knew, I gave him the second chance, the opportunity to make it right.

"Blow off your gig tonight. Take me to dinner, come to my apartment and explain."

Tammy stayed standing to the side, waiting to see how it all played out, but I only had eyes for Anderson.

His face went through a rainbow of emotions, cycling through relief, happiness, and anger and eventually landing on dismay.

I knew his answer before it even started to leave his lips.

"I want to." I didn't even wait, starting my embarrassingly underdressed walk to his bedroom to get my shit and get the hell out of there.

"Easie."

"Don't," I said, shaking off his hand on my arm.

"But—"

I turned to him in a flash, pointing one angry finger directly in his face. "If you're going to say anything other than yes, I don't want to hear it."

The silence that followed probably hurt the worst of all.

With shaky hands, I whipped off his shirt, unable to get out of it fast enough, feeling the fabric burn through my naivety and set my heartbroken skin on fire.

I thought I'd known better. I thought I'd been prepared to protect my heart from someone I knew would break it.

I was wrong.

Anderson seemed distraught, the roots of his fantastic hair nearly pulled all the way out with his tugs, but I tried my best to ignore him. He got lost in himself too, pacing and mumbling and even dropping into the occasional distressed squat.

It didn't take me long to gather my things, and once I finished, I didn't look back.

It wasn't to be cruel or to make some kind of statement.

It was because I couldn't.

Scooting out of the bedroom and down the hall, Anderson followed me, but he did it silently. No explanations were offered. No pleas to get me to stay were made.

The end was really happening.

I waved a small hand at Tammy, but all she could do was cringe in return.

The door opened easily enough, but the weight of it closing behind me nearly took me all the way to my boney knees.

Larry was right.

My guts were fucking everywhere.

Chapter 23

Anderson

AS SOON AS THE door closed behind her, I got sick. Vomit and mess all over myself and the floor, I didn't even make it to the bathroom.

I accepted the inescapable reality of cleaning it up as my penance.

"God, would you look at yourself?" Tammy asked, offering me a wet wash cloth and a pound of unsolicited advice and criticism. "You are the biggest fucking moron. All of this so that you could hold on to the ghost of a kid who's never coming back."

Her words stung, licking my fresh wounds with salt and rubbing it in with each truth.

"I should have just told her."

"No fucking kidding," she huffed. "I'm pretty sure I told you that from the beginning."

Pushing back from my mess and leaning back into the front of the couch, I hiked up my knees and let my face drown in the comfort of my hands. "I can't explain it," I whispered, knowing that Tammy would get close enough to hear me no matter how low I talked. "Every time I started to say it, the fear of letting it all go was paralyzing."

"You mean the fear of letting him go?" she whispered.

All I could do was nod.

She settled onto the floor next to me, shoulder to shoulder and bumped me lightly with the weight of her body.

"That's just it, Andy. You've served Evan well, but he's not coming back. No matter what you do. But Easie is here now, and she makes you happy. I've seen it with my own gorgeous eyes. Give her a chance to get to know you. God, give her a chance to be the priority."

"I don't even know who I am anymore," I admitted, lifting my head to meet her eyes. "How can I show her what I don't even see?"

Tammy shrugged, made it all seem much simpler than it was. "You can learn together."

I shook my head in shame. "There's no way she'll listen to me now. She gave me more than enough chances, and I blew every last one of them."

"Anderson. The woman told you she was falling in love with you in the middle of a heated and humiliating argument. If you do it right, truly make an effort to rectify the mistakes you've made, she'll let you back in."

Hope bloomed in my belly and inflated my posture closer to normal. I wanted that so badly.

It wasn't a snap realization—changing years of feeling one thing to another in no more than a mere second. It was a come to Jesus moment, an event that made one inescapable fact true. I'd lost the one thing that Evan wanted for me the most—the chance to live freely and do the things that made *me* happy—because I couldn't let go of the ghost of him. Until Easie left, my brain had never been able to make the distinction. Fulfilling Evan's dreams made me feel a sense of accomplishment and contentment. Easie made me feel euphoric. Easie made me feel *loved.*

"You'll probably have to give her a free shot at your nuts, but she'll let you back in."

"God, I don't know."

"The least you can do is try. Unless you're happy with living without her for the rest of your life?"

My stomach rolled again, threatening to make me clean up two times the mess.

"I'm definitely not happy without her for the rest of my life."

"Then start from the beginning."

"What's the beginning?" I asked even though I was pretty sure I knew the answer.

"Evan."

She was right.

"One thing's for sure. She can't know you without knowing him. No one can."

"So I'll start with Evan."

Tammy scrunched up her face and plugged her nose. Looked over her shoulder and back to me.

"Correction. Start with the fucking vomit. Then move on to Evan."

Practical advice, I moved into the kitchen to get a roll of paper towels and a bottle of cleaner. I made quick work of it, hoping to never, ever get sick outside of a toilet again. Cleaning it up under these circumstances was bad enough. I didn't ever want to have to repeat it.

Once done, I showered, feeling the need to wash away not only the filth but the morning, the toxicity of my inability to change making me stink with regret. I couldn't believe I'd let it go that far. That the thought of giving up a single day of a hobby I didn't even enjoy nearly had me losing the potential love of my life.

At least, I hoped it was nearly.

Clean and ready to face the day, I went back to the living room, pulled the envelope from my cabinet and rifled through each of his letters one last time. His words were choppy and cheerful, the wistful innocence of his fourteen year old self ringing soundly off of every page.

To this very day, I still couldn't believe it had come to this, that he'd actually died. I never believed it, not even once, and the picture that Easie found haunted me every day since.

When Evan was struggling to form his last breaths, that's where I was. Taking that picture, smoking a cigarette, believing everything would be fine, and spitting in the face of my brother, who'd wanted nothing other than a healthy pair of lungs and the opportunity to use them.

Chapter 24

Easie

"WOULD YOU LOOK AT yourself right now?" Ashley said, taking in my sprawled position on our couch, a bag of Cheetos leaning against my hip and at the ready. My hair was sticky with the oil of a beach day and sexy night and yet another day without care, and my clothes were the same ones I'd left Anderson's apartment wearing. I hadn't really slept, but I hadn't cried either. Instead, I'd been nearly unshakable, watching marathons of NCIS and Law and Order and shoving every available food into the hole in my face.

But I hadn't smoked one goddamn cigarette. I'd quit more than a week ago, but Anderson either hadn't noticed or hadn't deemed it worthy of mentioning. Bastard.

If I wasn't lighting up right now, I was pretty sure I had it kicked. In fact, I was doing pretty fucking well, considering.

"What?" I asked, avoiding the issue like a pro and redirecting the focus to her. "You don't like Mark Harmon? I thought older men were your thing."

"Dear God," she whined, leaning closer to get a better look and swimming well clear of my bait. "There's old food on your shirt." She sniffed. "What . . . Is that rotten milk?"

Her nose turned up in disgust.

"Fuck you and your hygiene," I barked, flipping her off like the delicate lady I was. "I had cereal."

I looked down. Pretended to dust off some of the crumbs. The food couldn't be that old. Fourteen hours or so, max.

"And what? Attempted to *pour* it directly down your throat?"

"Shut your pie hole. This has nothing to do with you."

"Like hell it doesn't! I have to live here and watch this disgusting display. I have to somehow manage you, get you to a set of a show where this douche also works, and it'll be easier to do it if you don't smell like a fucking gutter rat."

"Douche?"

"Well, he's obviously done something wrong. You were a fucking smitten kitten a day ago."

"Maybe I did something wrong," I muttered just to be petulant in the face of her omniscience. It was pretty immature, even for me.

"I'm sure you did."

"Hey! I didn't do one fucking thing!"

"I'm not in the mood to argue with you. Anderson made you really happy. It was obnoxious, but you were actually pleasant. I'm betting he deserves at least one more chance."

"Samsung Galaxy meet iPhone."

"What?"

"It's my new, cooler version of pot meet kettle. AKA, you're a fucking hypocrite. I haven't been seeing much of your 'I'm smooching with Larry' face lately. What's up with that?"

Midnight blue eyes shot straight to the ground. "We're talking about you."

"Hah! I see how it is."

Diverting my attention, she changed the subject. Like sister like sister, apparently. "A package came for you."

"Fuck that." I waved her off and turned my eyes back to the undeniable chemistry of Tony and Ziva. Bullshit writers. Always making you wait a million years for the happy ending. "It's probably a free sample razor or something. I have no reason to shave for the rest of my life. You can keep it. Consider it a gift."

"What? That's it? One failed relationship and you're going to be a spinster for the rest of your days?"

"Yes," I agreed sullenly.

"Will there be cats?"

"Of course there'll be cats. What do you think I am? Some kind of second rate spinster? Fuck that shit and your fucking free razor package."

She rolled her eyes.

"I have a sneaking suspicion you want to look at this one."

"Why?"

"Because the return address is one block up, you obstinate broad."

I shook my head, clucked my tongue, and ignored the raging beat of my stupid, forlorn heart. "That actually means I want it even *less* than the free razor. Good sales pitch. Your boss wants a meeting. You're fucking fired."

"Could you be mature for five seconds? Jesus."

"I tried the whole mature relationship thing. Look where it got me." Besides, comedy numbed the pain. At least temporarily.

She growled in frustration. "If you don't open the package, I'm opening it."

"Be my guest," I offered, calling her bluff.

But she wasn't bluffing, ripping into the tape on the small box and pulling back the flaps only to find an envelope. My heart was in my throat as I watched her. This was the worst possible time for the package inside the package inside the package prank.

If there was another envelope inside the envelope, I might start ripping people apart.

Ashley opened it, and thankfully, there wasn't another trick inside. A bundle of folded, rough-edged notebook paper came out first, followed shortly by one pristine, new, flat piece of paper.

She didn't say anything aloud, but her face said it all.

"Let me see it," I demanded, holding out a shaking hand.

She handed me the new note, and like a starving woman, I ate up the words as quickly as possible.

Easie,

I know this isn't the way to do this. You deserve an in-person explanation, and you deserved it a long time ago. I still want to give you that, so I won't say much here. Just know that these are my most prized possessions. I hope when you read them, you'll give me the chance to explain.

It feels like a lifetime that I've been making all of my choices based on these.

When you gave me the chance last night, I should have chosen you.

Anderson

Anger flooded my veins at the lack of information and his cloak and dagger technique. Enough secrets. I just wanted to know what the fuck was going on.

Hand still shaking, I held it out and waited for a silent Ashley to fill it again.

When the paper met my hand, it was soft like butter, a feel acquired by someone running their hands over it a million and one times.

It felt like a ticking bomb as I unfolded the first flap and then the second, sinking down to the couch so I didn't have to hold my own weight anymore. Anticipation and nerves were making the simple task seem nearly impossible.

Immediately, one very specific word stood out. *Brother.* Reading as fast I could without losing comprehension, I dove in, eating up the words and losing my breath a little more with each one.

Dear Anderson,

Hey, Big Brother! How's college?

Mom keeps telling me that college is bound to be the best years of your life, but I have a hard time believing it. Seems to me all of that time in a classroom would be a waste when I could be out there living my life!

Exploring and teaching myself all of the important stuff through hands on experience.

That's what I'm going to do when I'm living free and breathing easy.

I'm going to hike all the time and learn about as many plants and animals as I can while I do it. It just seems more fun that way.

Yeah, I'm definitely not going to college. I've got way to much other stuff to do.

Anyway, I miss you, but you know that.

Love,
Evan

PS- Don't tell mom about the no college thing.

A brother. He had a brother I'd never fucking heard about. Carefully moving that letter to the bottom of the stack, I read the next one.

Dear Anderson,

How's college? Have you seen any live music?

I'm so into it lately. Ever since Hunter Holston came and performed for us here at the hospital, I haven't been able to get enough. His fingers moved so fast on the strings of his guitar, and I still can't seem to figure out how he manages to sing and play at the same time. It looks almost impossible, but I won't let that stop me.

That's what I'm going to do when I'm living free and breathing easy.

I'm going to put in all the time it takes to master singing and playing guitar at the same time, and then I'm going to perform somewhere. Even if I just got to do it every once in a while, it'd be worth all of the effort.

Anyway, I miss you, but you know that.

Love,
Evan

When the same words jumped out at me again—living free and breathing easy—I moved faster, taking in the familiar activities and words to live by like a steady stream of water. Over and over the words smacked me in the face, a heaving pile of letters and letters filled with plans and dreams. All of these things were the Anderson I thought I knew. But these letters were *to* him. These weren't *his* words.

That's what I'm going to do when I'm living free and breathing easy. I'm going to learn to surf and ride as many waves as I can fit into a day.

That's what I'm going to do when I'm living free and breathing easy. I'm going run the Rio Del Lago 100 Mile Endurance Run.

That's what I'm going to do when I'm living free and breathing easy. I'm going to paddle board from Malibu to Santa Monica.

I'm going to enter a dance marathon and keep going until the end.

I'm going to join a basketball league and keep playing like a kid well into adulthood.

I'm going to learn to wakeboard in the water and ski on the slopes and do it as much as possible.

I'm going to be an actor and live as many lives as possible.

Slowly, I flipped through the letters, watching with a freaky kind of detached emotion as my tears splashed onto the surface of each page. All of them read the same, with Evan speaking words of positivity and planning the rest of his years. And he was going to be busy.

Until the very last one.

Dear Anderson,

I guess you've heard by now. They don't have any lungs for me.

Turns out I'm never going to live free and breathe easy. It's kind of freaky to think that I won't be around to talk to you. You were always the easiest person to talk to because you actually listened.

Plus, you never, ever told me I couldn't do all of the things I wanted to do.

At first I was pretty bummed that everyone else's warnings proved true, but then I realized they hadn't.

I may not ever get to do any of these things for real, but I've lived a thousand adventures in my dreams. Mostly because you never told me to stop dreaming.

More than most other people ever come close to experiencing before it's too late.

So I'm okay with it.

Now, I'll just have to dream about you doing it for me.

Live Free. Breathe Easy. Do it every day.

Anyway, I'll miss you.

But you know that.

Love,

Evan

I could barely breathe by the end, and I certainly couldn't speak. Which is why I waved off Ashley's pleas to clue her in.

A sob lodged in my throat, cutting off my air for just moments—something Evan had apparently dealt with for too much of his very short lifetime.

"Well?" Ashley prodded, still trying to get an answer that I couldn't produce.

I shoved the papers in her hands and sank my head between my knees, dizzy with the overwhelming news.

Anderson had a little brother and lost him. I was beyond devastated for him—for his very obvious ongoing battle with the loss. He still lived his brother's words every day, that much was clear.

What wasn't was why he wouldn't have told me about it.

"Why?" I stuttered, forcing my nerves to slow their flutter and meeting Ashley's eyes with my own. "How could he not tell me? I don't understand."

Ashley folded the letters carefully closed, one, solitary tear running over the swell of her cheek and down off the cliff of her jaw.

She took my hands in hers, ignoring the wet trail on her cheek and instead focusing on erasing mine. "Do you think you really know yourself, like you really show who you are to other people?"

"Of course," I answered automatically.

"Easie."

Gahhhhh. I clenched my eyes tight and rolled my head, but despite any form of verbal confirmation, Ashley knew she was right. "I have a theory about you, and I've had it for a while."

"This should be rich."

She skewered me with a look.

"Sorry."

"It's not that you aren't this snarky ball of fire that you kick around every day. It's that you're *more* than that."

I rolled my eyes.

"I'm fucking serious," she snapped, getting annoyed with my obvious dismissal. "You can't find the medium between this and who you used to be. You have a lukewarm heart underneath all that sarcasm."

"Ouch."

She laughed, just barely smirking and sinking little dimples into her cheeks. "You care. I know that, you subconsciously know it. But does Anderson know it?"

"He fucking should!"

"Easie."

Chastised again. "Sorry. Look, I don't know what he knows or doesn't. But I wouldn't have judged him. I wouldn't have . . . I mean, I don't even know. What is it that he was afraid I would do?"

"I'm pretty sure that's a question for him, don't you?"

"You know, Ashley, I'm not sure I'm liking all of this fucking wisdom from you. It's starting to freak me out."

"We've established this. I've *always* been the smarter one. Just accept it and move on."

"Mom and dad seemed to think I was pretty smart," I mumbled.

She laughed. "Hah! They think I'm smarter too."

"Nuh uh!"

"Would you like to call them? Ask their opinion?"

I glared. "You know I don't."

She shook her head. "That's another one of your issues. But it's one to tackle on a different day."

She was definitely right about that. Man issues today. Mommy and Daddy issues . . . well, not now.

Decision made, I stood up quickly, ignoring the crumbs that fell from my shirt to the carpet below.

"I'm going over there. Right now."

"Whoa, whoa, wait a minute," Ashley rushed out in a panic. "Not like this."

"What? He sent me these letters," I said, shaking them, "He obviously wants me to show him I'm ready to talk about it. So I'm going over there."

"No," she clarified. "That's not what I mean."

"Well, then what do you mean?" I demanded to know, my impatience seeping through me like the ooze of syrup through bread.

"I mean you can't go over there like that. You look horrendous and you smell even worse. Trust me on this. This is not the kind of look you want to be sporting should make up sex become an option."

"I'm not going over there to sleep with him," I argued. We had issues to fix.

She rolled her long-lashed eyes. "No one ever goes over there *intending* to fuck in situations like this. It just happens."

"It just happens?"

"Yes."

"What? Somehow we're both naked, he trips, and his penis lands straight in my vagina?"

She narrowed her eyes and cocked a hip. "You know that's not what I mean."

I shook my head, but heeded her advice, talking as I shoved past her and headed down the hall to take the world's quickest shower.

"Ignoring your questionable knowledge on the subject, let's just pretend you know what you're talking about."

She walked along behind me, and when I looked over my shoulder to check on her progress, she raised scrunched her forehead and inclined her head toward her right ear to indicate she was waiting.

"Everything you know about what's happened here, the obvious lying, the complete disillusion between who he is and who he thinks he should be . . . the fact that he's shown no sign that he'd actually be willing to choose me as his number one priority ever . . . what about all of that makes you think that we'll be able to make up at all, much less be jumping each others' bones in a showing of angry and aggressive sex?"

A snort-like giggle choked in her throat and a grin brought the corner of her mouth toward her eye. The line of her neck shortened with one cute shrug of her shoulder.

"Simple. You love each other." My hands fell to my sides and my lungs expanded at the realization. I may not have been the one to say it aloud, but I sure as hell admitted it to myself.

"And love conquers all."

Chapter 25

Anderson

FROM THE VERY MOMENT Easie left my apartment, I didn't.
I hadn't gone out to train, I hadn't gone out to surf, and I hadn't
gone to work at El Loco. In an interesting turn of events, Tammy
was covering *my* shifts for a change. And the brief taste of freedom had
me craving another.

I knew all of the decisions wouldn't come so painlessly, but the
one to quit working at the restaurant did. It didn't have any value to me
or Evan and overcrowded an already bursting schedule. And now that
I'd gotten paid for the first few episodes of Quirks and Kinks, I didn't
immediately need the money.

The next time I left my apartment, it would be to give my notice.
Or to go to Easie if I got too impatient while I was waiting for her to
come to me.

Based on that, I figured I'd be here for at least another five minutes.

Roughing my hands through the scruff of my hair, I jumped up
from the couch and then scrubbed a palm down the front of my face.

Christ, it was hard waiting to know what would happen—if I'd ever get a chance to see if Easie could fall in love with the real me. Whoever that was.

My stomach hadn't calmed down, so I'd avoided food. I didn't want to chance getting sick again. The humiliation from the first time was more than enough.

Three paces back and forth down the length of the coffee table was all I managed before giving in and storming to the kitchen counter to grab my keys. The metal felt cool but damp in my sweaty palms, and the edges of each key dug into the skin of my palm because of the tension in my grip.

Forcing my fingers to relax, my open hand gave way to several imprints of keys. Each ridge and dent mocked me, the small sliver of skin covered by my ring the only thing untouched, for the distance between Easie and I didn't even require a drive.

I stormed the door, angry footsteps pounding the old hardwood floors of my apartment and slapping an echo into the otherwise stagnant air. The door came flying as I ripped it from its hinges.

And revealed a completely startled, wet-haired Easie in its wake. Bags pulled at the darkened skin underneath her eyes, and her makeup free cheeks flashed red with exertion.

Once she'd decided to come, she'd done so quickly.

"Easie," I breathed, her name weighty and mined straight from my chest.

"That *is* my name," she said, her words sharpening right along with her eyes. I'm pretty well convinced her eyes would have started in that position had I not surprised her by opening the door before she could knock. "Is Anderson yours?"

My chin jerked back, surprised, but she didn't make me wonder for long.

"It's just that there have been so many lies, I figured we better start from the very beginning."

Ouch.

Clearing my throat, I forced myself to nod. "That's fair."

"You bet your tight ass it is."

A small, disbelieving puff of air shot from my nose. At least she still liked my ass.

"So," she prompted, sticking out her tiny hand. "Easie Reynolds."

Clarity hit me like a ton of bricks.

Fuck, this was not going to go well.

"Anderson Evans," I replied, grasping her hand and holding on tighter than normal. I knew when I said the rest, she'd be tempted to let go. I visibly winced. "Though, technically, I'm also Anderson Aranda." Her face started to shutter, closing down and pulling back, but I charged on, speaking a truth I scarcely even admitted to myself. "I changed my legal last name after Evan died. Aranda is the name my father gave to me by blood."

She opened her mouth to say something, but ended up floundering and closing it again. She repeated the process several times before a syllable successfully escaped her lush lips. Throughout it all, I held tight to her hand.

"Well, I guess that goes better with your appearance. I wondered briefly how a guy who looks like you ended up with a last name like Evans."

"A guy who looks like me?"

"You know you have a hispanic flare."

I did. And it probably wasn't the best time to mess with her, but old habits die hard. "My father is Honduran-American. My mother is a southern California blond of Irish descent."

She nodded briskly before blurting, "And I'm sorry to hear about your brother."

My thumb stroked the skin on the back of her hand. "Thank you." She started to pull back again, so I further tightened my grip. "Come in."

She looked to the empty hall behind her and then back to me. Indecision was ripe in the air all around her.

"Please," I whispered, scared to say everything I had to say, but wanting the chance to say it more than anything.

"Alright," she agreed, making me notice the envelope tucked under her arm for the first time by tightening it to her chest. All I'd been able to see up until then was her face.

"Thanks for bringing my letters back," I murmured, ushering her inside with a hand at the small of her back. My other hand still held onto hers.

She nodded slightly, noting, "They're well worn."

I laughed a hollow, self-deprecating chuckle, staring at the floor in front of me as we headed for the couch. "I've read them every night for almost six years now." Turning her to help her take a seat, still holding on to her hand, I met her eyes with my own. "I'd say they've held up pretty well."

"Will you start at the beginning? Tell me everything?"

"Of course I will."

"Good. Not telling me before means you're stupid. Refusing to tell me now would have made you an asshole."

"I'm not rejecting you, I promise. You deserve answers. Honestly, you deserved answers a long time ago."

"No kidding."

"Easie—"

She wrestled her hand out of mine and put its clammy remains over the line of my mouth. "It's done. Just tell me now."

Closing my eyes, I took a deep breath in through my nose and blew it out my mouth.

"Evan always had trouble breathing. At first, my parents just thought it was asthma. That because I was seven years older than him, he was just trying too hard to keep up with me."

She gripped my hand now, rubbing at the edge of my ring.

"But his symptoms didn't plateau. In fact, they kept getting worse no matter how much they relegated him to the sidelines—which he *hated,* by the way. He was really spunky. A lot like you."

One tear pooled in the inside corner of her eye and slid down, leaving a glistening path down the line of her cheek and hanging precariously off the edge of her jaw. At the same time, a tiny smirk pulled at the opposite corner of her mouth.

"It took months of doctors visits and several examinations to diagnose him with Idiopathic Pulmonary Fibrosis. Scar tissue grows and builds up on the inside of the lungs and robs you of the ability to breathe. Apparently, some people get worse slowly, while other unlucky ones degenerate extremely fast. Evan was in the second category."

"My parents tried to tell me several times how bad it was, but I never believed them. You see, Evan, he was always so upbeat. Such a goddamn dreamer. And it all happened so fast. I thought, at the very least, I had more time."

"You weren't there," she asked, but she said it like a statement. She already knew.

I shook my head, covered my mouth with a shaking hand. I fought the tears, rubbed at my eyes furiously. But I couldn't seem to stop them. Like flooded lakes, both eyes overflowed, forming tiny streams down my cheeks, curving through the forest of day old stubble that lived there.

"That picture you saw?"

She nodded. There was no questioning which picture I meant.

"He died that night."

"*Anderson.*"

"His last letter came the next day."

She covered her mouth with one hand and squeezed my fingers with the other. My ring cut into my skin, but I welcomed the pain.

"I took it as a sign, you know? Like he was telling me what to do, how to turn it all around. I obviously didn't want to be the person I was anymore." I shook my head, ran a ragged hand through the back of my hair. "God, being out partying like that—smoking a fucking cigarette? Even if I didn't realize how bad it was, I knew I had healthy lungs and he didn't. I may as well have spit in his fucking face."

"So that's how you felt about me smoking. Like I was spitting in it too," she incorrectly surmised.

"No," I corrected, wiping a fresh tear from her cheek with the back of my knuckles. "It was *me* disrespecting him again."

"What? How do you figure that?"

"You didn't have all the information when you were making that choice. I knew exactly where I'd come from, what Evan had been through, where I'd been when he died, and I still made the choice to find you irresistible."

She laughed a little, gave me a mischievous but still sad eye. "Well, come on. You really had no choice. I *am* irresistible."

"And unwaveringly humble."

"That too. I'm all the good things."

I smiled and brushed my thumb across the apple of her cheek. "That much I know."

She grabbed my hand from her face and pulled it away. Disappointment bloomed in my chest, but leveled off when she didn't let it go.

"What's the ring?" she asked, running her fingers along the ostentatious outline of it. "You never take it off."

"Ha," I laughed. "It was his." I shook my head. "He loved flashy shit."

She smirked. "You don't?"

"Not so much," I confirmed honestly before dropping the volume of my voice to a murmur. "But I like things that remind me of him. I took it when he died . . . had it engraved."

Slipping it slowly from my finger, I revealed the obvious tan line and turned it over so that she could read the inside.

"Live Free, Breathe Easy," she whispered aloud as she did.

"He wanted that more than anything."

"For him . . . or for you?" she questioned insightfully.

"I don't know. I guess both of us."

She grabbed my hand. Slid the ring back on my finger.

"So you've spent all your time achieving all of the things he didn't get to."

"Silly, huh?"

She shook her head, looked down at her lap, and twisted the fingers of her two hands together. "No. Not silly at all."

"I'm sorry, Easie. I really should have told you everything. I should have made time for you—for us—"

"Anderson," she cut in. "I forgive you. Really, I do."

Energy surged through my body, and before I knew it, I was reaching for her face and doing my best to touch my lips to the peachy softness of hers.

She backed away gently. Gave me a sad smile. "But I don't think we're ready to be together."

I could feel her slipping away, sliding back out just as easily as she'd insinuated herself in. Desperate, I fought to hold on, grabbing onto everything I could and digging in my figurative fingernails to keep her from sliding through my grip. "I am, Easie. I'm ready," I implored. "I choose you."

She laughed, but it wasn't with humor. It was the earth shattering sound of near devastation, a sob nearly choking her as it lodged in her slender throat.

"Yeah, I got that from your letter." She shook her head with disappointment.

I didn't understand. I'd thought that's what she'd want to hear. I'd thought it was what she deserved. I'd thought it was romantic.

I'd thought wrong.

"If you'd given me the chance to know—to know you *and* Evan—you never would have had a choice to make."

"Easie—"

"I wouldn't make you choose, Anderson. Not ever. If you think that I would, you don't know me either."

I started to deny it, a matter of a means to an end, a path to having what I ultimately wanted—her. But she was right. I had never once thought there was the option to have both. That I could hold on and move forward at the same time.

Not once.

"I . . . God, Easie. I'm sorry."

"I am too."

She stood up, each inch of her now towering height breaking my heart a little more.

"So this is it?"

She leaned down and touched her lips to mine, and then left them there, each word she spoke weaving its way directly from inside of her straight to the heart of me.

"Not a chance, Anderson Evans. This is just the beginning."

"The beginning?"

She nodded. "The beginning of us. The beginning of Easie and Anderson."

It took me watching her walk out the door, a near panic attack, and the lingering feel of her skin on mine to understand.

Neither of us really knew the other. The picture had been too well obscured by insecurities and secrets.

But it was never too late to start now.

Chapter 26

Easie

S OME LESSONS ARE LEARNED; others are earned. Anderson and I earned ours.

I needed to embrace my soft as well as my hard, and he needed to start living for himself. If we wanted to be happy together, we needed to be happy alone first.

But by the grace of good God almighty, I hoped we found our lonely happiness fast.

I already missed the bastard, and it had only been two weeks. It wasn't that we hadn't kept in touch—we obviously had. Anderson had made a real effort to cut back on all things Evan in his life and even went out to visit his parents for the first time since he'd died. I was a little disappointed that he hadn't asked me to go with him, but I understood. And frankly, the circumstances of our relationship were strictly of my making.

Every day, Anderson sent me a good morning text and called me mid-morning. He talked about his plans for the day or asked me if I had something on my schedule that I wanted him to be included in. My answer was always yes. If he asked, I accepted. No matter what.

He was working hard to weed through years of learned habits to find out what he actually liked and what he didn't. Everything had started out as a way to validate Evan, but a couple of things turned out to be real passions. He'd admitted to me that he'd become really fond of surfing, but he liked it a lot better when he did it on his own schedule. He hated singing and playing guitar, claiming that the attention was all together too much.

Of course, that conversation—and the fact that we were still working together frequently—led to a discussion about acting.

I'd read the letter. As much as it broke my heart, I knew it wasn't some fate-destined notion that we'd chosen the same careers. Evan had chosen his.

But the jury was still out about how he felt about it. Apparently, getting to work with me every day clouded his ability to judge the trade for its most basic properties.

And, with all the work he'd put in, he was still planning to run the 100 mile run in just three months time.

That left me with a hell of a lot of work to do and not a lot of time to do it.

"I have to be able to run how much?" I asked Tammy, stretching out my stride and trying to match hers. It didn't help that she was a foot taller than me.

But so was Anderson. And that was the whole point.

"Twenty miles."

Shit.

"Fuck my face, this was a bad idea."

"He's gonna love it," she encouraged, smiling genuinely as she did.

"Fucking hell."

"Run faster too. You're going to need to be able to run a consistent ten minute mile."

"Fuck you and your natural inclination for athleticism. Don't you know I've been smoking for the last ten years of my life?"

"The cancer sticks are your fault."

True enough. But the running made me cranky, and Tammy and I had only grown closer over the last couple of weeks. She was my kind of woman. Crude, brutally honest, and gifted at inappropriate humor. It hadn't been love at first sight, but we'd definitely formed a Womance now.

"Did you have surgery yet?"

"What?" she guffawed and stumbled before picking her natural stride back up. "Don't ever ask a transgender person that. Completely inappropriate."

"Which side of the line of appropriateness does it look like I normally walk on?"

Her head inclined and a smirk enhanced her face all the way to her eyes. "Point taken."

"Besides, I was just trying to figure out how to threaten you when you really piss me off. A penis punch or a twat tap?"

"A twat tap?"

"Tara Sivec. Read it. Learn it. Love it."

"You're such a woman."

"Newsflash," I called dramatically, trying not to trip as I pushed my hands out to the sides to form an imaginary banner. "So are you!"

"The only difference is I know what it's like to be both."

"And?" I asked when she didn't actually make a point.

"And that means I'm wondering why you're making this poor guy suffer. You both want to be together, so why the fuck aren't you together?"

"I'm just waiting for him to be ready," I explained halfheartedly. I wanted us to be together too.

"He's ready."

I shook my head. "He needs more time to live for himself. He needs to figure out what's important to him."

"God, you're an idiot."

"Fuck you!"

"Easie," she called slowing to a stop and pulling me to one next to her. "He knows what's important to him."

I shook my head.

"You, you moron. So is Evan, and so is making a difference in other people's lives. He doesn't want to let anyone down like he thinks he did Evan."

"Thinks?"

"Pffft," she huffed before confirming, "*Thinks*. Evan loved him. Thought Anderson hung the stars and the moon and created all the air in between. There wasn't one day that that kid was disappointed in his big brother, the day he died included."

I tilted my head in question, struggled to catch my breath.

"Anderson may have wanted to be a better person after that, but Evan already thought he was. After all, he was doing the one thing Evan really wanted to do."

"And what's that?"

"*Living.*"

God, she was so fucking annoyingly right. I wanted to wipe the smug smile right off her too pretty face. I might have been nicer if I hadn't missed Anderson so much.

"Are *you* dating anyone?" I asked with a sneer, turning away from her and breaking into a walk. One hand squeezed at the stitch in my side while the other pushed the hair that had escaped my ponytail out of my face.

"I was seeing a guy for a little while, but eventually it got serious and I had to tell him I'm transgender."

"You think that's something you *have* to tell people?"

"Me?" she gestured, sticking a painted fingernail in her chest. "Yes. Honesty is a big part of a relationship." She tipped her head meaningfully to remind me what the lack of it had done to mine.

"I don't know about other people. But, for me, I need someone to know everything, and still be able to accept it."

"It doesn't upset you that some people *can't* accept it?"

"Of course it bothers me. But part of being completely tolerant is accepting that there is, and always will be, intolerance. Hurtful words and callus remarks are never okay, but having your own opinion is. I can't begrudge anyone their right to free thought anymore than they can begrudge me of mine. *That* is freedom."

"You're tolerant of the intolerant?"

"Exactly."

Picking our pace back up into a jog, I couldn't help but whine. "How much further do we have?"

"Since we've just now passed the one mile mark and the goal for today is three, pretty much two miles."

"I can do simple math, thanks," I grumbled.

"Hah!" she laughed. "You're in trouble."

Yeah, yeah. But I was determined. I was doing it for him.

For him *and* Evan.

"Good thing that's where I'm used to being."

Chapter 27

Anderson

"ANDERSON," MY MOM GREETED, running out the front door with her blond hair flying behind her and ending up with her arms around my neck.

I hugged her back, squeezing her tight for the third time in the last two weeks. Or in the last six years, depending on how you looked at it.

"Hey, mom," I said back, looking up and over her shoulder to find my dad leaning in the open doorway. Apart from his eyes, I looked just like him, from our dark hair and skin, all the way down to the way we held our bodies and the quiet, reflective spirit inside.

Evan had been a carbon copy of my mom.

"Come in, come in," she cheered. "Dinner's just about ready."

I pulled away from the hug, but kept her tucked under one arm. "You don't have to make dinner every time I come home, Mom. I promise I'll come either way."

Tears filled her eyes like a flash flood, and she tucked her head down to avoid showing me.

God. Of course, she didn't think I'd keep coming.

Reeling her in slowly, I wrapped her back in a hug and whispered directly into her ear.

"I'm sorry."

She tried to wave me off, but I could hear the uneven waver in her breathing.

"Come on, let's go inside." I ushered her forward, careful not to rush her up the steps and then handed her off to my dad. Once he had her settled under his arm, he reached out with his other hand to shake mine.

"Son."

My throat spasmed on the word. "Sir," I replied respectfully. A tiny smirk engaged a half-dimple in his cheek.

Conversation lulled as I followed the two of them into the dining room and sat down at the table. My dad sat down with me while my mom shuffled back and forth from the kitchen with dishes of all varieties.

Normally, my dad would have been helping, but judging by the uncomfortable way he sat in the chair and watched her, I was guessing my mom had given him strict orders to stay in the dining room and keep me company.

Or make sure I didn't escape.

It was slightly funny, but I was the one who had caused it, so that pretty much negated every last ounce of humor.

The table finally weighted down with too many pounds of food, my mom took her seat beside my dad.

"Let's pray," my dad commanded, making me bow my head and fidget my uncomfortable hands in my lap. I'd largely given up organized religion six years ago. And I hadn't been that stringent to begin with.

"Bless us, O Lord! and these Thy gifts, which we are about to receive from Thy bounty, through Christ our Lord. Thank you for the blessing of our son, Anderson, and we humbly ask that Evan may rejoice in Your kingdom, where all our tears are wiped away. Unite us together again in one family, to sing Your praise forever and ever. Amen."

"Amen," I mumbled, looking up into the eyes of my expectant mother.

I knew I'd created this awkwardness, so I hoped with all I was that I could set it right again.

I would. It would probably just take time.

"We've been watching your show," my mom chirped, holding out a plate of pot roast for me to take.

As I took possession of the offered plate, my dad's eyebrows climbed all the way into his hair line.

More awkwardness.

But, this time, it was the fun kind.

"Oh yeah?"

"Yes," my mom confirmed, blushing. "You're very talented."

"Thanks, Mom."

"And your costar. She's pretty spunky, huh?"

Hah! She had no idea. "Easie," I said, feeling like she deserved to be known by name. "And yeah, she's great."

My dad's expression turned from traumatized to knowing.

I cleared my dry throat. Took a sip of water. "She's actually the reason I'm here."

My mom's face caught up with my dad's.

"She's the reason I'm ready to move on."

"You're together?" my mom asked, trying to be nonchalant.

"Not at the moment," I answered honestly.

But we would be.

Pursed lips worked at each other before flattening out once more. She glanced to my dad and then back to me. "Well, we'd like to meet her one day."

My next words were a promise. "You will."

"What are your plans for the rest of the night?" my mom asked as I stepped over the threshold and onto the stoop an hour and a half later. Conversation was stilted but there. We'd get better at it every time. Of that, I was sure.

Confidence influenced my smile, curling up the edges and turning it into a full face experience. Cara Aranda came alive at the sight of it.

"I'm gonna go get ready to claim my woman."

Chapter 28

Easie

TODAY WAS THE DAY.

It was time to take back my man. We'd been separated for four weeks now, and that was enough. I couldn't stomach even one day more.

I mean, we'd been happy on our own for nearly a month. I knew self-discovery took time. I was rational. I, however, *wasn't* a masochist.

And I missed his touches so bad it was starting to hurt.

And, as a bonus, I'd seen on the news the night before that Ryder had been arrested. Something about Public Misconduct and Resisting Arrest. I couldn't help but feel like it was a sign of good things to come.

"Are you ready?" Ashley asked, startling me enough that I made the makeup lady make an unplanned streak of eyeshadow across the apple of my cheek.

Annoyed, she sighed, reaching for a makeup remover wipe and starting over again.

Paying little attention to her, I studied Ashley, wide-eyed, until she grew impatient and prompted me again. "Well? Did you read the script?"

Right. She wasn't talking about my little internal love affair. She was talking about the show. The huge, enormous, all-important finale that we were set to start filming in the next twenty minutes.

Vegas, baby.

She was talking about my job.

"Uh, yeah, I'm ready," I semi-lied. I'd done my best to prepare, but when there were as many crazy things going on in two days as there were during today and tomorrow, you could only really be ready for a little at a time.

'The ten most popular fetishes,' Larry claimed. But I chose to take it with a serious grain of salt. There was no telling where he got his information.

Dressed in my outfit for the intro, I was thrilled to be starting from number one and working our way down the list instead of the other way around.

In popularity order, we planned to explore the following:

1. Domination and Submission
2. Sexual Role-play
3. Rubber/Latex/Leather
4. Voyeurism and Exhibitionism
5. Spanking
6. Foot Worship
7. Cross-Dressing
8. Water Sports (Including, but not limited to, Golden Showers)
9. Swinging and Group Sex
10. Adult Babies

You can see how an outfit from number one might be more appealing than one from number ten.

"She's ready?" Ashley asked the makeup artist, pulling me out of the chair as she did.

"She's as good as she's going to get."

"Ack," I choked on a scoff. *Excuse me?!*

Ashley immediately slid into damage control, dragging me down the hallway before I could get into a hair-pulling cat fight with the makeup lady.

"What a little bitch!" I shrieked while Ashley did her best to smother me. "Can you believe her?!"

"Easie—"

"I mean, what does she expect? I know I didn't talk to her, but she's new and I have a lot on my mind!"

Ashley rolled her eyes. "Simone's not new. She's been here for the entirety of the show."

My head jerked back and my mouth fell open, agog. "Well, *shit.* I guess I'm the bitch, huh?"

"You're both bitches, really. But I'm pretty sure she's mad at you for two reasons."

"And those are?" I asked as she pulled me around a group of crew members and pushed me toward the set. A window on the left revealed the lights and life of the strip.

"Your resting bitch face—it's bad—and the fact that Anderson has such an obvious boner for you."

"What's she want with Anderson's boner?" I snapped, instantly jealous.

"I'm pretty sure you can answer that for yourself."

Back to blaming her, I repeated myself. "That little bitch!"

"Let it go," Ashley commanded. "Focus."

Before I could say anything else, she shoved me forward on my tiny heels, careening and tripping my way onto the wood floor of the set.

Anderson stood waiting for me, and when he noticed the gracelessness of my entry, he moved to make sure I didn't eat it.

"Thanks," I murmured, pulling my hair out of my face and unsticking it from my red lipstick.

His eyes were hidden behind the dark lenses of his aviator sunglasses, and the tan of most of his skin was hidden underneath the line of his neatly-pressed tuxedo. A bow tie sat perfectly at the base of his corded throat, and a million watt smile nearly made me cover my sensitive eyes.

He looked dapper and dashing and happy and like everything I'd ever dreamed of. And I . . . well, I was in a corset and handcuffs.

It was a romantic setting for the most timeless of story books.

Both of us opened our mouths to say something when Howie stepped right between us.

"Hey, kids."

Taking disappointed steps back, both of us mumbled some form of, "Hey, Howie."

"Anderson, I want you to face camera full front. Easie, you're going to hook your arms—"

He grabbed them and put them where he wanted them.

"—here. Like you're cuffed through the curve of his arm, okay?"

I nodded.

"Keep your body angled toward him, but make sure to give the camera your face.

I nodded again.

"Okay," he said cheerfully. "Just let me do a lighting check and we'll be ready to roll."

He disappeared quickly, walking to the edge of the set and talking to several of the guys.

Alone again, Anderson and I both started to talk.

Him: "Easie—"

Me: "Anderson—"

Simultaneous: "Go ahead."

Him: "I—"

Me: "I—"

I sunk my head in my hands. "Fuck."

Cycling one breath in and out, I looked back up again, and we met each others' eyes. We weren't just looking at one another, we were *seeing.*

Once more, we spoke at the exact same time, except this time, I didn't mind.

"*I love you.*"

"*I love you.*"

I'd never seen Anderson smile so big, and I had a sneaking suspicion he wasn't the only clown-faced party in the room.

Our minds still moving as one, we met in the middle, lips to lips. Lips turned into tongues, and with each second that passed, the kissed deepened even further, Anderson's hands coming up to cup the back of my head and tilt it the opposite way as his.

By some stroke of luck, everyone must have realized what a pivotal moment for us, the absence of catcalls and invasive questions giving us the time to not only finish our kiss, but get out the vomit of words that had been climbing in our throats since the moment we'd laid eyes on one another.

"I know exactly who you are, and that's because you haven't hidden that. You're open and kind, and you've been nothing but supportive of me. Even when I was a judge-y bitch. And everything you've done for your brother may have been about him, but the fact that you cared enough to do each one says something very specific about *you.*"

Carrying on his own, very separate conversation, Anderson purged all the thoughts crowding each other on his chest. "I should have been honest from the beginning because I knew early on that you were going to be the one. Evan became an excuse instead of a beloved memory, and I'll regret the time I wasted between us for the rest of our lives."

"No," I demanded. "No more regrets. Not for me or for Evan or for anyone else. The three of us are moving forward together."

"Three?"

"Evan is always going to be a part of you, and you're a part of me. Package deal, baby. Luckily, I'm little so the shipping cost shouldn't be too outrageous."

"Ahem," Howie cleared his throat from frighteningly close.

Both of our heads whipped toward him.

"I'm loving this reunion, guys, truly. But do you think we can move on to the show? As much as I hate it, none of this heartfelt conversation is filmable material. And according to Larry, the studio bills by the hour."

Matching smiles growing on both of our faces, Anderson and I looked to each other and back to Howie as one, linked our hands together, and gave speaking in unison one more try.

"Fine. We don't need to talk about it anymore."

Me: "It's done."

Him: "It's settled."

Simultaneous: *"We're happy."*

Chapter 29

Anderson

CRACKED ROCK AND UNEVEN soil roiled beneath my feet as I ran, daring me to keep going and challenging me to manage it. So many emotions consumed me, each step felt like a lifetime and a blink of an eye at the same time.

I kept my eyes active, eager to live each moment—every tweet of each different bird, every bubble of each stream. I didn't want to miss even one piece of it because I didn't want Evan to miss even one thing.

I could feel him with me, pushing me further, helping the air to rush in and out of my lungs on schedule the way he so helplessly couldn't do for himself. And at the same time, I could feel my drive to change, each step putting me closer and closer to my goal to conquer this challenge and move on.

After two months of bliss, the day had finally come to fight for one of my most difficult achievements to date.

Sweet Easie had kissed me goodbye and sent me on my way an earth shattering seventy-nine miles and almost fourteen hours ago.

Everything about me ached and begged for the chance to cry uncle, but I tuned out the pain and the fatigue and pushed forward anyway. I'd been privy to some of the most beautiful scenery I'd ever witnessed and every last runner in the race encouraged me when I encountered them. But most of the time I was on my own, with nothing to keep me company but my thoughts and whispered murmurings from a would-be Evan.

I could practically feel him there, running with me, coaching me to keep going, but as an incline built under my feet, his voice seemed to fade.

Tammy was supposed to come in as my pacer for the last twenty miles, and frankly, it couldn't come soon enough. I needed someone there, pushing me, pleading with me, and I needed to feel their physical touch.

The drive to finish for Evan was slowly ceasing to be enough.

I'd crossed several bridges and run through the thick of wooded trails, but the sight of open space ahead of me waved like a mirage, easily becoming the most beautiful thing I'd seen all day.

A portrayal of Easie stood there, waiting for me, stretching her tiny, toned legs and winking as I approached.

I shook my head to clear the dream, but no matter how many times it went back and forth, Easie still stood there, beckoning me toward her with a flirty jaunt and a bend toward the ground that had her heavy breasts making an appearance at the top of her tank.

Knowing I shouldn't, that I didn't have the reserves necessary, I ran harder anyway, eager to get to her whether she was real or fake or the call of my very near death.

When I got within range, she shuffled into a jog, gradually picking up speed as I approached and matching me step for step by the time I came up beside her.

"Easie—"

"Don't talk," she told me, throwing up an arm and putting one pretty finger to her lips. "Not yet, anyway." I sealed my lips but waited for at least a basic explanation. When the excitement settled and my overly rapid heartbeat finally abated, she laid it all out for me, though it should have been obvious.

"I'm here to pace for you, that's it. Let's finish this thing."

"Easie—"

"Shh."

"Just one thing," I told her, holding up one rejuvenated finger in an accompanying gesture.

She inclined her ponytailed head and pursed her lips—pretended to think about it.

And then winked. "Okay."

Grabbing her neck, I kissed her as we ran, slowing our pace to just enough to be maintainable without falling. I pulled away but never let go of her eyes.

"I love you."

"I know," she assured me, facing her eyes to the front and officially shutting me out.

I smiled to myself and watched her as she ran, thanking Evan for sending her to me. A blessing like her could only have come from him.

She focused her breathing, working through the pain that started to kick in at her ten mile mark, and pushed herself harder to keep the pace I needed.

I started to slow down, but she caught me, shaking her head no and forcing me back up to my planned pace.

I watched her work for every step, push for every quarter of a mile. And she was doing it all for me.

Looking down at my finger, I knew exactly what I had to do, that I couldn't live another day without making sure she knew where we stood, and I knew just the moment to do it.

Three hundred yards from the finish line, as she started to pull away to give me the glory of my photo finish, I grabbed onto her hand, laced our fingers together, and refused to let go.

"Anderson—"

"Hell no, baby. We're going to finish this together. I wouldn't be here without you."

She smiled sweetly, the sweat from twenty miles of pushing herself to her limit and beyond sticking a strand of loose hair to her forehead and down the line of her cheek.

She didn't try to remove it, the energy to do so nothing but a wasted effort.

I barely pulled my eyes away from hers to watch where I was going, raising our hands in the air together for the last five yards and the dash across the finish.

In an effort to keep moving we walked hand in hand, and when that wasn't enough, arm in arm. By the time we made it to the end of the line of cheering spectators and loved ones, she'd burrowed her way under my arm completely, burying her face in the stank and sweat of almost eighteen hours of physical exertion. If that wasn't love, I wasn't sure what was.

Euphoric and exhausted, I wanted nothing more than to have my lips on hers, so I made it so, leaning down and twisting her until the front of her body met mine.

She didn't fight it, meeting my tongue stroke for stroke with her own, and pushing her body as deeply into mine as she could manage.

"You're crazy," I told her, breaking the kiss to catch my breath despite not being anywhere near close to getting my fill.

"If you need to run, I'm gonna run too. And if you want to hold on to Evan for the rest of your life, you'd best just scoot over and make some room for another set of hands."

Her lips met mine again, nipping and biting and licking away at the exterior before delving inside. I worked hard to keep up, but by and large, now that I was still, the fatigue had started to overwhelm me.

And I wasn't ready for it.

"Easie."

"I love you."

"You, the inventor of the hamster mile, the hater of all things physical, the ex-smoker self-proclaimed couch potato, just ran twenty miles, *for me*. Yeah, baby, I *know* you love me."

Her eyes went soft at first, and then transitioned to wide as I sank to one knee and pulled Evan's ring off of my finger.

"Oh my God," she cried, making me smile and hold onto her hand tighter.

What I wasn't expecting were the four or five "Oh my Gods" that followed, each voice pulling at some distant place in my subconscious.

Closer than expected, several familiar faces stared back at me.

Ashley and Tammy. Larry and Howie. My mom and dad. And a woman who looked exactly like the love of my life, but older, huddled under the arm of an attractive man. *Easie's parents.*

Easie saw me notice our audience and shrugged. "I would have warned you."

It wouldn't have mattered.

"Easie Reynolds, will you marry me?"

For once she embraced seriousness and expediency and answered nearly before I'd finished the question. "Any day. Any time."

There was no thinking about it. No nerves choking the path from her vocal chords to her mouth.

We both knew it was right.

The ring swallowed her tiny finger, but aside from the sizing, I'd never seen anything fit better.

I pulled myself to my feet, pressed my lips to hers, and then moved my mouth to her ear. "And the wedding night? Think you want to try something kinky?"

Her arms tightened almost to the point of pain and her chest swelled to twice its normal size.

"You bring the helicopter, I'll bring the kitten."

Epilogue

Easie

"**D**O YOU HAVE TO rub the same spot on my skin over and over like that?" Anderson asked as we cuddled on the couch like a couple of perfectly crafted spoons.

"It's comforting," I defended.

"It feels like you're going to wear right through."

For a guy who was so preachy about 'to each his own' and 'live and let live,' he sure was good at nitpicking my ways of showing affection. "Aren't you supposed to yearn for my every flaw? Covet every idiosyncrasy?"

"I could," he agreed, pursing his lips and pretending to ponder. "But then we'd be that annoyingly perfect couple. By my recognizing your flaws for what they are, I can still love you beyond anything else in this world, and yet, other people won't be afraid to hang out with us."

"I don't buy it."

"Okay, how about this," he offered stretching his neck from side to side as if preparing for a fight. "Enjoying your flaws would only magnify my affection for you. As my affection for you already inhabits some of the very highest portions of the "affection chart," any more would likely lead to codependency. I wouldn't be able to eat without you, sleep without you. I'd lose all interest in looking after my own welfare in your absence and eventually it would lead to my death. In turn, you'd be so despondent at the loss of me that you'd turn to alcohol and drugs, a sort of whiskey lullaby if you will, and in the end you'd die too."

I stared at him, wide-eyed.

"Do you want us to die?"

At my silence, he asked again. "Do you?"

I shook my head in wonder.

"I, for one, am against it. So, you see, I point out your flaws for our welfare." His face was grave. "I'm doing this for us."

He'd really come into his own since he'd proposed, joking more than ever and even taking the opportunity to relax every once in a while. Before our blowout, you would have never been able to find him on the couch, snuggling and watching TV. If he wasn't sleeping or fucking, he wasn't horizontal. But not anymore.

Though, he made plenty of time for those too.

Now he lounged. Now he loved.

And I loved experiencing every minute of it.

Anderson

Years had been leading up to this moment, the night before my wedding with my future bride in my bed. Everything about her enhanced everything about me, and I couldn't wait to make her my wife.

But, as always, Evan had been on my mind, but it was even more than usual.

I didn't know if it was the momentous nature of the occasion, or if he was trying to tell me something, but I'd spent the last forty-five minutes in bed, trying to figure out what it meant and what that meaning meant practically for me.

Finally, like the flipping of a switch the answer hit me, and I knew what I needed to do. Easing myself out of the bed without waking her, I padded down the hall, into the living room, and pulled open my standing cabinet.

Paper and pen were easily accessible, kind of as if they had been there waiting for me to use them.

I pushed the cabinet door closed with a soft click, made my way to the dimly lit couch and leaned forward onto the sturdy coffee table.

Pen in hand, deep breath in lungs, I put pen to paper and wrote.

Even I was surprised by the way all of my emotion poured out.

Dear Evan,

Hey Little Brother! How's Heaven?

Is it really and truly a better place? Everyone says it is, and trust me, with you there, I'm hoping they're right. But for the first time ever, I'm not really sure.

See, I finally understand the point of everything you said to me while you were here.

Since you left, I've been making sure to live all of your dreams for you. I hope you've seen me. I hope I've made you proud.

But none of them made me dream bigger, made me live a whole life outside of my body.

Something, that just recently, I finally managed to do.

I'm in love.

You'd really like her. She's fucking hilarious. And she loves it when

I tease her. She pretends not to, but her eyes light up and get soft. I've never really seen anything like it. And I've had the absolute best time learning all of her looks and cues. Even the ones that mean she's seriously pissed off at me. In some ways, those are the best expressions of all.

I guess what I'm saying is I'm finally living free and breathing easy. Well, I guess technically, I'm breathing Easie. That's her name. Can you believe that?

I'm hoping you can feel it—that God will make it count for the both of us.

I'll always miss you.
But you know that.

Love, Anderson

Sneaking back into our bedroom on quiet feet, I tucked the crisply folded paper into the breast pocket of my tuxedo.

Evan would walk down the aisle with me tomorrow—walk with me on my on my journey one last time—as I officially transitioned from living his life, to mine.

The End

Acknowledgements

I'm extremely fortunate to have tons of supportive people in my life. But, as always, the first person I have to thank is my mom. She's the first person to have eyes on my book, even when it's in pieces, and is an invaluable source of encouragement and wisdom. And she's not a bad editor either. Lol! Thanks, Mamalicious!

Alison and Kelly—Thanks for beta-ing for me. You did a terrific job. Or, you did a terrible job, and people can blame you for this shitty product. Just kidding!

My proofreaders! I can't even. You're too much. I expect T-shirts within the next week.

My author friends. There are a ton of you, and you're all AWESOME. Thank you for sprinting with me, pushing me to keep writing, lifting me up, and assuring me that I really COULD do this. M. Mabie, Aly Martinez, NA Alcorn, and Tara Sivec: I feel like I was separated at birth from all of you.

Book, B*tches, & Balderdash ladies. You guys are SO much fun! I legiterally have no words for you. None. I think I ran out of all of them talking in our group. Thank you for being some of the MOST awesome people I've ever met. Fuck Isaac!

Blogs. Um, hello, none of us could do this without you. I *definitely* couldn't do this without you. You all work so hard, and so many of you have supported me in ways that I can never thank you enough for. But I'll try. Thank you, thank you, thank you! I'd list you, but then I'll forget someone and be devastated. Bad mojo.

You. The readers. Sweet baby Jesus, you guys are awesome. Every message, every comment—they mean *everything* to me. I spend hundreds of hours working on these books, and just one message from one of you—someone who saw something in my book, was touched in some special way—makes it worth it. Every word written is mined from me, but I go in search of them for you. Please keep reading. I'll love you forever.

And, of course, I have to thank my family. My husband and son sacrifice the most, going without food and attention in order to let me push through to my deadline. The BIGGEST reason I fear having a stalker is that they would see how messy my house is through the windows. Thank you for your support and for believing that this book is going to be something big.

About the Author

Laurel Ulen Curtis is a 28 year old mother of one. She lives with her husband and son (and cat!) in New Jersey, but grew up all over the United States. She graduated from Rutgers University in 2009 with a Bachelor of Science in Meteorology, and puts that to almost no use other than forecasting for her friends and writing a storm chasing heroine! She has a passion for her family, laughing, and reading and writing Romance novels. She's also addicted to Coke. The drink, not the drug.

LAUREL'S SOCIAL MEDIA:

http://www.facebook.com/laurelulencurtis
http://Laurelulencurtis.blogspot.com
www.twitter.com/LUCurtisAuthor
www.pinterest.com/Laurelcurtis/
https://www.goodreads.com/author/show/6912103.Laurel_Ulen_
Curtis

Other Books by Laurel:

The One Series:
The One Place
The One Girl

Huntsford Hearts:
Impossible

The A is for Alpha Male Series
A is for Alpha Male
Secret Alpha
Accidental Alpha

One Last Night: A Novella

Hate: A Love Story

Coming Soon or In the Works:

Ellie's Beat (A Hate Prequel Novel)
Untitled (A is for Alpha Male, #4)
Trigger
Fated (Huntsford Hearts, #2)

. . . and Ashley and Larry's story. Title to come!

30298996R00170

Made in the USA
Middletown, DE
19 March 2016